LOVE FORTUNES

and other

DISASTERS

KIMBERLY KARALIUS

Swoon Reads New York

A Swoon Reads Book
An Imprint of Feiwel and Friends

Swoon Reads books may be purchased for business or promotional use. For information on bulk purchases, please contact the Macmillan Corporate and Premium Sales Department at (800) 221-7945 x5442 or by e-mail at specialmarkets@macmillan.com.

Library of Congress Cataloging-in-Publication Data

Karalius, Kimberly.
Love fortunes and other disasters / Kimberly Karalius.
pages cm
Summary: Devastated by a "love fortune" indicating that she will be a spinster, fifteen-year-old Fallon decides to take control of her own fate, even if it means working with Sebastian, a notorious heartbreaker.
ISBN 978-1-250-04720-5 (paperback)—ISBN 978-1-250-06360-1 (e-book) [1. Love—Fiction.   2. Fate and fatalism—Fiction.   3. Magic—Fiction.   4. Adventure and adventurers—Fiction.   5. Friendship—Fiction.]   I. Title.
PZ7.1.K36Lov 2015
[Fic]—dc23
2014049323

Book design by Ashley Halsey

Feiwel and Friends logo designed by Filomena Tuosto

First Edition: 2015

10 9 8 7 6 5 4 3 2 1

macteenbooks.com

To those searching for love.

THE BARGAIN

Love stopped at the town of Grimbaud, weary and limping upon a twisted ankle. "I've been trying to help people," she said, struggling out of her dirty sneakers, "and no one is listening to me."

A stray cat cocked its head, her only audience. She sat on the edge of the canal. Her right ankle was pink and swollen, but the pain eased as soon as she dipped her feet into the cool water. Boats bobbed on the canal, and windows flashed glimpses of families preparing dinner. Love came in many forms, but that day, she was a whiny thirteen-year-old with a sunburned nose. Her scalp itched under her baseball cap.

Every year, Love backpacked through the entire world to take inventory. She rode on the backs of motorcycles and slept on benches. Sometimes she even took private jets if the champagne was sweet enough. But not this year. This year the spreadsheet tucked inside her backpack proclaimed that there were too many broken hearts in the world.

"They make themselves miserable," Love whispered,

glaring at her reflection. "I wish I could just tell them how to love."

At that moment, a woman wearing a tattered wedding dress walked up the street. A veil covered her face. Her clasped hands loosened when she saw Love. "You weren't at my wedding," the woman said ruefully.

Love consulted her spreadsheet and shrugged. "Sorry, Zita. I was late for all my appointments today because of this useless ankle."

"Is that so?" Zita smoothed her lace-trimmed bodice. "Looks like you have a bigger problem than that."

"I was never good at accounting."

"And?"

"People are ignoring their instincts," Love pressed her fist to her heart. "If they knew what their romantic futures held, they wouldn't suffer so much."

Zita considered this. "What if you just talk to them like you're doing now with me?"

"Brides can see me on their wedding day. You won't recognize me tomorrow." Love sighed. "Usually, no one sees me."

"Why don't we use that to your advantage?" Her veil stirred. "Use me as your megaphone. Use Grimbaud as your testing ground."

Love stared hard at her reflection in the water. The surface wavered and she thought she could see a universe of wrinkles on her face. She was tired of being subtle, of having people guess wrong. "Let's talk."

chapter 1

TICKER TAPE

Fallon Dupree was fascinated by people in love. She noticed how easily some couples fit together like puzzle pieces, fingers laced, matching smiles, and the same small, deliberate strides. But thinking of herself as a puzzle piece felt entirely unromantic, so she preferred to focus her excitement on the year ahead. She knew, with the same certainty that Duprees were born with, that she would meet The Boy in high school. He would feel familiar, and new, and their hearts would become beautifully tangled. She couldn't wait.

On the Friday before school started Fallon cracked open the window in her apartment and inhaled deeply. Grimbaud always smelled like roses—the red kind, she thought, purchased by lovers.

The peace shattered when a wail erupted from the first floor. "Open this door," said a girl's voice, followed by banging. "We're not through, Bastion!"

Not again, Fallon thought. She shut the window with a snap.

Moving into the student housing complex a month before school started had been, for the most part, a smart idea. Fallon had never been without her parents or brother before; she loved exploring Grimbaud each day on her own, with only herself to please. But as more students moved in over the past few weeks, the complex grew rowdy, and no one caused more ruckus than a boy called Bastion— or rather, his ex-girlfriends, who came and went like clockwork.

He never once opened the door to any of them; Fallon was disgusted, especially when she could hear those girls crying or shouting threats through her walls. She hoped that if the crying began, the girl would notice the tissue box Fallon had left underneath the staircase.

After smoothing any last wrinkles out of her coral shirt, Fallon locked the door behind her. She checked her watch, noting that it was still too early to meet Anais. However, on *today*, of all days, she refused to stay inside and listen to Bastion's ex. Grimbaud could amuse her this morning instead.

She walked through the cobblestone streets of Grimbaud with her face soft from moisturizer and her brown hair neatly parted in the middle in a bob ending at her jaw. Unusually polished for a fifteen-year-old, she earned a few respectful nods from policemen patrolling the street corners. Grimbaud was made up of webbed canals and buildings dating back to the medieval era. Stone cupids and storks, sometimes painted and generally gaudy, huddled in the spaces between windows. Smokers spilled ghostly hearts from their mouths. A café owner handed Fallon a coupon for couples seeking brunch. With a smile, she folded the coupon and tucked it in her skirt pocket; she'd add it to the list of activities she'd do with her future boyfriend, the top being taking a boat ride through Grimbaud's famous Tunnel of Love.

Her attention turned toward the spires piercing the sky, the belfry tolling, and the market squares holding hungry wanderers in search of pralines and hot, twice-baked fries.

Charm-makers sold their wares in shops that looked like gingerbread houses. Fallon's skin prickled as she stopped to stare at the charms on display. A man wearing key chains on his belt promised that buying one would improve her exam scores. A little boy poured green liquid into a bottle labeled CREATIVITY: ONE TEASPOON WITH YOUR COFFEE.

She purposely avoided Verbeke Square. The temptation to get her love fortune early, rather than wait for Anais and Nico, would be too much to bear if she got a look at Zita's charm shop now. Instead, Fallon turned around and walked all the way back toward the complex, stopping a block away to go inside a corner drugstore.

The door jingled when she stepped inside. Her feet made sucking noises on the sticky tile floor. Rows of plastic-wrapped chips and cookies gleamed in the fluorescent lighting. Fallon tucked her hair behind her ears and headed toward the produce section.

She inspected the pears, blueberries, and lemons. White fuzz grew on the fruit. She drew back, her breath coming in short gasps.

"Ah. I see you're admiring the fruit. We have trouble selling produce," said a voice coming from the cash register, "since, you know, most of our customers are high schoolers."

Fallon frowned. "That's still not a good excuse, Anais. Your dad shouldn't let this fruit rot."

Anais stepped out from behind the register and wiped her knees. The girl was tiny, with fluffy blond hair and rosy cheeks. The mischievous curl of her lips dampened her adorability, as well as the peach-colored sweats and stained apron that was her work uniform. "Lucky Grimbaud's health inspectors aren't as dedicated as your parents," she said. "We're not scheduled for inspection until December."

Mr. and Mrs. Dupree were health inspectors, feared by all restaurants and eateries in Fallon's hometown. Her parents had seen enough disease-riddled restaurants and factories that they never let Fallon or her older brother, Robbie, touch anything mass produced in stores. Once a week, her parents had taken them out to eat, using the outings as a chance to conduct blind raids. She had a stockpile of memories of her and Robbie sitting at tables, neatly peeling crayons, while her parents searched kitchens for dead rats and solidified grease like pirates hunting treasure.

Robbie was six years older than Fallon and had gotten to taste freedom first by attending Grimaud High. It was then, when Fallon slept over in his apartment one weekend during his senior year, that she had met Anais Jacobs, the drugstore owner's daughter. With no fresh market within walking distance, twelve-year-old Fallon had braved the drugstore with her brother. When Fallon almost hyperventilated over the clumps of dust and decaying broccoli, Anais had raised her eyebrows and called her "snotty."

They had become friends on the spot, staying in contact first through phone calls, then through letters when both girls were old enough to care to write them.

Anais took a rag and wiped the cigarette case down. "What are you doing here so soon? Are you nervous about your fortune?"

Fallon shrugged. Her toes twitched again. "I shouldn't be, but I am."

"That's a normal reaction, especially the first time you get one." Anais blew a speck of dust off the corner of the case. "But I'm not worried. My relationship with Bear is secure. Whatever Zita has to say about my boyfriend has to be good."

Fallon smiled at that. "When are you going to introduce me to him?"

"When school starts. He'll be back from his judo tournament by then." Anais balled up the rag. "You want to get going now? I told Nico to save us a spot in line."

"Has he been worried?"

"Enough to lose some of his hair. Poor guy."

"Then we'd better go."

"The sooner I can take off this paper bag, the better," Anais said, untying the apron.

While Anais dashed upstairs to change, Fallon tried to ignore the way her heartbeat crawled into her ears, setting off a steady alarm that no one but her could hear.

⊶▷

A line snaked through Verbeke Square, curving through a maze of café tables and around vendor stalls. The line began in front of Zita's Lovely Love Charms shop, the only shop in a row of old brick buildings that sold something other than lace.

Zita's shop had been painted a shade of pink lemonade and featured bow windows with a second story used only as a backlit display of Zita's finest love charms that glittered with gemstones and gold. Sunlight made the shop gleam beside its drab companions. No one looked at the lace while they waited for their fortunes.

"Nico better be at the front of the line," Anais said. "My sandals aren't made for standing."

Fallon glanced at her friend's flat, faux-leather shoes. They looked like they had been cobbled together by a blind shoemaker, if not a factory, and she doubted that the straps would last the walk back without breaking. "I'm sure he's got us a good spot."

The majority of the line consisted of Grimbaud High students. Tradition dictated that every high school student should get a love fortune before the beginning of each school year. This particular love fortune was different than the other charms sold in Zita's shop: it foretold your romantic future for the entire school year. Zita's 100 percent accuracy kept the townspeople coming back to her shop.

The line moved, releasing a smattering of students trying to process their fortunes. Some cried—happy tears or sad—while others stared at their ticker-tape fortunes with stunned disbelief. The students with the best fortunes glowed like stars, one step away from dancing on the cobblestones. Nico stood in the middle of the line, twisting his damp shirt in his tanned fingers. He had brown hair, burned gold from the sun, and a sinewy body.

"Couldn't you have gotten here earlier?" Anais said, pinching Nico's arm.

"Hey! It doesn't make a difference. The line's been here since dawn. Just be glad you're not in the back of the line," Nico said, "because I'm nice enough to let you cut me."

"Did you eat breakfast?"

"Nah. I can't stomach it." Nico rubbed the back of his head; his fingers paused over his thinning hair.

Fallon and Anais squeezed in front of Nico in line, much to the consternation of the students behind him.

"After we all get wonderful fortunes," Anais said, "we'll have to indulge in a good brunch."

Nico pressed a hand to his mouth. "Please don't talk about food."

Fallon worried about the green tinge of his skin. "Sit down right now," she said, placing her hands on his shoulders. "Put your head between your legs."

Nico obeyed. He gulped down a few deep breaths before struggling to his feet again.

"Could you be seasick?" Anais teased.

"Not possible. Sailing the canals is nothing like the sea. The water's smooth, like gliding on mirrors."

"The better to see your bald spot with."

Nico rolled his eyes. "I'm just excited, okay? And out-of-my-mind nervous. This could be the year I get Martin's attention. Or not. Oh god, or not."

"Deep breaths," Fallon warned.

"You don't understand," he said. "Martin broke up with Camille over the summer. I might have a chance."

Fallon had only known Nico for a month, having been introduced to him through Anais, but she already felt invested in his longtime crush on Martin Pauwels, the student government president. As a sophomore, Nico had secured the unwanted position of treasurer, enabling him to work side by side with Martin during the new school year.

Nico's full name was Nicolas Barnes, of the Barnes family that owned the most popular canal cruises in town and the famous tourist attraction, the Tunnel of Love. Nico spent his days cleaning the boats, manning the Barnes' and read it herself. "It's true. It really says that. Fallon, have you been holding out on us? Is there a boy you like? Someone from your hometown, maybe?"

It took a few seconds for her throat to work. "No."

Anais cursed.

Fallon forgot how to breathe. The word "never" scared her. It held the weight of forever.

Her fate was sealed.

Fallon broke away from the machine, ignoring Anais's and Nico's shouts as she ran straight into the shop. Despite the warm lighting, the layout of Zita's shop had the ambiance of a perfume department. Marble counters and shelves displayed booklets on how to kiss and how to plan a perfect date. Bins of innumerable pocketbook charms, potions, and amorous gifts reserved for adults overwhelmed her. The scent of a dozen roses stuffed up her nose and tickled her brain. She imagined holding hands with a boy alongside the canal at midnight. Sharing secrets. Stepping on cobblestones. Exchanging kisses as decadent as truffles. Her heart pounded like a wild thing. She breathed through her mouth and stumbled toward the nearest counter.

"Try not to breathe too deeply," warned the girl at the counter. "The scent they pump in here takes a long time to get used to. It makes you daydream."

Before Fallon could speak, someone approached from behind. "Lucie, remember your training. Don't tell our customers such things."

Lucie shrunk behind the counter. "Sorry."

booths spread throughout Grimbaud, and sometimes giving tours when the cruises were booked low. Over the weeks that she had gotten to know him, she had learned how to speak above the roar of boat engines. Nico had mastered that skill long ago and had no trouble bemoaning Martin's now ex-girlfriend and the fact that, as far as anyone knew, Martin didn't like boys.

The line continued to move, and each step brought them closer to the moment of truth. Fallon could see Zita's storefront now, adorned with slanted gold lettering. The windows revealed a shop lit with warm, round lights. Love potions in glass-blown bottles gleamed in the windows. A rack holding prewritten love letters spun like a carousel while charms molded like cupids sat in baskets labeled HALF PRICE. Fallon tore her eyes away from the enchanting display.

The love-fortune machine was built into the wall on the left-hand side of the shop. Like the storefront, it was painted the same shade of pink and rimmed with golden swirls. A series of cogs, kept behind rose-colored glass, moved each time the machine printed a new fortune on paper strips. The boys in front of them shoved their coins one by one into the slot; Fallon heard Nico swallow loudly when the last boy, shouting with victory, brandished his good fortune and walked away.

"Who's going to go first?" Fallon said. Her hands shook.

Anais rolled her eyes. "Me. Otherwise we'll be pelted for holding up the line."

She slipped her coins into the machine and placed her hand on the scallop-edged heart in the wall. The heart pulsed as the cogs turned. No one knew exactly how the love-fortune machine worked, but it was clear that the heart read who you were—somehow. Fallon felt a slight tremor under her feet. As if Zita herself were underneath the cobblestones right now, reading Anais's heartbeat and scrawling her fortune.

The ticker tape slid out of the machine facedown. On the other side, written in red ink, was the fortune.

Anais squealed. "Good news for me. *Your love life will be fruitful as long as you are true to yourself.*"

Fallon let go of the breath she didn't know she'd been holding.

Nico frowned. "What does that mean?"

"If I'm myself, I'll get to keep Bear as my boyfriend."

"If," Nico said, "you actually let him see you in your work uniform."

"Never."

"What about the biscuit tins? I'm sure he'll think you're adorable when—"

"No way. No boyfriend of mine needs to know about that." Anais pushed him forward. "You go next."

Nico put his hand on the heart. He shuddered so badly that the printing of his fortune seemed miraculous. Nico scanned the fortune, one, twice, and muttered, "Oh no. Oh no."

Anais plucked it before he could drop it. "*Your will go unnoticed by the one who matters.*"

Fallon rubbed his shoulder, at a loss for words. "Nico

His eyes grew red with unshed tears. "No big deal, rig I expected this."

"Shut up," Anais said, drawing him into a hug.

Fallon wished she could tell him not to give up, but th wasn't how Grimbaud worked. Zita's love fortunes were al ways right. The red ink was clear enough; Nico would do better forgetting Martin once and for all. Easier said than done. Fallon squared her shoulders and stepped forward, taking her turn at the machine.

She placed her hand on the scallop-edged heart and closed her eyes. The cogs turned in a symphony of clicking and clanking. In that moment, Fallon swore the earth absorbed her heartbeats like sunlight and saw the truth in them. Her fate. She almost forgot to reach for the ticker tape as it slid out of the machine.

"Fallon, read it," Anais said, her voice soft with new worry.

Fallon opened her eyes and tore off the strip. The red ink made a long scar on the surface. "*Your love will never be requited,*" she whispered aloud as she read each word.

Her stomach dropped out of her.

Nico rubbed his eyes, turning green on her behalf. "Are you sure?"

Anais gently pried the fortune out of Fallon's hands

"Why don't you stock the love-letter stationery." It wasn't a question.

After Lucie left her post, Fallon turned around to meet none other than Camille Simmons. She wore a pink-and-white uniform consisting of a tight dress and shiny silver shoes. Her name tag read ASSISTANT MANAGER. If beauty was a reason to like Camille, then Fallon could see why Martin had dated her for so long. Camille's hair was parted down the middle, long and straight as a pressed sheet. Her caramel skin seemed to glow, and her lips, always painted a shade of dark chocolate, drew admiring glances from boys. And she knew it.

"Can I help you?" Camille said in a bored tone.

"I need something to help with my fortune," Fallon blurted.

Camille's lips twitched. "Let's look you up in the computer first."

"You don't have to."

"Protocol."

Camille slipped behind the counter and asked for Fallon's name. She only knew who Camille was because Nico complained about her constantly, calling her his rival for Martin's affections. After a few moments, Camille paused over the keyboard. "Oh. Our shop can't sell you anything."

"I don't understand."

"Your love fortune can't be tampered with." She shrugged. "We're saving you money, you know, by refusing to let you purchase something. Because it won't change anything."

Fallon's legs turned to jelly.

Camille studied Fallon. Then she flashed a sympathetic smile that didn't quite reach her eyes. "I'm not Zita, but here's some advice: if you want to be more attractive, there are magazines for that."

chapter 2

PAMPHLET

Sweet butter waffles did nothing to raise Fallon's spirits. The doughy waffle got stuck in her throat, making it hard for her to swallow, and she had to stop between bites to wipe at her eyes.

"Maybe . . ." Anais said softly, biting off a chunk of waffle, "maybe *my* fortune isn't that great anyway."

Nico snorted through his tears. "Don't be jealous."

She punched him in the shoulder.

Fallon managed a smile as she watched them. After parting ways, she kept her head down as she walked through the streets, hoping that no one would notice her red cheeks and the damp handkerchief clenched in her fist.

The student housing complex was a welcome sight. The wide, stone building, framed by a low twisting fence, was split into twenty separate apartments for boarding students. Languishing potted plants populated the inner patio, where students could study under the stars. She unlatched the wooden gate and climbed up a small set of stairs to her apartment on the second floor. Wind blew in over the water—the coastline was only a few blocks away—and she could almost see the stretch of blue between the rooftops when she reached the top of the staircase.

"Why does the school year feel over already?" she asked the town.

A door opened on the first floor, revealing the caretaker, Mrs. Smedt, lugging a full trash bag.

Fallon sighed and let herself into her apartment.

Numerous antiques shop visits had allowed Fallon to decorate her white-walled apartment quickly. Her parents had bought her a complete set of expensive pots and pans, along with glassware and stainless-steel utensils. She'd also bought a tape player that would allow her to listen to the cassette tapes she'd smuggled from home; sometimes the radio wasn't enough. The vintage restaurant posters she'd hung up reminded her that restaurants existed in time and space that her parents hadn't investigated.

Fallon had saved room on the corkboard over her desk for Zita's fortune; it was already crowded with photos of her, Nico, and Anais pulling faces. Her fortune was still in her pocket, curled around the coupon she had been given during her morning walk. The thumbtack shook between her fingers as she pinned the ticker-tape fortune to the board. The coupon, useless now, was thrown in the trash. When her gaze landed on Robbie's wedding photo in the corner, her breath caught.

Robbie and his wife, Morgane, were so young in the photograph; he barely filled out his tux, and Morgane's bouquet looked too heavy for her thin wrists to hold. They had married the day after their high school graduation.

Fallon remembered starting middle school at the time, struggling to deal with the age difference between her and her brother. Until the wedding, it was easy to pretend that they weren't six years apart. He came home from Grimbaud High on vacations and captivated her with stories of living in the student complex and receiving Zita's love fortunes each year. Nothing had changed, until suddenly he grew a mustache and moved out after getting accepted to a two-year quality-control management program after graduating.

"I knew Morgane was the girl for me, thanks to Zita," Robbie said at the wedding, evoking a few laughs. "My freshman year, I got a fortune that simply said: *Wear red.*"

The story always caused a lot of laughter and happy sighs. Eager to fall in love, Robbie followed Zita's instructions by buying tons of red shirts, inadvertently beginning his discovery of what kinds of clothing pilled or bled or broke too easily. The bright color came in handy one evening when he was studying on the patio. Morgane lost her glasses and was retracing her steps—an impossible feat when she could barely see an inch in front of her nose. She tumbled behind a potted plant, but was able to call Robbie for help because she saw the fuzzy tomato red of his shirt through the leaves.

Fallon dreamed of following in her brother's footsteps

when it came to love—that was one reason why she insisted on attending Grimbaud High. Generations of Duprees had either lived in or boarded at Grimbaud, falling in love during their high school years. Fallon had fully expected to receive Zita's guidance to lead her to the boy who would make her heart dance.

And it didn't happen.

"It won't happen, ever," Fallon said, pinching the bridge of her nose to stop the tears. Her face hurt and her eyes felt sandy. She had planned to call her parents and brother after receiving her fortune, but she didn't reach for the phone. What could she possibly say?

With some struggle, she pushed the fortune out of her mind. School started on Monday. She dragged out her ironing board to press her school uniform and double-checked that her backpack was fully stocked for the fresh semester.

Her comfortable routine was only vaguely interrupted by the sounds of soda cans fizzing and music drifting out of open windows. The student housing complex was alive again. *The school year will continue,* she thought, running the iron over her blazer. A year full of possibilities and closed doors.

Fallon blended in with the other Grimbaud High students trekking to campus on Monday morning. Her white blouse and pleated skirt in browns and gold kept her warm, paired with her dark chocolate blazer and matching knee-high socks. Uniforms provided her the perfect mask; no one could tell her that her clothing was boring and expensive. Still, she couldn't help but take care of her uniform while most students let theirs wrinkle.

A group of boys walking in front of her pushed each other and laughed. The boys' uniform choices rarely deviated from cream-colored polos, crew-neck sweaters, blazers, and brown pants. Though she noticed some boys wearing their pants either rolled up to the ankle or with hems dragging on the ground. Robbie wouldn't have appreciated seeing that. Treating well-made clothes terribly was a high crime in his book.

Grimbaud High was a humble stone building that had once been used as a gate marking the western end of town. Since it had become an academic institution, two wings flanked the original gate. The gate created a tunnel that led to the greenbelt that separated Grimbaud from the next town over. Anais waited for Fallon in the tunnel, talking with a tall boy who held her backpack.

"Good morning," Fallon said, giving fair warning as she approached. She didn't want to interrupt.

Anais grinned. "Look who I ran into. He still hasn't changed into his uniform, but I assure you, he's a student here. This is Thom Janssens."

Fallon introduced herself and shook hands with Thom. Her hand, while not particularly dainty, got swallowed up in his. "Nice to meet you."

"You can call me Bear," he said while blushing. "I think everyone will, the longer we're dating."

"See? He's smart too," Anais said with a laugh.

Bear's white judo uniform clung tightly to his body, revealing his broad back and muscles bunching under the fabric. He said he had been up since sunrise practicing with his team. His hair was shaved close to his head, accentuating his big ears and the acne scars marring his cheeks. He had a gentle way of looking at Anais, as if he couldn't believe that she was standing beside him.

"I hope you told your team that we're dating," Anais said. She clung to his arm, sighing a little when her fingers found muscle.

Fallon knew that look and tried not to laugh.

Bear stiffened. "Why?"

"So they know who the girl in the back is during competition," she said. "I'm making a poster that I'm going to wave around. I've also got three ideas for a cheer."

He went pale.

"I'm kidding." Anais patted his arm with her free hand. "I don't want you to lose because of me."

Bear rubbed his head, bemused. "I know. I'm just a little slow."

"Everyone's a little slow with Anais," Fallon added, surprised by his attitude. Did he always put himself down so easily? "You'll get used to her. She's actually very sweet."

He relaxed a little. "She is."

When the first bell rang, freshmen were directed around

the back of campus for orientation. Tables lined the grass. After writing her name on the sign-in sheet, Fallon looked up to find a piece of casserole shoved under her nose.

"Don't forget your piece," said the woman manning the table. "Principal Bemelmans's fennel-and-endive casserole is exquisite."

"Exquisite" wasn't the word she would choose. The casserole was undercooked. Fennel leaves floated like tiny longboats in the soupy mess. The cheese on top hadn't even melted. Fallon refused to take the paper plate from the woman. People started to stare. "I'm sorry," she said. "I can't eat that."

The woman's skin turned blotchy. "You *must* try it."

Fallon dropped the plate on the table, already inching away. She apologized again.

The woman read the sign-in sheet. "A Dupree," she nearly shouted. "No wonder."

The back of Fallon's neck burned with embarrassment as whispers followed her. Upperclassmen leaned out the windows, watching the new students below. Had they heard the woman shout her name? Fallon kept her eyes on the grass. She didn't want to know.

The owners of charm shops occupied the tables on the left. Grimbaud High didn't teach charm-making (probably to keep the old campus intact, Fallon thought), but offered coveted apprenticeships instead. The shop owners were ready to conduct interviews on the spot for any freshman already interested. Charm-making wasn't a career or hobby she wanted to pursue, so she explored the tables on the right, consisting of honors classes and academic clubs.

The office-experience program drew her attention. Mr. Drummond ran the program, a middle-aged man with a curly mustache. "You can trade your study hall for one of these jobs," he said, handing her a list. "Not much left this year. Upperclassmen get first picks, and answering the front-office phones is as popular as ever."

Fallon scanned the list. Most of them had already been crossed out, but she found a job as a library assistant toward the bottom.

Mr. Drummond nearly snatched the list from her hands. "Are you sure? You'd be working with the head librarian, Ms. Ward."

"Is something wrong?"

"She's a spinster," he said, lowering his voice.

Fallon's eyebrows shot up. The way he spoke, spinster-hood sounded like a contagion you could catch through the air. In a town preoccupied with love, the idea of being single was fairly terrifying—especially when Zita confirmed it through the fortunes. Her own fortune slid through her brain and down her throat, demanding tears. *Your love will never be requited.*

"Then maybe I'll like her," she said, blinking fiercely as she wrote her name on the list. Before Mr. Drummond realized what she had implied, she turned away from the table.

Orientation finished with a few words from the

student-government president, Martin Pauwels. Rejoining Anais and Bear, Fallon waited impatiently to finally see Nico's crush.

"Grimbaud High welcomes you," Martin started, his calming voice amplified by a microphone. He had a pale complexion, thick glasses, and floppy black hair. As Martin outlined the student conduct handbook, he spoke tentatively, as if dreading the yawning and daydreaming overtaking the freshmen. "You'll be going to your first classes in just a few minutes, but let me assure you that the next four years are not all about romance. Consider your dreams. Strive toward them by doing well here. Please accept the school pride T-shirts our staff is handing out."

Members of student government appeared with shirts slung over their arms. Fallon didn't see Nico, but ended up with a medium-size shirt.

"Cute, right?" Anais said, admiring the hand-drawn rendering of the crest printed on the shirt.

The fabric didn't have much give. She held the shirt pinched between her thumbs and index fingers, as if it would squirm. "Some people have reactions to wearing polyester," she said, louder than she'd intended.

This time she couldn't miss the stunned looks she got from the other freshmen. Fallon took out her schedule book for something to stare at.

Because orientation had counted as homeroom for the day, Fallon headed to her first-period class: speech and debate with Mrs. Heymans.

A squat old woman with a fondness for wearing brooches, Mrs. Heymans wrote rules on the whiteboard as Fallon entered. The sharp scent of the marker, mixed with dusty wood, made her feel strangely at home. She hadn't expected to see any familiar faces in her classes, let alone electives, but there was Nico, already seated and fanning the front of his shirt, which was still damp from working on the canal. His eyes rose to meet hers without a smile. "It was there before I arrived."

"What was?" Fallon asked.

Then she noticed a pamphlet sitting on top of her desk.

The rest of the room went quiet, as if everyone inhaled at the same time and sucked the room dry. Even Mrs. Heymans stopped writing on the board; she left the period off Rule #10: No throwing paper balls. They all watched her.

Fallon sat down in her chair, the cold of the plastic bleeding through her skirt, and stared at the cover. SPINSTER VILLAS: A HOME FOR YOUR HEART was written in bold calligraphy. It depicted a group of pretty women holding hands and laughing together as if they had nothing better to do than revel in their stagnant fates. Identical whitewashed buildings stood behind them. If she squinted, she could see a bee sitting in one of the rosebushes underneath a window.

She opened the pamphlet. Words swam on the paper.

Over and over, she saw women of indeterminate ages looking content. These women played croquet in the gardens,
formed a knitting circle in front of a cozy fireplace, and
posed with cats draped over their shoulders like scarves.
The Spinster Villas claimed to offer a happy, comfortable
life to those doomed to a life without romantic love. They
need not suffer. The world had so much more to offer.
Come join them. On the Contact Us page, the list of numbers included Zita's shop; it was common knowledge that
the Spinster Villas, as well as the Bachelor Villas, were
owned by Zita. Remembering yesterday's fortune made her
stomach twist. Fallon slowly folded the pamphlet, her face
hot.

Mrs. Heymans was the first to speak. "I'm sorry. I left
the classroom unlocked this morning."

Fallon placed her hands on the desk, taking deep breaths.
"It's true. My love fortune turned out this way."

The class hummed with sympathy. Students got up out
of their chairs to rub her back and offer kind words. The
attention was overwhelming but expected in a way. Zita's
love fortunes brought people together. High school was no
different. Soon enough, students would start sharing their
own fortunes, passing them back and forth like found ob-
jects lost on a sandy beach. Puzzling over them, trying to
help each other, celebrating together. She couldn't have
escaped the first day of school without everyone knowing
about her fortune, but it shouldn't have happened like this.

"Who found out?" said a girl. "It wasn't any of us."

Nico slumped in his seat. "I can think of someone."

Fallon frowned. "You can't be serious. I don't even know her."

"That's exactly the point!" Nico crossed his arms. "Camille has to be behind this. She's the only one who knew about Fallon's fortune, since she works at the shop. Wasn't it Camille you spoke to in the shop? She looked your name up in their system."

Mrs. Heymans rolled her eyes. She must have been used to hearing his conspiracy theories regarding Camille Simmons.

"That may be, but I haven't done anything to attract her attention. I was just one of many unlucky girls yesterday."

"And someone decided to make you feel bad about it."

"Sit down, everyone," Mrs. Heymans said.

"How about you, Barnes?" said a boy in the back. "Bad fortune?"

Nico didn't shy away from answering. "My crush won't be noticing me this year."

Another round of pitying glances and murmured words. A girl wearing her hair in braids said, "If you actually tell us who you like, we could devise a way for you to get noticed."

"By embarrassing me? No, thanks." Nico's mouth slid into a grin. "Looks like Mrs. Heymans really wants to go over the rules. Let's indulge her."

"Thank you, Mr. Barnes," Mrs. Heymans replied dryly.

For the duration of class, Fallon tried to picture the

future she was tumbling toward. She'd never had pets, so the idea of owning even one cat, let alone a dozen, seemed like a daunting task. The special events held each week sounded like torture: watching romantic comedies together on Friday nights and touring museums on a giant purple bus. But, if the women in the pamphlet were any indication, living at the Spinster Villas was supposed to be fun, like a never-ending sleepover party.

"Living in the villas is supposed to be a good option," Fallon said after class ended.

The hallways were mazelike, including the enclosed bridges connecting the added-on buildings to the gate, but everyone took their time heading to second period. The school gave a generous fifteen minutes between classes for such a small campus.

Nico adjusted the strap on his shoulder bag. "You should just ignore the pamphlet. Locking yourself up in the villas isn't going to make you happy."

"You make it sound like a cage."

"It could be. Look at Ms. Ward, our librarian. She got a bad fortune like yours, went away to college, and came back here for some reason. If you're thinking of following in her footsteps, at least do that. Go see the rest of the world."

Fallon smiled wistfully. "There's too much to love about Grimbaud."

Nico shrugged. "I get that."

They walked in silence for a while. Her parents traveled a lot due to their reputation; they often flew planes across the globe to train other health inspectors or to attend conferences. That lifestyle was partly the reason why she and Robbie got to go away for school. No one would be home otherwise. Fallon didn't think the rest of the world could compare to a place that made her feel swaddled in surprises and charm. Giving Grimbaud up was inconceivable.

"Are you feeling better?" Fallon asked.

"No. It's just hard keeping a miserable face when everyone's so happy."

"When does student government start?"

Nico flushed. "We have the first meeting on Thursday."

After throwing himself into campaigning last spring, he'd won the position of treasurer. Nico wasn't particularly popular, but it helped that everyone knew the Barnes name; he had told Fallon about how close he had been to bribing people with free rides on the canal for votes and she was thankful that it hadn't come to that. Nico now had the opportunity to spend time with Martin—as long as Camille, as vice president, remained civil. Breakups were a messy business, fortunes or not.

As students disappeared into classrooms, clearing the halls, Fallon noticed a pair of peculiar girls leaning against a row of lockers. Watching them. The girls had to be related somehow, but they looked nothing alike. Fraternal twins, she guessed, after spotting how they both wore their blazers' sleeves rolled up at the elbows and styled their hair in coiled ringlets that fell down their backs.

"The De Keyser twins," Nico said under his breath. "Mirthe's on the left. Femke's on the right."

"Hello, you two," Mirthe said, her brown eyes flashing.

Femke linked arms with her sister, blinking her green eyes slowly. "You're carrying some unfortunate fortunes."

"How do you know?" Nico said.

"Can't you hear the whispers?" Mirthe's nut-brown face brightened. "Well, it doesn't matter. Plenty of people were in line yesterday at Zita's shop. I must say, I've never seen such a dramatic display of emotion. Running into the shop was a bold move, Fallon."

"What else could I have done?" Fallon said, lifting her chin.

"That's precisely what we want to talk to you about," Femke said.

"Zita's love fortunes weren't kind to either of you this year. In fact, from our observations, they must be set in stone," Mirthe said.

"Only mine."

Nico squeezed Fallon's shoulder.

The twins cocked their heads at the same time. Femke said, "So you're going to give up?"

The floor tilted. Femke's question burned in her ears and pressed against her heart. Fallon waited for the pain to stop, wishing that she could just go back in time. No terrible fortune. No invasive questions. But she couldn't go backward. Nor did she want to just fold her dreams away in a dark closet. Her future of living underneath a pile of cats cracked in the middle, but it was Nico who spoke first.

"Never," he said, swallowing thickly. "Not until I share my feelings with Martin."

When Fallon found her voice, she said, "I don't want this to be the end. If I can find love somehow, some way, I want to take it."

The warning bell went off, leaving three more minutes before second period was supposed to start, but no one moved.

Then, finally, Femke and Mirthe flashed matching mischievous smiles. "We can offer you help as long as you work with us."

Femke tore a piece of paper out of her notebook and scribbled down the time and place of the meeting. When Fallon took it from her hands, she felt the featherlight presence of hope stirring.

chapter 3

CHARM-MAKERS

Convincing Anais that Fallon had to stay behind after school wasn't so hard. Fallon claimed that she had to stay behind to ask her history teacher some questions concerning the syllabus.

"Ever the studious pupil," Anais teased. "When you get home, drop by the store."

Fallon drifted through the afternoon, caught between breathless anticipation and dread. She didn't know much about Femke and Mirthe besides what Nico had told her before the tardy bell rang: their family ran a respectable weather-charm store and they kept to themselves. One twin was never without the other, and sometimes their attempts at looking alike came out strangely. Nico had told her that the twins came to school once wearing the same electric pink eye shadow and cat-eared headbands. After hearing that, Fallon was surprised that they had left their little bubble to talk to her and Nico. What were they planning?

The meeting would take place in the basement of the school. The science classrooms were dimly lit; jars of eyeballs and other animal parts were on display as if arranged by an interior designer. Fallon's labs in the past had been limited to solving equations in her notebook and measuring melting points and recording phase changes. Not very exciting compared to the creepy atmosphere these rooms boasted. However, the science classrooms seemed to fit the unease she felt as she wandered through the basement.

She heard the sound of laughter and talking coming from one of the open classrooms. She paused in the doorway to find the chairs arranged in a U-shape facing the teacher's desk. Femke and Mirthe sat on top of the desk. Nico was already sitting, and she didn't know the other student, a miserable-looking girl with clumpy, unwashed hair.

"Don't just stand there, holding the doorframe up. Come on in," Mirthe said. "Say hello to Hijiri Kitamura."

Hijiri sat up in her chair, but she wouldn't look Fallon in the eye. In fact, she seemed incapable of lifting her gaze any higher than her ankles. The girl had to be a freshman because she held her class schedule in a death grip.

"Nice to meet you," Fallon said.

Hijiri spared a wobbly smile.

"We're just waiting on one more person to join our merry band," Femke said.

"That's it?" Nico asked. "We're the only ones with bad fortunes?"

"Some of the people we spoke to were too scared to join," Mirthe said with a stubborn wave of her hand.

"They weren't desperate enough," Femke added.

"Well, that doesn't make us sound too appealing, does it?" Nico rested his chin on his fist.

"Desperation is a good thing," Fallon said. That feeling allowed her to take baby steps in the past, inching out from underneath her family's shadow. She wouldn't be surprised if its electric-nauseous energy helped her out again.

"That's right. What other feeling could compete with a town that embraces its chains?" Mirthe said.

Mirthe glanced at the wall clock. "Almost time."

"He'd better be here."

"If he skips out on us, we'll leave a rain charm in his apartment."

"Clever." Femke opened her notebook and scribbled it down. "Why haven't we tried that yet?"

Like any charm in Grimbaud, they either worked or didn't—it was the risk the buyer took when purchasing a charm. A rain charm was supposed to be used to attract rain, usually bought by farmers or garden enthusiasts. But if the twins planned to use it the way she thought they did, the charm would trap a rain cloud within an apartment. The wood flooring would be ruined, she mused. An expensive prank.

Her thoughts scattered when a boy entered the room. Fallon knew who he was immediately, from the few times she'd seen him leave his apartment at the complex. He was, without a doubt, the boy called Bastion.

"Sebastian Barringer," Mirthe said with a mock bow. "Nice of you to join us."

Sebastian surveyed the room with indifference. "So this is the place."

Fallon didn't want to like this boy or even be remotely friendly to him, but she could understand why girls kept crying outside his door. He had narrow shoulders and a slim build. His hair was styled to look disheveled. Sebastian's eyebrows were dark, dramatic slashes, making him look either perpetually annoyed or bored. Yet, paired with a smooth smile, he could make a girl's pulse quicken. Fallon's own heart had been startled awake the few times she'd passed him at the complex, but she knew better than to take her feelings seriously.

Mirthe pointed to the seat next to Fallon. "Since you're late, why don't you start us off by sharing your fortune?"

Sebastian didn't blink. "No."

Fallon watched as Sebastian slid into the chair; he rested his hands on his thighs, but the tight pull between his shoulder blades gave away his discomfort.

"This is an important discussion. If we're going to work together, we have to be honest." Mirthe hopped off the desk and grabbed a marker and an eraser. She wrote the word "Love" on the whiteboard. Then, with the precision of a surgeon, she used the corner of the eraser to slice up the word. "Zita has stolen the same thing from all of you. You may think it's love, and while that's part of it, the bigger picture is that she's taken your freedom. You can't possibly risk going against your fortunes. Why? Because it will bring you heartache and misery?"

"Yeah," Nico answered, despite it being a rhetorical question.

Mirthe quirked an eyebrow. "Life is about making mistakes. If you don't take chances, blindfolded and frightened as you are, you're not really living, are you? Heartache makes you stronger. Misery is the stuff of good poetry. You're denying yourself much more than the bad things in life by listening to Zita's fortunes."

When all eyes turned back to Sebastian, he remained placid. "I won't share my fortune. The fact that I'm here should be enough."

Femke pursed her lips. "Leave it be, sister."

Mirthe chopped the "e" into indiscernible pieces with a big sigh. "Fine. How about the rest of you?"

Nico started, revealing the fortune that predicted his invisibility for another year. He looked a little less sick than yesterday and grew more comfortable when he told them about Martin and his ex-girlfriend, Camille. "He doesn't like boys," he explained, running a hand through his hair. "That's just another obstacle for me. But I thought that, maybe if he got to know me . . . well, that's what I believed before this fortune."

Femke took notes quietly while Mirthe paced the front of the classroom.

"My love will never be requited," Fallon said, the words heavy on her tongue. She stared at her hands, tracing each knuckle with her eyes.

"Ah," Hijiri whispered, "the spinster fortune."

Fallon's face grew hot. "I don't . . . I don't have anyone I like. That's why it feels worse. Even if I end up having feelings for someone in the future, it's frustrating to know that it would be pointless."

Seeking reactions from the others, Fallon caught Sebastian looking at her with a curious expression on his face. She wondered why, discreetly touching her lips in search of crumbs from lunch.

"A death sentence, huh?" he said with a smile.

Her mouth mimicked his. "Close enough."

Sebastian turned to the twins. "What about your fortunes?"

Mirthe and Femke wore matching, self-satisfied smirks. Mirthe spoke up. "We've lived in Grimbaud all our lives and we've never gotten love fortunes. Zita's cronies won't find us in her database. We remain blissfully ignorant of our romantic futures."

Nico gasped. "How can you stand not knowing?"

Femke shrugged. "Because that's the way love's supposed to be."

"And personally, it pisses us off that Zita had driven other love charm-makers away. Once the accuracy of her fortunes was established, the other love charm-makers lost business and had to leave," Mirthe added. "That's a lot of history and competition gone. Terrible. So we think of our boycott as a nod to those whose love charms are gone now."

But Zita had done more than chase other love charm-makers out of town; she owned other properties in

Grimbaud. Fallon's guidebooks stated that Zita founded the Spinster and Bachelor Villas, and the shops in Verbeke Square paid rent to her. She turned her attention back to Hijiri as they continued sharing their fortunes.

Hijiri smoothed the fortune on her lap, stalling, until fat tears rolled down her cheeks. Her chin dimpled as she fought for words. After Femke handed her a tissue, Hijiri took a few gasping breaths. "*You can't inspire love in others if you don't change yourself.*'"

Fallon flinched. Robbie had told her about those fortunes. The boys and girls who usually received that message were the ones already attracting bullies. Their clothes were stolen in the locker rooms, their desks carved with foul language. Invisible but noticed.

Each fortune was worse than the last. Fallon didn't know how they would be able to leave the room when the air was so thick with sorrow.

"I don't know what to do," Hijiri cried, touching her oily hair. "I've always looked like this. Why can't someone love me like this?"

Femke set the notebook down, her face as quiet as Mirthe's was stormy. "Why shouldn't you be loved?"

Like a hook sinking into a fish's mouth, the pain of her words startled them. A different kind of pain.

"That's right." Mirthe said. She tossed the eraser in her hands, getting ink all over them. "That's exactly the point. Zita will win, just like she always does, if you don't ask yourselves questions."

Hijiri blew her nose. Nico perked up, his eyes blazing.

Sebastian kept his cool gaze on the twins. Fallon drew a breath, waiting.

"The five of us are starting a rebellion," Mirthe said.

Rebellion. The word made Fallon shiver. She would make a terrible rebel and she knew it. How did the twins look so confident, so sure that all of them could do this?

The twins explained that their grand plan for putting a stop to Zita involved three phases, however, they promised only to reveal one phase at a time, since overwhelming a group of "depressed, heartsick teens" would not be smart. "The less you know, the better," Femke said with a pleasing smile. "But it'll make perfect sense the further along we get."

"The first phase has to do with love charms," Mirthe said, writing on the board again. She drew a giant heart. "As I said before, Zita's shop has been around since our grandparents were in school. She's had years to wipe our town clean of the love charms that others have left behind. This is bad for us. We need love charms, and we can't use Zita's. Do you know of anyone else selling love charms in Grimbaud right now?"

Everyone shook their heads.

"How about books and magazines?"

Nico said, "Not one."

"You can't even buy them from Zita if you get a bad fortune," Fallon said, remembering what had happened after she ran into Camille in the shop.

"Exactly! So if Zita won't give you charms to fight the

fortune *she* gave you, what chance do you have of changing your fate? It's the perfect tactic. She's boxing us in."

Femke added, "That's why finding love charms is step one of our plan."

Fallon listened carefully as the twins explained how the charm gathering was going to work. Using whatever resources were available, each member of the rebellion had to collect love charms. Charms were organized into three different forms: object, verbal, and potion. Love charms were no different. Successful charms were usually written down for safekeeping, so finding books and magazines seemed like a good start. Femke suggested searching the library archives for forgotten charms; it was worth looking into for anyone who thought they could get a peek. Fallon wrote that down in her planner. She had already registered to volunteer at the school library anyway this year, so she'd work on befriending Ms. Ward.

"If your parents send you generous pocket change, you could buy the magazines that are being printed now. You'd have to pick them up yourself, though. Delivery is too risky," Mirthe said.

"That makes sense," Nico said. "Even the mailmen are dependent on Zita's fortunes. If they knew what we were ordering . . ."

"We'd be caught," Mirthe finished. "You can take a bus out to neighboring towns, but if you have your own transportation, that would be better."

"Mirthe and I share a moped," Femke said.

"Then it sounds like buying the new charms will be up to you," Sebastian said dryly.

Mirthe ignored him. "There are other ways to find old love charms. You have to keep your eyes and ears open. Write them down if they're not already captured on paper. Learn to squeeze the charms out of people."

"Don't forget to organize them," Femke said as they packed up their belongings.

The energy in the room hummed. No one had ever tried to shut Zita's shop down. This was new territory, and the task ahead had not quite sunken in. Fallon pushed whatever doubts she had aside. Her fortune reminded her of what lay ahead if she sat by and did nothing.

At first, Fallon thought she was alone walking back to the student housing complex. Her thoughts flickered and glowed like fireflies. She imagined eating whatever entrées were cooling on tables at the outdoor cafés, as if judging their quality was not a habit she'd been bred to follow. *I could eat whatever I want*, she thought, *and pick each dish just by what smells good. My nose isn't as developed as my parents'*. She liked that flaw. The sky darkened, allowing the streetlamps to cast golden shadows on the streets.

As she approached a footbridge, Sebastian walked beside her. He had a languid stride, even while carrying his schoolbag over one shoulder. He didn't look at her for quite some time. He stared straight ahead, chin up, with that incorrigibly bored expression on his face.

"You could have waited," he said. "I live at the complex too."

Fallon wasn't sure what to say. When the meeting ended, her only desire was to return to her apartment. There were clothes to lie out for the next morning and she needed to use the potatoes she had bought for her dinner tonight or else they would go bad. "My mind was on other things."

"What things?"

She tucked her hair behind her ears. "Nothing important."

The canal below their feet made gentle lapping sounds. Two little girls ran across the footbridge, shrieking and throwing leaves at each other.

"I've heard about you." He watched the leaves as they tumbled out of the girls' hands.

"Me?"

"Fallon Dupree, Grimbaud High's princess."

"I've only been in school a day. How could I have a title?"

"News travels fast. I heard that you wouldn't eat the principal's casserole at orientation. That caused quite a stir. Along with the T-shirts. I guess you won't be wearing one on our school spirit days."

"The quality's poor," Fallon said. "Wearing cheap material makes my skin crawl." Robbie had all but burned away any desire she had to wear cheap clothes after he became a clothing inspector.

"It's not a Dupree thing to do," he said.

"What do you know about my family?"

"What everyone else knows. Duprees are sleuths. They inspect everything. They also live up to their own quality standards, be it food, clothing, or dating. This is a small town, isn't it?"

Part of her wanted to turn the tables on him. Sebastian had to have been gossiped about at school, if his track record of girlfriends over the past month gave any indication. She was willing to bet he dated and dumped girls no matter the season.

As if sensing her thoughts, he said, "Barringers have been coming to Grimbaud for years too, but we don't have a reputation. Until now. I'm doing an awfully good job. You've seen the girls at my door this summer?"

"I'm not that nosy."

He snorted. "You've been leaving tissue boxes."

Her breath caught. She hadn't expected him to notice such a small thing.

Sebastian flashed a lazy smirk. "I have a lot of ex-girlfriends. That's kind of you to leave them tissues. You keep buying the expensive ones."

"They need the extra care, with you breaking their hearts," Fallon said softly. "Go away."

If Sebastian heard her, he didn't give any indication. He matched her pace, keeping his gaze on the other side of the footbridge. His bangs fell into his eyes. "I'm bored, Fallon, and dating is as fun a game as any."

Fallon's voice turned bitter. "I have a talent for ruining fun. You're wasting your time."

Sebastian took one long step forward, flashing the white of his ankle. His leather shoe came down hard on the leaf resting there. The shattering sound made a group of crows rise into the air. "You didn't jump."

Fallon blinked. "Was I supposed to be scared?"

Sebastian cocked his head. He looked back at her over his shoulder. "I don't know. That's what's interesting about you. You don't act like a princess."

"Are princesses scared of leaves breaking?"

"Of course. Princesses are delicate creatures. The sound reminds them of bones shattering in a dragon's mouth. But you're made of stronger stuff."

Fallon sucked in her breath. Her body felt leaden. The shadows shivered and danced around them, the light from the streetlamps stinging her eyes.

"You could try me out sometime, you know, with the dating thing." His tone was teasing. "Who knows? We could fall in love."

She tried to smile as they started walking again, if only for her own sake. "I doubt it."

"Maybe."

"Sebastian," she ventured. "It doesn't matter what my fortune says. I'm not interested in dating you."

His mouth twitched. "More like passing the time."

"I think you'd have more fun with a real princess," she said.

When they reached the student housing complex, Sebastian opened the gate for her. She thanked him, but tucked the gesture away in her brain. She didn't need to remember nice things like that, coming from a boy who would date anyone.

chapter 4

OVERDUE

Sebastian's words returned to plague Fallon on her walk to the school library the next day. Nothing about her was princesslike. Nothing at all. Fallon lacked classic beauty, an affinity for animals, and was not, as Sebastian insisted, delicate, no matter how well she cared for herself. Okay, so even after a morning of rushing from class to class and sharing her homemade lunch with Nico and Anais, her hair remained perfectly parted down the middle and her nails were clear of dirt. But she was no princess. Rather, Fallon decided as she walked into the library, she'd make a good clever maid, the one in fairy tales who always got her mistress out of trouble.

A clever maid wouldn't be scared of crushed leaves.

Ms. Emma Ward, the head librarian, stood on a chair against the back wall of the library, adjusting one of the many inspirational posters encouraging teens to read. The angle was a little off, so Ms. Ward kept leaning forward and backward to gauge whether she had straightened the frame. The chair wobbled with each movement.

"Lift the left side about a half an inch," Fallon suggested.

Ms. Ward squinted through her cat-eye glasses. "Are you sure?"

"It's easier to tell, standing back here."

Ms. Ward shifted the frame accordingly and managed to climb down from the chair. Her long black pencil skirt and conservative sweater didn't allow her much room for movement. Ms. Ward was in her twenties, with gentle features that were sharpened by her angular jewelry and glasses.

Fallon handed her a purple slip of paper that came from Mr. Drummond. "I'm Fallon Dupree. I've been assigned to be your helper during this period," she said. She wasn't much of a reader, even though she took great care of the golden-bound picture books she had since childhood. More often than not, she buried herself in her parents' old quality-control textbooks in an effort to find loopholes in their strict lifestyle. What excited her about work at the library was the system itself: she loved the idea of a card catalog holding all the knowledge in the room, and the distinct pleasure of being able to reshelve a book to its assigned spot.

The plastic-covered library books at Grimbaud High had wrinkled pages and were tattooed with illegible margin notes. They smelled like sadness and temptation, drenched in dust motes that drifted like tiny stars. Many a bored teenager had trampled the ancient carpet. Gum hardened underneath the wooden tables. Nooks and unpopular stacks provided ample cover for secret make out sessions. Fallon winced. She didn't relish the idea of watching other students live out their good love fortunes, and she hoped Ms. Ward didn't either.

"A helper," Ms. Ward repeated. "Yes, that's just what I need. I didn't think Mr. Drummond listened when I requested being part of the program."

"What should I do first?"

"You should probably shadow me. I'll show you how the library works. A library, no matter how big or small, is a careful balance of love and responsibility. A machine, if you will, cranked by those who care most about reading. What a wonderful balm it is for the soul."

Fallon smiled. The drab library looked more cheerful after hearing Ms. Ward's ardent speech.

The hour passed quickly as Ms. Ward showed her how to shelve returned books, properly stamp and register a book being borrowed, and how to pretend you know more about the card catalog than the students searching for a particular title do.

"It's so simple to use," Ms. Ward said, "but I can't tell you how many students stare at the catalog as if it's a monster waiting to bite their fingers."

The boy sitting alone at a table looked up. He had smooth, dark skin with eyes large and brown like twin dark chocolate truffles. The veins running along his skull stood out. A broken key hung from his neck. He was too young to be a high school student, so Fallon figured that he must have been one of the teacher's sons in need of a babysitter. The music pouring from his headphones sounded like a tango.

"Quiet in the library," Ms. Ward sung, tapping her fingers on the boy's table as she passed.

The boy shrugged and lowered the volume on his tape player.

"He says his mother fries mozzarella sticks in the cafeteria," Ms. Ward said when they stepped into the history aisle. "Is that true?"

"I don't know."

"I mean, does the cafeteria really serve mozzarella sticks?"

Fallon brought her own lunch to school, so she wasn't sure.

Ms. Ward gave a tentative smile. "It's just funny. It seems like a childish food to serve teenagers. You're all almost adults."

A lump formed in Fallon's throat. She couldn't miss the longing in Ms. Ward's voice, how her words were gingerly spoken. The librarian was lonely. And no wonder. The entire school knew how her love fortune had turned out.

"I think that's all for today, Fallon. Fifth period swiftly approaches." Ms. Ward led them back to the circulation desk. Behind the desk, out of sight from students, were some photographs. Each one depicted the same group of women caught in the middle of activities: knitting, watching movies, playing croquet on the lawn outside the Spinster Villas.

"Your friends?" Fallon asked when she felt Ms. Ward watching.

"Yes." Ms. Ward smiled sadly at the photographs. "They're lovely women."

Fallon wanted to know why, after traveling the world, she had decided to return to Grimbaud. But asking her about such a touchy subject would have been rude. "Those are nice pictures," she said instead.

Ms. Ward thanked her. They spent the remaining minutes awkwardly standing behind the desk, shuffling loose book pockets.

If the twins were right, only the deepest, most abandoned archives of the library might hold charms made by the old love charm-makers. Fallon doubted that the school library had such a back room. Grimbaud's public library was the next stop.

After school, she explored the stuffy stacks of the public library, finding private collections that the librarian working the front desk assured her had more to do with historical records than charms. "We don't keep back issues of magazines," the librarian said, looking down her nose at

Fallon, "but our charm-making books are on the second floor."

"What about love charms?" Fallon asked.

The librarian cast a sidelong glance at the policeman guarding the doors. "You must be asking about *Zita*. You won't find her charms in any book. A chef doesn't give away his secret recipes, now does he?"

"Of course not," Fallon said. "Sorry."

As Fallon left the public library, she noticed a pink rose pinned to the collar of the policeman's uniform. She could only describe the shade as pink lemonade. The same color as Zita's shop. *Why that pink?* She thought, tucking her hands in her skirt pockets. *Does Zita have something to do with the police?* Grimbaud's emblem was a cupid, not a rose, and no officers in her hometown wore extra embellishments on their uniforms. She'd have to ask the twins about it.

Her feet took her to Verbeke Square, where she spent an hour drinking hot chocolate at one of the outdoor cafés. The drink clung to her tongue, thick and creamy; she managed to relax a little. Zita's storefront was active, drawing an older crowd. A few stragglers still waited in line outside the shop to get their love fortunes, but most of the town must have already received theirs.

"How can you wear such a sad face when you're drinking hot chocolate?" asked an unfortunately familiar voice from behind her. Fallon turned to look at Sebastian.

Dark jeans hugged his legs and a green V-neck showed

off his collarbone. He wore a navy-blue plastic bracelet on his wrist, but Fallon couldn't make out the words printed on the outside. It looked old, the writing cracked with age. Sebastian lifted his eyebrows. She swished the cooling hot chocolate in her cup. "Well, look at my view."

He smirked and pointed at himself.

She sighed.

Sebastian grabbed a chair from another table and dragged it right next to hers. He sat close enough to touch her but was wholly focused on seeing what she was seeing. "Zita's. Nice choice. You must enjoy feeling miserable."

"Honestly, I was hoping for some inspiration. I don't know how I'm going to find charms."

"We'll find some."

"How are you so sure?"

Sebastian rubbed his lower lip. "Zita wasn't the first love charm-maker in Grimbaud. She couldn't have erased the marks left behind by other love charm-makers. We just have to look harder."

Verbeke Square lit up pink and orange as the sun bled through the clouds. Fallon pictured the ghosts of the past dancing through the square, selling crude charms, dueling on behalf of love, and exchanging encouragement and advice as old as the world itself. Could one woman really erase all that past? Sebastian had a point. Maybe there were other ways of coaxing Grimbaud's lost love charms out of the cobblestones. She stared at him, wide-eyed. "I can't believe you just said that."

"What?" He blinked. "Did I surprise you?"

Fallon's cheeks flushed with shame. "I was under the impression that you didn't think so deeply about . . ."

"Important things? Well, I do. When I have to," he said gruffly. "And this Zita business is a serious problem."

Over the last month Fallon had figured Sebastian out: he was a smooth-talking, shallow boy with no concern for a girl's feelings. She knew boys like him in her hometown. But Sebastian had surprised her twice already since she met him at the meeting. He showed a bit of depth in the way he had spoken about princesses (whether she agreed or not) and now about the town she adored. She wanted to understand him.

"Serious problem for who?" she ventured. "You don't seem to be having a problem with romance."

He stiffened, curling his fingers into fists. He seemed at once to lock himself up, door after door slamming over each feature. A key turned, sealing his lips shut, and he shifted away from her.

Her cup of hot chocolate was suddenly fascinating.

"Sorry," she said, though she wasn't sorry for asking. Everyone in the group who had love fortunes shared them. Except for him. She didn't have much to go on. Rather, she was apologizing for saying the wrong thing.

"What I do is my business."

"But if it hurts you, then it becomes my business too. The entire group's business. We're all working together now."

"I know."

"Then?"

"Not yet." He cracked a weak smile. "Don't forget that you have your own secrets, princess. I think we're even."

Fallon drank the rest of her hot chocolate. "So. Charms."

"They can't all be on paper," he said. "Try listening and see what you find."

Fallon tried keeping her ears open on her walk home, but she only heard the wheels of food carts crunching leaves and tourists snapping pictures of the canals. The red light on her answering machine waited for her. She knew without having to look that the message was from her parents.

"Call us back," her mother said, her voice thick with impatience. "Your father and I are waiting for the good news."

Her hands shook while she peeled the last of the potatoes and made a cold salad with them. The vinegar she used as dressing stung as she chewed. Her eyes wandered around the apartment. There was so much she could do instead of calling. The tile floor needed scrubbing. The ceiling fan needed dusting. The hole under the armpit of her favorite pink cardigan needed mending.

Outside the apartment, students chatted on the stairs or brought their homework outside to the patio. A tiny jingle nearby meant that someone had already bought a charm. She couldn't tell from the sound whether it was a charm for financial prosperity or excellent test scores, but she knew from past visits to see Robbie that the complex would look like a small shrine by midterms with all the hanging charms fluttering from railings and roofs.

Her phone rang and she nearly jumped out of her chair. She answered without thinking. "Hello?"

"There you are," her mother said. "We thought we'd try calling you again. Eating dinner?"

"Yes."

"What did you make?"

She knew the real answer. "I bought potatoes and green beans from the market. They still had soil on them. Very fresh."

"Good, good."

Mr. Dupree spoke next, asking her briefly about her classes, but then the conversation turned sour as her parents started making assumptions about her fortune. "We found a nice bakery that would be a superb place to order your wedding cake from. It's called Sweet Crumblier," Mr. Dupree said. "They passed our inspection with flying colors. A hard thing to do, as you know. Their specialty is violet macarons, which might actually make a good alternative if some of our guests don't like chocolate cake."

"Finding a dress will be much harder," Mrs. Dupree said. "We'll need Robbie's help. We don't want you walking down the aisle in polyester, do we?"

"What are you going on about? I haven't even told you my fortune yet."

Fallon felt choked by their expectations as they planned the imaginary wedding they expected Fallon to have. Like her brother. Like the rest of the family, who consistently married young.

"Well, go on then," Mrs. Dupree said with a sniff. "It will be easier to talk about cake and dresses when we have something tangible to work with."

"I agree. Tell us. What did your fortune say?" Mr. Dupree said.

Fallon's jaw worked. The truth wouldn't come out. It was stuck in her throat, digging its heels into her bones.

"Fallon? Are you still there?"

"Yes," she croaked. "Zita's fortune said I had to be patient."

"You're kidding," Mrs. Dupree said.

"I guess I won't be meeting my future boyfriend this year," she said, trying to joke.

"There must be something wrong with the machine," Mrs. Dupree said. Her words spun faster as worry and annoyance interlaced. "How could my little girl be denied our family tradition?"

"Maybe she's not our child," Mr. Dupree said. A bad joke. It only upset Mrs. Dupree more.

"It's okay," Fallon insisted. "There's always next year. It's not a bad fortune, after all. There are worse." Like the fortune she really got.

"It's a stale fortune," Mrs. Dupree said. The sound of her blowing her nose rattled through the phone. "It means you're stuck, Fallon. You shouldn't be stuck."

"I know, Mom. I know."

"I worry about you. Next thing I know, you'll be back for winter break with a suitcase full of prepackaged sandwiches."

Fallon snorted. "Not going to happen. I'm following your rules. Always quality."

"Always quality," Mr. Dupree repeated with a proud voice. "There now, dear. Nothing to concern yourself over. We'll have to be patient, just as Zita says."

Just as Zita says. Fallon gripped the receiver tighter.

By the time she got off the phone with her parents, Fallon felt achy all over. A shower would solve the problem, she thought, so she quickly grabbed her nightclothes and let the hot water melt the knots in her shoulders. Gradually, her sweet lemon body wash distracted her from thoughts of her parents' premature wedding plans. Suds hid her skin. Her eyes burned from soap, not tears, and she had to stand under the showerhead for a few minutes before she could open her eyes again.

An idea came.

She emerged from the shower in a hurry, her short hair clumped and dripping, and threw on the first thing at hand. Her pajamas were boyish, with pink-and-purple stripes shot through with silver. Fallon took the velvet bathrobe her mother had bought her for her birthday last year and slipped it on. She tied the sash snuggly at her waist. Even though the bathrobe had set her mother back a paycheck due to its authentic crushed velvet material, Fallon didn't think anything of the fact that it dragged in the dirt on her way to Anais's.

chapter 5

READING MATERIAL

Anais's father received a lot of strange deliveries as a drugstore owner. "Look at it this way," Anais had explained, "a drugstore is a weird and wonderful place. You never know what we're selling. And yet, we always sell what you need. How do you think that happens? It's not magic. It's persistence."

Persistence in the form of small-time inventors and companies plaguing Mr. Jacobs with shipments of their products. Every Monday morning, a truck would park outside the store with a new set of boxes and manila envelopes. Mr. Jacobs carefully opened everything, considered the products, and usually wrote back brisk rejections in the same day. Mondays were slow.

Sometimes Mr. Jacobs liked what he'd been sent. Last year, he had decided to carry tweezers shaped like Zodiac animals. He sold ready-made sandwiches from down-on-their-luck chefs and shower caps patterned with monster trucks (those hadn't sold very well). Yet, much to Anais's annoyance, her father kept every sample he ever received. The stockroom was hopelessly cluttered.

Mr. Jacobs might have saved love-charm contraband, whether he knew it or not. Since Fallon had no other leads at this point, it was worth trying out. The night was surprisingly warm, or maybe it was the insulated weight of the bathrobe. She checked the clock hanging in the window of an antiques store and was startled to find that it was almost 11:00 P.M. People still roamed the streets; some gave her strange looks as she passed, but she understood the attention. If this had been any other night, she would have already been asleep in her bed. She tightened her sash and entered the store.

The drugstore's atmosphere was oddly sleepy for a weeknight. Her shoes stuck to the tile floor. A fluorescent light above the freezer section flickered like a twitching eye. Voices from Anais's portable radio whispered through the aisles. She found Anais with her head bent toward the little radio.

"Is your father asleep?" she asked.

Anais nodded. "If he wasn't, I'd be blasting this station. Hard-boiled Hal's talk show is coming up in a few minutes. I hate having to listen like this. Makes me feel like I'm doing something covert."

Fallon wanted to laugh at that. Just yesterday, she'd joined a rebellion.

Anais peeled her eyes away from the radio long enough to take in Fallon's clothes. "What's wrong?"

"Nothing's wrong."

"Uh-huh. Then how do you explain the bathrobe? And are those pajamas underneath? The Fallon I know would rather eat the cafeteria's frozen chicken nuggets than show up in public with her jammies on."

"I have a favor to ask."

Anais's lips curled. "I'm intrigued."

"If you have time," she started, noticing that no one else was in the store, "please let me into the storeroom. I want to see if your father saved any old magazines or books sent to him."

"The storeroom is a mess, but Dad's got his own system. He might get upset if you move things around."

"If I find what I'm looking for, I'd be happy to pay for it."

"Of course you would. I'm just not sure if . . ." Anais's thought strayed when a three-note tune announced the beginning of the talk show. She inched the dial up further and Hard-boiled Hal's amiable voice filled the store:

You won't find anything sappy on our show. Stick around, grab a beer, and we'll talk about the other things that matter in life. Yes, other things do matter.

"He says that every night," Anais explained, chuckling. "I wish you'd stay up sometimes. You don't know what you're missing. I may be happily dating someone, but even I can appreciate Hard-boiled Hal's no-romance policy. It's awfully refreshing."

Fallon knew she wouldn't get anywhere with Anais glued to Hard-boiled Hal's voice. They listened for a few minutes. Grimbaud's high schoolers loved his radio show, ironically titled *Hard-boiled Hal's Practical Guide to Love*. His show had nothing to do with love except for the avoidance of it; he urged his listeners to embrace their unromantic sides. Words like "pink" and "hearts" and "pet names" were banned from vocabulary. He even had a monthly segment where he talked about the merits of farting and burping in front of the opposite sex. "Zita would powder me in glitter and candy if she knew who I was," he said, chuckling. "Too bad for her. I choose to remain happily unwashed and unappealing, a constant thorn in her side. Just the way I like it."

Fallon knew the appeal of such a show. Hard-boiled Hal served as a shrewd, pragmatic conscience in a town practically dotty with thoughts of love. He offered the townspeople relief from the pressures of Zita's love fortunes—as long as his identity remained secret.

As Hard-boiled Hal divulged his opinion on why giving lace as romantic gifts was a terrible idea, the front door jingled.

Anais, a smidge taller behind the counter, turned a deathly shade of white. "I'm not here," she said, ducking underneath the counter.

"What are you talking about?"

"It's Bear," she hissed. "Don't let him see me!"

Fallon stood on her toes and saw Bear enter the drugstore. Sweat darkened his muscle shirt. He wiped his upper lip with the back of his hand and headed straight for the fridges. Headphones covered his ears, keeping him insulated in his own world—he hadn't even turned his head to look at the counter when he came in. "What do you want me to do?"

"Pretend you work here."

"In my bathrobe?"

"Make something up!"

Fallon sighed and turned down the volume on Hard-boiled Hal's show.

Bear grabbed a drink from the fridge and made his way to the counter. His eyes widened when he saw Fallon, as if waking from a long sleep. "Hey, Fallon, right? Anais's friend?"

"That's me," Fallon said as cheerfully as she could.

"I didn't think you'd work in a place like this," he said, taking a second look at the sticky floors and flickering lights.

Fallon's cheeks burned, and for once, she was thankful that the lighting was unreliable. If Bear was surprised, her parents would have been mortified. "I know what you mean, but I'm trying some jobs out. I can already tell that I'm not cut out for being a drugstore cashier. It's kind of scary to be working by myself in the middle of the night."

"Oh. How long is your shift? I can wait for you."

Fallon felt Anais's hand squeeze her ankle from under the counter. "Thank you, but that's okay. I have to grow up sometime."

"But not from doing this job," he said, smiling.

"Right."

Bear slid the blue drink across the counter toward her; it was one of those energy drinks that left you wide-eyed and ready for another round of grueling training in the sport of your choice. Before she could fumble with the cash register, he eyed a display on the shelf behind her and pointed. "Wait. Can I get one of those biscuit tins too?"

Anais let out a whine.

"Sure," Fallon said loudly. She stomped a little for extra coverage and stood on her toes to get the tin. "Chocolate-covered or plain?"

"Chocolate," Bear said.

Fallon hid her smirk. The rectangular tin fit in the palms of her hands, holding only about a dozen chocolate-covered biscuits baked by Peak & Brown's. Situated just outside of town, the factory gave off the scents of crumbly biscuits and bittersweet chocolate. Thankfully, the student housing complex was nowhere near the factory, so Fallon didn't have to be tortured daily by mass-produced temptations. Peak & Brown's tins were collectibles. The tin she took off the shelf was decorated with gold-and-turquoise filigree; in the center, a charming little girl with blond curls beamed.

"My mom collects them," Bear said, pulling money from his pockets. "I don't think she has that one yet."

"That's nice of you."

"You don't understand. Our dining room walls are covered in Peak & Brown's tins. I broke one of the shelves when I was kid while wrestling with my little brothers. When my mom discovered the bent tins all over the floor, she refused to speak to me for six months."

"Really?"

"Really. I hate them." Bear looked away, embarrassed.

"But I keep buying them because they make my mom happy."

Anais whimpered. Fallon tapped her fingers on the tin to mask the sound. "So not even the little girl can make you think kindly on the biscuits?"

"That face haunts me." He shuddered. "Can you bag that?"

Fallon tried recalling whatever memories she had of Anais and her father operating the cash register, but it was no use. "Sorry, I still can't get this thing to work," she said. Grabbing a piece of scrap paper and a pencil, she added up the prices, plus tax, and had Bear look it over. "I hope you don't need a receipt."

"Nah. It's okay." He took the bag and dug some coins out of his pocket for exact change. "I've got five more miles to run before heading home, so I better go."

Fallon waved and watched him leave. At the sound of the door closing, Anais popped back up. Her cheeks were smeared with tears.

"Did you hear that?" Anais blubbered. "He hates her. He hates me!"

"Don't overreact. It's just a tin."

"Peak and Brown's has ruined my life, I tell you." She plucked a tissue from her pocket and blew her nose.

"Didn't Zita's love fortune insist that you be yourself? You need to share everything with Bear if you want to keep him." Fallon gestured at the store and then the tins. "Everything."

"No way. I can handle this, Fallon." Anais mopped up

her face and fixed her hair. She still looked endearing, even with the splotchy red skin. "No one I date ever has to know my horrible secrets. I am simply Anais Jacobs, a normal girl whose face is *not* printed on biscuit tins."

Fallon shrugged. When Anais was stubborn, as she was most of the time, it was hard to get through to her. And it wasn't as if this was the first time they'd had a conversation about Anais's "horrible secrets." The first secret was, of course, her grubby father and the drugstore—no boyfriend of hers should ever know she was associated with it. But the bigger secret was that Anais was, in fact, the little girl on the Peak & Brown's tin.

When Anais was a toddler, she had been spotted by a marketing representative from Peak & Brown's. In the middle of the supermarket, the Peak & Brown's representative knelt down on one knee, examined the giggling toddler with a magnifying glass, and offered Anais's father a substantial amount of money if he'd allow Anais to become their mascot. She had been photographed and painted at least a hundred times over the course of a week so that her likeness could be preserved for the future history of the bakery. Anais's toddler-self haunted her over the years, a source of misery rather than pride. "I don't have such rosy cheeks," she'd say, stabbing at the tin with her index finger, "and I can't make my eyes twinkle like that anymore."

"I know you're upset," Fallon said, catching the last drop of mucus with her own tissue, "but your secret is still safe, thanks to me. Will you open the storeroom?"

Anais glared at the tins on the wall and nodded. "Remember what I said. Don't touch anything unless you're taking it with you."

Fallon woke with a paper cut on her cheek. Uncurling herself from her sheets, still tucked neatly at the corners, she sat up and scratched off the dried blood. The culprit lay on the pillow next to her: an ancient teenage girls' magazine boasting tips on how to dress for a first date.

She switched off her alarm and groaned, tired from hours of sifting through Mr. Jacobs's storeroom. Anais had been telling the truth about the storeroom: it was a mess, covered in cobwebs and piles that only just made sense if you looked closely at how items were grouped. Fallon had pinched her nose as she rounded corners, avoiding the cheese samples that reeked despite still being wrapped in plastic. Mr. Jacobs had a section for books, but the only ones he had been sent were humorous or useful like a turnip cookbook or a guide on five ways to mow your lawn with your eyes closed.

Fallon had taken magazines aimed toward girls and women. The magazines, full of advice, would surely contain charms to attract crushes or deal with exes. She had looked at a few men's magazines too, but they seemed focused more on hobbies than on doling out love advice. She had promised Anais that she would give back the magazines she didn't use, and pay for the ones she did. So far, Fallon feared that she'd have to give back the entire stack. No charms in sight.

After returning to the complex with her arms full of magazines, Fallon had washed her hands and face thoroughly and set to work, moving through the pile. She made it through three fat magazines before falling asleep. Her dreams had swarmed with designer shoes, exercise routines, and quizzes.

School would start with or without her. Fallon took a shower, prepared and ate breakfast, and barely made it out the door in time.

"How's the charm-hunting?" Mirthe asked.

Fallon pressed against the lockers, avoiding a flock of students newly released from gym class. "I was able to find some old magazines shipped from out of town. They've been decaying in someone's storeroom."

"Have you searched them yet?"

"Not all of them."

Mirthe pursed her lips. "Femke and I are going to start our own hunt tomorrow night, but we're going to need your help for that to work."

"How?"

"Well, our parents will be out all night. Thursdays are date nights for them. Tradition." She rolled her eyes but grinned. "Anyway, it's the perfect chance for Femke and me to ride our moped out of here and peruse Lambrechts's shops. There's just one problem. Student government starts up on Thursday night."

"Are you an officer?"

"You've never been to a meeting?" Mirthe cocked her head. "I would have sworn that someone like you would be in many clubs."

Fallon brushed off the remark. Since when did good grades and ironed clothes equate club membership? She was too busy for clubs. "Well, I'm not. Nico is treasurer this year."

"But since he's an officer, he can't represent a club. That's where you come in. Each club has to have two representatives attend each month's meeting. If we're not there, our club will be suspended. It's important that our cover be maintained. I've already asked Sebastian if he'll go and he agreed. We need one more person and Hijiri seems to have disappeared on me."

Her mood soured when she heard his name. "Are you sure this can't wait? I think I have something to do—"

Mirthe gripped Fallon's hands. "Not one second can go by. Consider everything we do urgent. The school year's just begun and the fortunes will have their way with us soon."

"Okay, okay."

"Good. The meeting's at seven in the round room. It's late, but you can always walk over with Sebastian."

Fallon grimaced.

"Represent our fine charm-maker's club well."

After school, Fallon spotted Sebastian out by the basketball court. He leaned against the fence with his hands in his pockets, his pant legs rolled up above his ankles. He had his eyes closed, as if savoring the taste of the breeze rolling through.

She started walking toward him. Maybe she could convince him to help her look for Hijiri, so that the girl could take his place at the student government meeting. Fallon decided that she wanted to support Nico, since he'd be facing both Martin and Camille that night. Sebastian couldn't have cared much about the meeting; it would be easy to talk him out of going. But as her feet took her closer to Sebastian, she heard giggling.

Three girls swinging their backpacks called out to him, "Bastion, what are you doing?"

He opened one eye and frowned.

One of the girls, pretty with blond hair in a braid, split from the group and placed her hand on his chest. She peered up at him, saying something that made him smirk. Fallon stared at the girl's hand, the way it rested over the fabric framing his heart. Sebastian drew the girl into a hug. Her friends stood there watching, giggling between their fingers, as if everyone had won an award by capturing Sebastian's attention.

Before Fallon could look away, she saw Sebastian lift the girl's chin. He kissed her with one hand still in his pocket, his face as smooth as a blank sheet of paper.

She felt sick. It wouldn't be so bad if he and that girl were dating, Fallon thought, swallowing hard. But she knew as well as anyone at school that Bastion only dated in pretense. He may have been a good kisser, but with her eyes closed, the girl couldn't see how little Sebastian cared. He was the kind of boy Fallon never rooted for in the movies. The boy who usually lost because his heart wasn't in the right place. Sebastian's heart was unknowable.

Fallon told herself not to worry. Bastion was strong, but she had an entire fortress around her heart. She refused to share it with someone who kissed girls freely and led them on, only to dump them when they got too close. He wouldn't get to her.

Sebastian wiped his lips on the back of his sleeve, causing the girl and her friends to yell at him. He saw Fallon. "Hey," he called.

Fallon turned on her heel. As she walked away, she heard Bastion's name turn to poison. Another girl disappointed in him.

chapter 6

THE MINUTES

" 'Here are three steps to making up with your boyfriend,' " Fallon read, staring at the glossy magazine page. " 'First, set up a time to meet alone. Friends will only get in the way if you want to have a real heart-to-heart talk with him.' "

She sighed. After spending the last hour wading through more magazines, she'd only found vapid advice articles and fashion spreads. The clothing interested her, with wide-eyed models lifting their legs like cranes in front of city buildings and forests. Based on the prices of the clothes listed on each page, one would expect high quality. But Fallon wasn't so sure. Price was an old trick. What would Robbie think of these clothes? With just one look, her brother would know which blouse was cheap and which pencil skirt was quality.

Since school had cleared out hours ago, Fallon didn't shy away from reading the magazine in plain sight. No one was around, save for a janitor mopping the floor at the other end of the hallway. With the door to the round room locked, Fallon had made do by sitting on the damp, newly cleaned floor.

The round room had been named after its donut-shaped interior, reserved only for special presentations or student government functions. Three rows of wooden tables situated in stadium seating surrounded the middle of the room where guest speakers took advantage of the great acoustics. She could understand why the administration wouldn't let students wear down the furnishings with everyday use.

"Are you here for the student government meeting?" asked Martin, walking towards her. Being the student government president gave him the privilege of using the spare key.

Fallon shoved the magazine in her bag. "Yes."

"First one here," he said, almost sadly. But then, none of the officers were there with him.

"Where's Nico?"

"Who?"

"Nicolas Barnes."

"Oh." Martin's confusion gave way to a smile. "Sorry. I didn't know he had a nickname. Nicolas said he'd pick up coffee for the officers. He didn't have to. That's very kind of him."

Not even the teachers called him Nicolas. Fallon bit back a laugh. "You should call him Nico, if you can. Everyone does."

Martin scratched the back of his neck. "Are you his friend?"

She nodded. "Fallon Dupree. I'm representing the charm-making club."

"You don't look familiar," Martin said. He unlocked the door. "Is this your first meeting?"

"Yes."

"Then you'll learn that everyone dreads these meetings. Even the officers. I try my best, but I can't seem to make them any less dull," he said.

She glanced at the clock in the hall. Almost seven.

"They'll trickle in late."

After Martin flicked the light switch, a dozen fluorescent lights buzzed to life. The round room smelled musty, a comfortable scent mingled with lemon cleaner. Photographs of Grimbaud High students from long past covered the back walls. Skylights, useless at night, revealed the darkening sky. Fallon took a seat in the front row and opened to a clean page in her notebook. Martin claimed the podium and unpacked his papers.

After ten minutes, students began filling the room. Conversations echoed. Officers shook hands and sat at the desk beside the podium.

Martin took off his thick-framed glasses and wiped them with his shirt. Since the room was already too loud, he turned on the microphone and warned everyone that the meeting would start in five minutes.

"Coffee's here!" Nico said, lugging a brown paper case

with six coffees. He caught Fallon's eye on the walk down to the podium and flashed a nervous grin.

With only a few empty seats here and there, she worried that Sebastian would have to sit on the floor. Where was he? She didn't think he was prone to being late, except perhaps for dramatic effect, but no one would be paying attention to him at this meeting. Too many clubs. Fallon turned in her seat and scanned the two rows behind her.

Sebastian sat in the last row near the door. He frowned deeply, as if she were the one who was late, and gestured to the empty chair beside him.

No way, Fallon thought. Why sit in the back when she had a perfectly good view of the officers? The seat to her right wasn't yet taken, so she pointed at it and then at him.

Sebastian mouthed, "I don't do front rows," and sat back in his chair.

"You'd better move," Nico said, resting his elbows on the desk. "Each club gets a chance to speak at these meetings and it'll be hard to confer when you're miles away from each other."

"Do you want him to win?" Fallon asked.

"Just trying to help. Meeting's going to start."

She lowered her voice. "Without Camille? I noticed she wasn't here yet."

"Don't remind me. I wish we could have just one meeting without her, but I doubt she'd leave Martin alone so soon after the breakup," he said bitterly.

Fallon chewed her lip. Nico's anxiety rolled off him in

waves. "Hey," she said, touching his elbow, "Did he like the coffee?"

"I'm not sure. I thought he did, but Martin kind of stuttered when he thanked me. Like he was going to say something else."

"I told him to call you Nico."

He let out a surprised laugh. "Yeah, it was when he said my name. I'm still Nicolas. My president's too proper for nicknames."

"Well, be persistent. Miracles do happen."

"Like you moving to the back row?"

She grimaced. "I guess I should set a good example for you."

As Nico returned to his table, Fallon grabbed her notebook and bag and climbed the steps up to the third row. She plopped down into the chair and refused to give Sebastian the satisfaction of seeing her frown.

As Martin started his welcome speech, Fallon caught Sebastian sticking his hand in her bag. He pulled out the magazine and placed it on the desk between them. "Research?" he asked.

Fallon slapped her hand on the page. "Do you mind?"

"Where did you leave off?"

She sighed. "Page fifty-five."

He flipped through the pages to find an advertisement for perfume. "Not quite a charm," he murmured, "though all fragrances promise romance, don't they?"

"Be quiet."

"We're in the back for a reason. That's what I like about it: being on the fringe of the action."

As Fallon jotted down notes, the door next to her seat opened. Camille Simmons stepped inside. She hadn't bothered to change out of her work uniform; Zita's standard pink dress and silver high heels sparkled under the fluorescent lights.

Camille crossed her arms and waited by the door, as if expecting the meeting to come to a grinding halt in her presence. But then she caught Fallon staring. "I remember you," she said, not bothering to moderate her voice. "The girl with the bad fortune. I see you took my advice about the magazines . . . yet, they haven't helped. Better keep reading."

Fallon's face burned.

Sebastian turned the pages loudly. He spoke to Camille with his typical bored tone. "This magazine has some great advice about handling exes. Maybe Martin would like to read it."

Camille's smirk shattered. She knocked the magazine off the table. The sound startled the secretary, who had been reading last year's final meeting minutes aloud. All eyes swiveled to Camille. "Sorry I'm late," she said loudly, rebuilding her false smile in seconds. She glided down the steps and shoved Nico's chair over so she could sit next to Martin.

Fallon touched her cheeks, feeling the lingering embarrassment there.

Sebastian calmly plucked the magazine off the floor.

Tension stretched thin as the student government meeting continued. The news of Camille and Martin's breakup was about as widespread as Sebastian's rotation of girlfriends. All eyes were on Camille as she pulled out a pink pen and chewed on the cap. Her arm and thigh pressed against Martin, but the president pretended not to notice. Nico sulked, his chin falling to his chest as he studied, perhaps too closely, the stack of bank statements in front of him.

Club representatives took turns talking about what their clubs did and any concerns they might have for the new school year. Fallon didn't know what Femke and Mirthe would have wanted her to say about the club, but she tried to make it sound as dull as possible.

After introducing herself and Sebastian, Fallon stood up like the previous representatives. "There are quite a few charm clubs already, but our club focuses on the study of how charms are created. We do this by gathering every week to go over formulas and recipes, as well as popular theories. By the time we're done debating these matters, we rarely get to make the charms themselves. So, I guess you could say we're focused on theory."

A few attendees groaned. Camille smirked and wrote something on her paper. She pushed it over to Martin, who turned away.

"What do you hope to accomplish this year?" the secretary asked.

To overthrow Zita, she thought. "We're actually planning

on making some field trips to meet other charm-makers in the community. Our copresidents Femke and Mirthe De Keyser agreed to give us a tour of their parents' weather-charm business, but we hope to find other members of the community to learn from as well."

Sebastian, still sitting, made a noise of approval.

The secretary smiled slightly. "Thank you. Next club."

Fallon's job was over now that she'd spoken for the club. Hopefully she wouldn't attract more members or any unnecessary attention from the student government officers. At least Nico was an officer; he could warn them if anyone, namely Camille, came snooping around the club.

When she sat down, Sebastian gave her the magazine. Jeans to fit all body types took up a six-page spread, but a quiz made her pause. The quiz was titled "How Visible Are You to Your Crush?" At the bottom of the page, beyond the point tally and evaluations, she found a small blurb that made her skin prickle:

Catching your crush's eye isn't as hard as you think. When your crush is near, say the phrase, "Confidence, Confidence, Unveil Me" out loud. Strength will flow through your body and that energy will capture your crush's attention. Just make sure to use the opportunity you're given!

This charm wasn't about attraction, but about building the confidence to act on one's feelings. She had no trouble expressing her feelings—not that she had ever had to do it romantically—but she didn't experience the anxiety that Hijiri evidently suffered when talking to people.

She didn't have a crush, but she decided to try the charm anyway. When the basketball club representatives boasted about last year's victory at the national high school competition, the room erupted in merriment. Perfect to mask her words. "Confidence, confidence, unveil me," she said. A surge of warmth spread through her body, making her fingers and toes tingle. A cobweb-like net lifted off her skin and she was naked and utterly fearless underneath.

Camille suddenly stopped cheering; her eyes narrowed and swept across the room.

"Look down," Sebastian whispered, slapping a folder over her magazine to hide it.

She dismissed his warning as soon as she heard it; confidence was a heady thing. Fallon cupped her hands over her mouth and let out a hearty cheer with the other students. She stomped her feet. When she shot a bold look at the student government table, Camille's eyes locked with hers. Fallon's breath caught. Camille's mouth curled. Dread poked its way through the charm's grip.

With the other officers distracted from the ruckus, Nico reached the podium and turned on the microphone. The feedback stopped the rowdiness; amplified by the acoustics of the room, it sounded like hundreds of crying cats at once. "Save your cheering for the games, guys! We don't want the administration hearing us," Nico said.

Martin stood up, knocking Camille off balance. "Thank you, Nicolas. It's a privilege to be using this room. Let's continue."

Nico's ears turned red as he shuffled back to his seat.

The energy from the charm drained out of Fallon. She sat back down.

"What were you thinking?" Sebastian hissed. "You can't do that, especially when one of Zita's employees is here."

Guilt filled the gaps where her burning confidence had been. Fallon swallowed loudly. "I didn't think it was real."

"Well, at least we know you found one," he said.

"Sorry."

"Don't apologize to me. I'm not mad, really. You just scared me."

Fallon couldn't imagine scaring anyone, though her family's strict adherence to quality was sometimes uncomfortable for people who didn't put limits on what they wore, ate, and lived in. Harder still was picturing Sebastian scared of her—the girl he declared a princess. "Did you sense it?"

He nodded. "There was something pulling at me. When I looked at you, you started . . . glowing."

Glowing? Did everyone see that? Was she exposed already?

"Not literally," he hastened to add.

"But you knew that I wasn't just me."

"That's right."

As the rest of the clubs took their turns, Fallon dog-eared the page with the charm and refused to read the rest of the magazine while Camille might be looking. Working at Zita's must have made Camille extra sensitive to love charms. Fallon rubbed her arms. Did Zita train her employees to sniff out stray love charms? What happened to those who were caught? No one in Grimbaud had used alternative love charms since her grandparents' day, and what she'd heard about Zita establishing such a monopoly was vague. *One day she set up shop and everyone loved her love charms and fortunes so much that they gave up all others. Simple. Or was it?*

The meeting wound down with the secretary reading the semester's meeting dates and times off the agenda. Then last questions and concerns. As chairs slid back and chatter rose, Martin asked for the officers to stay behind for a few minutes.

Fallon jumped out of her chair to meet Nico before the officers started their own meeting.

"How'd I do?" Nico said, leaning against the officer desk. "The microphone was a pain, but at least it woke up the gardening club representatives in the front. Who falls asleep in the front row, anyway?"

As the officers gathered around the podium, Camille stole Martin's attention. She leaned over the mike to stroke his hand as she talked about something that made him laugh.

"Are you okay?"

He shrugged. "I might buy coffee cake on the way home. Works better than ice cream."

"Good idea."

"This could take a while. Have Sebastian walk with you."

"I can go home by myself."

Nico crossed his arms. "It's after eight and a long walk back to the complex. Don't be stubborn."

She sighed.

"Besides, you look tired. Did something happen?"

Fallon resisted the urge to show him the magazine. Not with Camille standing only a few inches away. "I'll tell you tomorrow."

chapter 7

CATCHING QUIET

"Can we stop at this café?" Fallon asked. Her stomach growled. The evening was comfortably cool, but she still shivered underneath her blazer as they headed home. The beans and noodles she had packed in her lunch box would have normally been enough to hold her, but for some reason she was starving.

Sebastian stepped up to the window and read the advertisement. "Organic ingredients. Made to order. Wouldn't you rather have something greasy and freezer-burned?"

If her mother had heard Sebastian, she would have fainted dead away on the street.

"There's a food truck usually parked about a block from here."

"This is more my style."

Sebastian opened the door, releasing the scent of arugula and spices into the air. "After you."

The café wasn't too crowded, so Fallon and Sebastian

waited for their spinach-and-pepper quiche at one of the tables near the kitchen. Being inside the café distracted her from the fatigue that gnawed at her bones. He must have sensed her mood because Sebastian refrained from making any irritating remarks until after they had swallowed every crumbly piece of quiche.

"I feel better," Fallon said. She finished her cup of water.

"Student government meetings get the best of everyone," Sebastian said, "but you could be suffering the aftereffects of a charm. Have you ever used one before?"

She lowered her voice. "Not a love charm. What about you?"

"Never."

"Does your fortune prevent you from buying them at Zita's shop?"

Sebastian wiped his hands on a napkin. His voice fell flat. "Yes."

She knew better than to press him for more information. As much as he seemed to have enjoyed the quiche, it hadn't been magical enough to loosen his tongue. "That's too bad. Femke and Mirthe have clearly denied themselves the satisfaction, but I'm sure the shop would sell Hijiri something."

Sebastian's expression clouded. "What did Camille mean when she said she gave you advice about magazines?"

Maybe it was the cozy café or the streetlamps outside that shone so gently on the pavement that calmed her. Her heart wasn't beating in her ears. She told Sebastian about the day she had gotten her bad fortune and how she ran into Zita's shop, frantic for a solution. Camille had suggested that Fallon's lack of attractiveness was the root cause of the bad fortune. "After today, it's clear that Camille doesn't believe the magazine world can save me," she said.

He balled up his napkin. "Fallon," he said, "are you feeling well enough to take a detour?"

"I don't know."

"Come on. You found a charm already. I think I'm onto one."

If he was trying to make her feel better, he had an odd way of doing it. Fallon got up from her seat and stretched. Nothing ached. She felt awake and full. Plus, if she went with Sebastian, she might learn something more about what forms the old love charms came in. They couldn't all be in magazines. "All right, but we can't be out too late. I still have to make lunch for tomorrow."

Sebastian lifted an eyebrow. "Sandwiches don't take long."

"Is that what you bring to school?" She laughed. "I *cook* my lunch. Using ovens and pans. Things like that."

He seemed mystified by that. "I haven't touched a stove in years."

She doubted he cleaned them either.

⊱─▷

Far from the main roads, Sebastian led her through neighborhoods lit by streetlamps and windows. Low stone walls separated the houses from the street; most people let their gardens grow tall enough for flowers and ivy to hang over the sides. Both big and small houses modeled themselves off of Grimbaud's decorative architecture. Most houses were brick with paneled windows in shades of teal or coral. Cupids lounged above doorways. Front lawns usually had at least one wire stork, especially when a family lived inside. Fallon pictured the people living in the houses she passed; she didn't like to peek in windows—it felt like an invasion of privacy—but Sebastian held no such qualms. He stopped periodically to stand on his toes, leaning on the wall to scan the properties.

"What are you doing?"

Sebastian plucked a scarlet begonia and twirled it between his fingers. "I'm trying to remember the house. An elderly couple owns it. When I asked them for directions, they told me to look for the house covered in storks."

"But everyone has storks."

"Apparently, we're looking for an armada of storks. Can't miss it."

"Don't you have better directions?"

Sebastian's mouth lifted into a half smile. He leaned forward and tucked the begonia behind her ear. "They live right next to the middle school. We're almost there."

The begonia's petals felt like a kiss against her skin. Fallon blushed and plucked it out of her hair. Instead of dropping it on the ground, she put it in her blazer pocket.

Grimbaud Middle School did not have the appeal or history of the high school. The building was made of dull brown brick with small windows and a chain-link fence all around. Since she only came to Grimbaud to attend high school, Fallon didn't know what the inside of the building was like. *I didn't have to get my rotten love fortune so early either,* she thought with some relief.

Sebastian was a few steps ahead of her. He stopped outside of a white-brick house. The stone wall right outside it was decorated with little stork figurines. The figurines seemed to be melded to the stone; they wouldn't budge when Fallon tugged on one. When she lifted her eyes, she finally understood what Sebastian meant: storks besieged the entire lawn.

Sebastian opened the gate and they walked carefully up to the front door. Fallon almost got her skirt caught on the beak of a wooden stork. An old man wearing a beanie and a long white beard answered the door. "We've been expecting you," he said, introducing himself as Jonas Maes.

"I hope I'm not too late," Sebastian said. He wiped his shoes on the welcome mat.

"Not at all."

Fallon introduced herself to Jonas. She knew nothing of how this visit would bring them a love charm, so she decided to let Sebastian lead.

"Pleasure to meet you. My wife, Mathilde, and I are happy to share our story with you. Sebastian told us about his history project, gathering stories from around Grimbaud. We even found some photos of us when we were younger that can go into your presentation."

Sebastian shook his head. "We're not allowed to use photos, but thank you."

Despite the mustering of storks outside, the inside of the house was neat and welcoming. Floral wallpaper livened up the plain furniture and a large patchwork quilt hung opposite the television set. Fallon sunk into a brown chair that matched her uniform while Sebastian opened his schoolbag. He rummaged around until he found a silver tape recorder. Then he opened up a packet of blank cassettes and wrote on the first one with small, mashed lettering.

"For the project," he said, pinning Fallon with a don't-argue-with-me look.

Fallon shrugged.

Mathilde Maes emerged from the kitchen with a tray of glasses filled with apple juice. She had arranged the Peak & Brown's biscuits into the shape of a fan. Her hair was as long and scraggily as Jonas's beard. "Please get comfortable. We could be here for hours!"

"She's joking," Jonas said. He sat down in the chair beneath the quilt and scratched his head through the beanie. "Our love story is very simple, but nonetheless magical."

Sebastian sat cross-legged on the floor beside Fallon's chair and placed the recorder on the coffee table. The red button on the recorder glowed when he turned it on. "Jonas and Mathilde Maes, I understand that you met before Zita's shop opened. Can you tell us about that?"

The loose question allowed the Maeses to start wherever they liked, which, to Fallon's disappointment, meant rambling about their childhoods instead of about the shop. When they finally got around to talking about the charm that brought them together, she sat up straighter in her chair.

"Love charms were everywhere, for anyone to find and use," Mathilde said. "In some ways, it was harder being in love when we grew up because the temptation to use them all was great. Everyone had their favorite love charm shops. But for the most part, using them was risky. Love charms used to cause more trouble than good. The police couldn't keep track of the havoc caused by them, which used to be pretty funny to watch."

"They were more clowns than policemen," Jonas said, grinning. "Always getting caught in the cross fire of a lovers' spat. Then Zita's shop changed everything."

"Too bad I was already engaged when her love charms really took off. I would have trusted Zita with my money. Her love charms are more stable and powerful than the ones we had as kids," Mathilde said.

Fallon shifted uncomfortably in her chair. She had a hard time believing that love-charm production had been as chaotic as Mathilde said.

"I was the insecure one." Jonas said. "When Mathilde told me that she would be moving after graduation, the news tore me apart. I couldn't imagine being parted from her. So I used a charm that's been passed down through the middle school for ages. Too bad the young folks can't use it anymore."

Mathilde swatted his shoulder. "You don't know if that stupid charm worked anyway."

"It did! You didn't move after all."

"My father found another job in town. He was lucky," she insisted.

Sebastian waited patiently for their bickering to end. "What was the charm?"

Jonas explained that in middle school, it was tradition to steal your crush's lock off the locker and hang it on the northwest corner of the fence before sunset. If you did, you and your crush would end up together—and stay together always.

"You don't know how many thefts were made because of that charm," Mathilde said dryly.

"Were there any limitations on this love charm?"

Jonas nodded. "It only worked for middle schoolers. Once you graduated, it was too late to try the charm."

"Personally, I don't think it worked at all. It was just an excuse for bravery. Jonas seemed more relaxed after stealing my lock, so it was easy to get him to open up to me more. I fell more in love with him the longer I spent time with him. That's the magic."

"Oh, Mathilde."

Another question burned on Fallon's tongue. "Did you ever see Zita? In person?"

The old couple exchanged a glance. "No."

Sebastian turned off the recorder and held it in his hand as they walked out the door. Fallon looked back at her untouched glass of apple juice, wondering what brand it had been. *Never eat or drink anything you haven't seen in the packaging when you're a houseguest*, her mother always said. But part of her felt guilty to have ignored Mathilde's hospitality.

"The storks are quite a sight," she said as they said good-bye.

Mathilde flashed a sad smile. "Storks bring babies, so we thought that having a lot of them around would help me get pregnant. Collecting them became a hobby, then something desperate, and before we knew it, Jonas and I couldn't walk inside our house without stepping on one. So they're outside now, for better or for worse."

Fallon felt like she had to ask. "Did you have a child?"

The old woman shook her head. "It was impossible. But then, eventually we came to accept it."

"I'm sorry."

"Don't be. There are some facts you can't change."

A lump formed in Fallon's throat. Just looking at the storks made her want to cry.

Fallon's energy fell as soon as she and Sebastian had said good-bye to the Maeses. Whatever was in the quiche that helped her wake up had run out, and she found her vision blurring as they treaded sidewalks and ran across the cobblestone streets.

About three miles from the complex, Sebastian left the pavement just as they were going to cross a bridge.

Fallon blinked. "Where are you going now?"

Sebastian pressed a finger to his lips.

Maybe he'd found another charm. Curious, Fallon forced her feet to follow him.

Grass grew on either side of the bridge, mixed with infallible weeds and food wrappers. The ground dipped as it led underneath the bridge. Sebastian took off his blazer and laid it on the ground; he sat so that Fallon would have enough room to use it too. She felt, once again, as if her fairy-tale role wasn't right. Only trolls (or realistically, Grimbaud's homeless) sat under bridges. The water cast diamonds on the cobblestone belly of the bridge above their heads. Shadows of silverfish darted through the water.

"You didn't have to come," he said.

Fallon frowned. "You're supposed to walk me back. As in, all the way to the complex. This doesn't have to do with charms, does it?"

"It's a hobby of mine."

"Like collecting storks?"

Sebastian softened. "Yeah, just like that." He leaned against the bridge and grabbed another blank cassette from his bag. Labeling it would have been difficult at night without the streetlamps nearby, so he popped the tape straight into the recorder. "This is going to sound strange coming from me, but can you be absolutely quiet for fifteen minutes? I want to catch it while I can. I'll explain afterwards."

Fallon was about to argue, but he seemed so serious, so unlike himself, that she reluctantly agreed.

Once Sebastian pressed the record button, the world took notice. The steady wind that had been whistling under the bridge died off. Frogs ceased their croaking. Even the water murmured as softly as a mother around a sleeping child.

Fallon brought her knees to her chest and closed her eyes. The silence didn't make her drowsy, like she expected. Instead, thoughts swirled in her head like a flock of birds. When the fifteen minutes were up, a bicycle raced across the bridge; her eyes flew open at the sound of tires on cobblestone.

Sebastian craned his neck, grimacing at the bottom of the bridge as if he could see through it. "That's always the worse part. We're lucky a car alarm didn't go off. That happened to me once. I swear my heart jumped up into my throat."

She hugged her knees.

"Now you know a terrible secret about me," Sebastian said lightly. "Not the secret you want to know, but this is a good one. I've kept this from every girl I've ever dated."

"I don't think they'd understand."

"There are less bizarre ways to scare a girl off." Sebastian sighed. "I prefer the regular breakup speech. It's straightforward and quick."

"It hurts them either way."

He sounded bored. "Don't we break each other's hearts

anyway? That's our world. We're born with china toys in our bodies and we let people smash them over and over again."

She dismissed his comment as a defense. "So what does recording silence have to do with it?"

"Nothing. You were right before, guessing that this was a hobby of mine. I like to wander around Grimbaud at night when people are asleep. And whenever I find a patch of quiet, I record it."

"Why don't you just listen to blank tapes?"

"Too artificial. Sounds that sneak into the recordings mean something. They help the quiet seem real. They're probably sounds that you would hear even if this town never existed."

Fallon wished she could see his face better in the darkness. Who was this boy who spoke of such philosophical things? Did someone trade places with the cold heartbreaker she knew?

"I hated sitting still as a kid," he said. "I climbed trees despite scraping my skin on the bark, chased stray dogs until my lungs burned, and got a good few scars from tussles with the neighbors' kids." He rubbed the back of his head.

"You don't strike me as that kind of troublemaker," she said.

"I was unhappy then."

"What changed? Something did."

"I went to stay with my grandmother when I was twelve." She heard the smile in his voice. "She runs a veterinary clinic in Glastonberry. It's beautiful there; the clinic's overlooking the sea. Grandma Marion's a rough sort of person. She yelled at me regularly during the first few months, and I can't say I blame her. I stormed the clinic the same way I had done back home, opening cages and trailing cat feces into the house. But in the end, we developed a truce."

"So she straightened you out," Fallon said with a laugh.

"She made me care about myself. Then I became handsome."

Fallon snorted and covered her mouth.

"What? It's a fact. Remind me to show you pictures." Sebastian said. "Anyway, Grandma Marion is a believer in meditation. She used to make me meditate with her, facing the sea. I thought it was stupid until I moved here for high school. Finding quiet, so rare in Grimbaud, became a way to battle my homesickness. I feel like I'm back at the clinic with her when I'm listening."

"Don't you go home for the summer?"

"Yes, but it's not the same. Summer's a busy time for the clinic. Grandma Marion started signing me up for grooming classes last year. I spent my summer cutting terriers and poodles. They bite. A lot."

"No scars?"

He wiggled his fingers. "You can inspect them if you like."

Fallon snatched his hands before he could pull them back. If she couldn't see his face, maybe his hands could provide answers. His palms were rough and warm, a little slippery. Was he nervous?

"These hands have cut the hair of a hundred dogs. It's a privilege to touch them."

"You could have fleas." She dropped them.

"Don't be so quick to dismiss me," he said. "I can actually cut human hair too. I cut my own hair. If you ever want a trim or something, I could do it."

Fallon touched her hair. Her mouth scrunched into a frown. "I don't think so."

Sebastian grabbed his bag and stepped past her. Once he left the shadows of the bridge, he was visible again, if only dimly. "Sorry, that must sound like an insult—a groomer cutting a princess's hair. Well, if anyone needs grooming, it wouldn't be you. You've got that down to perfection."

She scrambled after him, unsure of how to answer. There was real hurt behind his words. And if she wasn't mistaken, the distant streetlamp illuminated his bitter smile.

chapter 8

ASPIRATIONS

On Friday night, Fallon stayed awake long enough to finish searching through her magazines. School had been a blur of quizzes and class discussions and talk of weekend plans. She had seen Sebastian in the hallway after lunch, but, surrounded by girls, he was as unapproachable as ever. Still, she had wanted to talk to him. How unnerving.

After the episode at the bridge, Fallon and Sebastian didn't speak. She hadn't been angry at him for suggesting that her hair was less than stellar in its current style. Her straight hair had always been an adversary, lacking volume and thin enough for her to worry about future female-pattern baldness.

When she was eleven, her mother had taken her to a posh salon with marble rinsing stations. The stylist, named something trendy like Lexi, had given her a simple cut: a straight bob ending at the chin. No bangs. Lexi had insisted that the style best suited her brittle hair. And since it didn't bother her, Fallon had kept it like that. While other girls at the complex worried about finding the perfect style, Fallon could walk into any nice salon and get a trim.

She'd never been dissatisfied with her haircut, but something about his sincerity made her pause. Sebastian had offered to cut her hair.

Then something worse replaced the dissatisfaction: an epiphany. "Sebastian Barringer is real," she whispered. He was human. He had feelings behind those cold, liberally given kisses and barbed jokes. Before he became "Bastion," he had a life.

Last night she had dreamed of his grandmother's clinic. The ocean roared in her ears as she walked twelve dogs through the grass. Sebastian waved at her with a pair of silver scissors. When she woke up, thinking one of the dogs was licking her cheek, she found a puddle of drool on her pillow.

Saturday morning greeted her with watery sunlight and the hum of her heater. The complex was quiet, as it usually was on weekend mornings. Only the joggers and the ambitious woke up before noon. Fallon rubbed her eyes and climbed out of bed. She took a shower, standing under the water longer than necessary, and emerged from the steamy bathroom with her hair in a towel. She brushed her teeth before breakfast. The last of her eggs bubbled in the pan. She ate slowly at the kitchen table, never spilling a crumb.

Her teachers hadn't yet assigned anything bigger than a one-page essay on how she spent her summer vacation. Fallon's essay had taken her only an hour to write since she hadn't done much over the summer. *I visited my brother and his wife,* she wrote. *I shadowed my parents on a few restaurant inspections out of town.*

Again, she thought of the clinic and Sebastian's dog-grooming lessons. How did his grandmother know that he would like cutting dogs' hair? Her parents just assumed, as they usually did, that she would follow in the family's footsteps and become a quality-control manager of some sort. They actually hoped she would become a house inspector, since that was the last chunk of uncharted territory left.

Fallon gathered the eight magazines containing charms. She needed to tear the charms out and put them in a binder for when Femke and Mirthe asked for them. The outdoors called to her, so she put on a thick cashmere sweater and walked down to the patio. The angle of the building blocked most of the wind, so she comfortably settled in a wire chair and smoothed the bent cover of the first magazine in her lap. The first charm she tore out was the one she had tried at the student government meeting. Touching the paper gave her the shivers, knowing how close she had come to being discovered by Camille. After using a hole puncher and slipping the page through the rings, Fallon moved on to the next one.

A rustling drew her attention. She leaned to the right in

her chair and saw Hijiri kneeling in front of the potted ferns in the corner. She cut the leaves off the ferns and put them in a plastic bag.

"Are you working for Mrs. Smedt now?" Fallon asked. The caretaker sometimes hired a student or two to help her do the chores.

Hijiri flinched and dropped her bag.

"Sorry," Fallon said, standing. "I didn't mean to frighten you. It's only me, Fallon."

Hijiri's shoulders slumped, but she still wouldn't look up. The girl was dressed in baggy clothes and stained sneakers. Her long, oily black hair fell into her eyes and hid her face. "I didn't know anyone else was here."

"Then you better watch out for me. I'm an early riser," Fallon joked. She wanted to put the girl at ease.

Hijiri cracked a smile.

"Why don't you sit over here, next to me? I'm doing some work for the club."

At that, the girl perked up. "I am too."

After Hijiri pulled up another wire chair, Fallon explained what she was doing with the magazines. "I didn't try the others, but I'm sure they're all love charms."

"Let me see, please."

She handed Hijiri the magazines. "I bookmarked each one."

Hijiri examined each charm eagerly. She sniffed the pages and rubbed her thumb over the print. Whenever she was done with each page, she nodded at Fallon before tearing out the page herself. "You've got good instinct. These are love charms."

Fallon grinned at the compliment. "Thanks. How about you? What makes you so knowledgeable about the love charms?"

The girl shrunk into herself again.

"Hijiri?"

She took huge, gulping breaths before speaking, her voice just above a whisper. "I make them."

"Charms? Like Femke and Mirthe?"

"Better." There was no arrogance in her claim—only fear. "I've been making love charms since I was little."

Fallon smothered her surprise.

"My parents noticed my talent early and wanted to enroll me in Grimbaud Middle School. But I wasn't stupid. I knew what was going on here with Zita's shop. No one but her is allowed to produce love charms. Even crafting charms in secret has risks, and I'm . . . not a brave person. I would have been content crafting my charms in my hometown rather than come here."

But now Hijiri was in Grimbaud. A high school freshman. "Your parents won."

"They wouldn't listen."

Fallon understood that perfectly. "Where's home for you?"

"Lejeune."

"Wow. That's so far from here!"

"I know. Yet my charms worked. Sometimes. That's how

I managed to survive school until now," Hijiri said, tugging at her hair.

Fallon pressed her lips together. She didn't want to steer the conversation into dark memories. The poor girl was already huddled in the chair, trying to compress herself into nothing. "Why haven't you told the club about your talent?"

"Grimbaud scares me. The way this town has been is not natural."

"Zita."

"Yes. This mysterious queen of love charms." Hijiri rubbed her nose. "I'm supporting the rebellion because I want to see this town free again, but I can't be a fighter. I don't know how I'll help."

"What about your own love fortune?"

"It's not surprising."

"But it hurts."

Hijiri ducked her head. "Making charms for others distracted me in the past. Now I have nothing to hide behind. But still, there's something I want to make. The ultimate love charm."

Fallon leaned closer. "What is it?"

"You'll laugh."

"I won't. I promise."

Hijiri wiggled the bag of fern leaves. "Did you know that ferns symbolize sincerity? That's a powerful component to have in this love charm. Only true words and feelings can make it work."

Fallon had never thought much about ferns. Mrs. Smedt kept the pots of ferns watered in the patio. "What kind of charm?"

"Something right out of a fairy tale. I want to make a true-love kiss."

Fallon bit her lip.

"I told you not to laugh."

"I'm not! It's just . . . wouldn't that be hard to do?"

"Love has called this town its home, so love charms made here are the strongest. I have a chance." Hijiri raised her head. Her eyes, uncloaked by her hair, were startlingly dark. "True love's kiss is a thing of stories. It doesn't exist yet, but I want to create it in the form of a charm. If I succeed one day, it will work miracles."

The complex stirred around them. Most students still slept, but someone's alarm went off nearby; the walls didn't stop such sounds from escaping into the patio. Fallon struggled to say something, anything, about Hijiri's grand dream. Her head told her that creating such a charm was impossible. That was why magic kisses only happened in fairy tales. But her heart leaped at the idea.

"Winter break will give me time to try some ideas," Hijiri said, drawing Fallon back. "I should make progress on the charm. I *will*."

"Thank you for sharing that with me." Fallon rested her hand on Hijiri's arm for a moment.

The girl smiled and looked down again at her feet. "Thank you for not making fun of it."

"I can't possibly do that," Fallon said thickly. "A charm like that would be too precious to laugh at."

In the afternoon, Fallon walked briskly over bridges and busy streets to the main Barnes Canal Cruises ticket booth. Tourists tended to take photographs of the peeling mermaid statue mounted on the roof of the booth. The mermaid's beautiful face was at odds with the two hearts she squeezed in her fists; Fallon didn't like the statue, but Nico insisted it was a relic. His parents would never take the old thing down.

Even in cold weather, the canal glistened and sunlight bounced off the hulls of the tied-up boats. Fallon spotted Nico reclining on one of the benches facing the canal, his nose buried in a newspaper. A cup of coffee cooled on the seat beside him.

"Did you secure us a boat, Captain?" she teased, dropping her bag onto the bench.

"Dad threatened to double my hours at the booth if I snuck off with one. We'll have to share space with the tourists."

"That's too bad."

Anais skipped her way over to the bench with a crinkly package of sweet rolls. "I got us a treat!"

Nico eyed the package with suspicion. The last time Anais got seasick, he was the one who had to mop up her mess on deck.

"What?" she said. "I'm hungry."

Nico folded his newspaper. "If you take even one bite, we are not getting on a boat."

"Come on, don't be stingy."

"It's self-preservation."

After some bickering, Anais reluctantly agreed to save the sweet rolls for later. Fallon handed Anais the stack of magazines she hadn't used.

When she tried giving Anais money for the eight she kept, Anais just told her to treat her with dessert the next time they went out. "Knowing you, Dupree, I'd be eating something flaked with edible gold."

"I don't know about that," Fallon said, laughing. Then she noticed that Anais's hands had turned white under the strain of holding the magazines. "Are you okay?"

Anais shoved the magazines into her backpack along with the sweet rolls and groaned. "I feel like I'm carrying a family of storks on my back."

Fallon laughed and steadied her friend when she tilted. "If Bear was here, he'd carry it for you."

"I know." Anais pouted. "That's why I asked him to pick me up after the tour's over."

"I see. You can't possibly return home unescorted," Nico said.

"Bear doesn't know where I live," she said, huffing. "We're going to wander the shops and have dinner. Then I'll find some way to say good-bye before we get to the drugstore. Bear gets positively light-headed after kissing. I like to use that to my advantage."

Nico clapped his hands over his ears. "Too much information! Let's go."

Fallon happily followed behind as they headed to the tour boat. The boat had an open-air deck and seating below for those who couldn't handle too much sun. The trio headed to the back of the boat for some privacy, squeezing past tourists already leaping from seat to seat, taking pictures. In the back, the engine drowned out everything, including the rave-reviewed commentaries from the captain.

The boat pulled away from the dock. They moved at a slow pace down the canal; Fallon admired the backyards of old brick buildings and waved with the tourists whenever they spotted someone. The boat shifted when the tourists rushed to gawk at the entrance to the Tunnel of Love. The tunnel had its own loop that other boats didn't enter. Fallon watched the happy couples climb into tiny boats, each one painted with hearts. *Experiencing the Tunnel of Love is another dream I'm fighting for*, she reminded herself. Her hair whipped back from her forehead, her eyelashes trembled. Autumn made the tour feel like an excursion.

The desire to talk about the rebellion stirred in her, but Fallon bit back the words in Anais's presence. Instead, she asked Nico about his first officer meeting.

"Did you make Martin fall madly in love with you?" Anais said, elbowing him.

Nico swatted at her. "Don't you remember my fortune?"

"Whatever. Entertain me."

"I'm just the treasurer. My life revolves around memorizing the numbers on the bank statements so that I can tell them quickly if an idea is in or out of budget."

"But you didn't join for the numbers," Anais said. "Come on. Did Martin look any different from last year? New glasses, perhaps?"

"He looks . . . more tired now. I think being president wears him down."

"Then take him on a vacation," Anais said, grinning.

Nico blushed and mumbled, "Not with Camille around."

"Are you serious? She's still there?"

"Camille's the vice president," Fallon said.

"That must be awkward."

"Camille's not over him," Nico said in a pained voice. "She's been ruthless in stealing his attention. It's awful."

"Martin can't want her back." Anais grabbed Nico by the collar. "Please tell me you've been listening to gossip. Does anyone know why he broke up with her?"

"No one knows for sure, but the breakup probably had something to do with Camille spending more time at Zita's shop than with Martin." His expression clouded. "Apparently, Camille had been told that she was 'meant for better things.'"

"Poor guy." Anais released his collar.

But Fallon shivered with unease. She raised her voice over the engine. "Who told Camille that?"

"Someone at work, probably. Rumor has it that Camille will be promoted to manager at Zita's shop after graduation."

Fallon breathed in the crisp air scented with the flavors of the town. She didn't like this strong connection between Camille and Zita's shop. The higher Camille climbed in the shop, the more likely she was a serious threat to the rebellion. This wasn't just about Nico's unrequited love anymore. As if sensing her thoughts, Nico stared out at the water in silence.

"What about you, Fallon? School's only been in session for a week and you're already in trouble," Anais said.

"What?"

"You've been talking to Sebastian." She said it more as an accusation than a fact. "Be careful. That boy eats hearts for breakfast!"

"It's not like that. We just happen to be in the same club."

"You joined a club?"

Fallon told Anais about the charm-maker's club.

Anais raised an eyebrow. "I didn't know you liked charms. Not enough to make them. Man, I wish my dad didn't work me so hard. Then I could join."

Nico panicked. "You wouldn't want to. It's a tiny, boring club. We don't do anything."

"You joined too?"

"Someone has to protect Fallon from Bastion," he said.

Anais nodded. "Well done, Nico."

The boat shuddered as tourists gathered on the right side to take photos of a bronze cupid statue. Fallon curled her hands around the railing. A week ago, she would have laughed along with them about Bastion. But now, she couldn't ignore her changing opinion of him.

The truth was disappointing in some ways because disliking him had been so effortless. The dog groomer in him had been an odd surprise, along with his fierce, quiet love for his grandmother. Sebastian remained a mystery, but as she beheld pieces of the real boy underneath, she felt her own heart give. Just a little.

chapter 9

QUALITY

"Boy, you look surprised," Robbie said with a grin.

When she heard the knock on her door Sunday morning, Fallon didn't think she'd find her brother standing on the other side. Panic flooded her chest. Although happy to see him, she hadn't prepared for visitors. Her dooming love fortune hung innocently on her corkboard. Fallon invited him inside but kept him standing near the door.

Since his employment as a clothing inspector, Robbie never left the house in less than quality. His mustache and slicked-back hair were perfectly oiled. He smelled of spicy aftershave when he bent down to hug her. The leather jacket and khaki slacks he wore molded to his body perfectly.

"What are you doing here?"

"Checking up on my little sister." He looked at her strangely. "You didn't call. I got worried."

She'd forgotten. With everything that had happened

this past week, Fallon had been lucky to remember calling her parents. "I'm sorry. School's been taking over my brain."

"Enough to distract you from sharing your love-fortune news with me?" He shook his head. "I have a hard time believing that, but I understand. Mom and Dad told me about the news. You're stuck waiting, huh? How unusual."

"Zita's only reminding me that being patient is part of my romantic journey," Fallon said. Her pulse quickened, but the lie came easily.

"Mom and Dad sounded pretty upset, but there's nothing we can do if that's your fortune. I asked them if they were holding out on me— Is Fallon adopted or what? The joke hadn't gone over too well, as you can imagine."

A rush of guilt overpowered Fallon. She was the only member of the family who hadn't found love early. Maybe she *had* been adopted.

Robbie reached over and tousled her hair. "Hey, now. Don't worry. I'm here to cheer you up. How about we spend the day together?"

Since getting married, Robbie hadn't gone anywhere without his wife. Fallon fought the urge to look behind him. "Just us?"

"Morgane's spending time with her friends."

Fallon managed a smile. "Just a second."

They spent the morning wandering the streets around the complex, sharing stories of their experiences along the way. Robbie told her about the time he and Morgane snuck into the belfry after hours, taking photos with each of the forty-eight bells. She didn't have anything as exciting to share, though sitting under the bridge with Sebastian came to mind.

"I have a friend who likes collecting silence," Fallon said. She turned her face away so that Robbie wouldn't see her cheeks burning. "He runs around town recording pockets of quiet. I went with him once."

Robbie stopped at a storefront to examine a knitted scarf. "I didn't know Grimbaud was ever quiet."

"There are gardens and little cafés. Places where couples can have privacy." But, she realized, such parts of town were designed to cater to people in love. The everyday townsperson had to be more clever to find peace away from stolen kisses under yew trees or over shared desserts.

"Not thrilling enough," Robbie said, crinkling his nose at the scarf. "You'll be a senior before you know it!."

"Not for another three years."

"Still. Maybe you better start planning something."

Fallon sighed. "Aren't you a responsible adult now? Don't tell me to break rules and risk arrest."

"Arrest? Who said anything about that? Maybe next year you'll get a better fortune and you and your boyfriend can work together."

"Yes. Maybe," Fallon said wistfully.

"What's going on over there?" Robbie asked, pointing at the construction cones across the street.

She couldn't tell. "We need to go that way anyway for

lunch," she said, thinking of taking him to a café that served excellent omelets.

They crossed the street and turned the corner, finding a small crowd of curious onlookers standing in front of a park that served as a miniature shrine to Love. People dropped coins into the gurgling fountain and enjoyed the topiaries shaped like hearts. The main draw was the statue behind the fountain named *Love Being Cherished*.

The marble statue depicted a voluptuous woman as Love, her naked body and tumbling hair positioned just right to be inoffensive. A teenage boy stood on marble steps to her left; he kissed her cheek while shedding lovers' tears, a bouquet of roses and a poetry book chiseled into his hands. The teenage girl kissed Love's other cheek daintily, with wide-open eyes; her hands curled outward, accepting whatever blessings came her way.

Fallon thought the statue was beautiful; she understood why people came to this patch of earth just to admire it. But today, no one was allowed near the statue except for the construction workers. The workers finished securing iron beams underneath the statue. A truck waited on the street.

"That statue's being removed," said a woman standing nearby.

"For refurbishment?" Robbie asked.

"No. For good."

Robbie's face flushed with outrage. "How could that be? This statue's been here for generations. It's a relic."

The woman shrugged, but she looked just as upset. "Nothing belongs to the town anymore, does it? Zita bought the land the statue sits on, and she can afford to remove it. I don't know why. It's offensive to touch something made in honor of Love."

More than offensive, Fallon thought. The statue symbolized the townspeople's connection to Love. Removing the statue felt like a slap in Love's face. Tension rippled in the air as the construction workers continued preparing the statue for the move. Robbie asked around, but no one seemed to know where the statue was being moved to. The workers remained tight-lipped, even when someone threw a water bottle at them.

Underneath the unease, Fallon heard the faint sound of a tango. She scanned the crowd and found a familiar boy standing on the outskirts with giant headphones covering his ears. He was the same boy from the library. The boy's hands curled into fists, his eyes stormy.

Fallon couldn't catch his eye, but she wanted to make him feel better. *It's just a statue, after all*, she thought, but it felt like a lie. Dread made her toes tingle. She grabbed her brother's arm. "Robbie, let's go."

Witnessing the historic statue's removal had shaken up the Dupree siblings. Robbie ignored the clothing shops as they walked to the café. He made no snide remarks about the tattered skirt the woman in front of them wore. He didn't even blink when they passed a toddler wearing a drawstring hood that was against clothing regulations. Fallon should have been grateful that Robbie wasn't prattling on about his job, but at what cost?

"What are you thinking about?" Fallon asked gently.

Robbie rubbed his mustache as they waited to cross the street. "Just shaken up."

"We both are."

"But you're still making memories here," he said. "And Grimbaud is changing. Part of me knows that change happens—I mean, even regulations on buttons change—but mostly I'm worried about returning to Grimbaud and finding nothing familiar about it. That my four years here only exist in a dream."

"They can't take the belfry away," Fallon said.

Robbie's eyes widened. "Do you know if Zita owns the belfry?"

"No."

He muttered a curse. "I hope that omelet is as good as you say."

Now more than ever, she wanted it to be. Thankfully, the oozing cheese and spicy sausage ended up being delicious enough to drag her brother from his melancholy. The café's perky goldenrod roof and outdoor seating offered a corner view of an old church and the gardens surrounding it. Fallon cut into her omelet and worked especially hard to distract him. She even voluntarily asked him about work—something she knew would start him off on a tedious ramble.

"You wouldn't believe the stack of sweaters I inspected last week," Robbie said with his usual verve. "They looked normal enough at first glance, but I found a stray needle buried under the armpit. The stitching was broken at the neckline. The labels were even missing their identification numbers."

"I don't think most people notice that on their clothes," she said for argument's sake.

"Be that as it may," he said, dabbing his lips with a napkin, "tracking clothing is important. We must always know what business produces even the lowliest blouse."

"So you know who to blame."

"In some cases, but it's for the customer too. Those people who love shopping at off-price retailers can benefit from checking the label. If they recognize the number, they'll be able to tell whether they're really buying the brand they want. You'd be surprised how often shops like that switch the tags around. The labels stay."

Fallon finished her omelet, feeling both overwhelmed by her brother's apparel adventures and relieved to have him back to his regular self. She didn't know how Morgane could stand listening to him every night when he came home from work. It was Zita's doing; if not for the red clothing, Robbie and Morgane might not have met. They could have spent their four years at the complex without ever having spoken to each other.

Yet, instead, Robbie was happily married, another greased cog in the Dupree family wheel. She loved her brother and parents, but she felt more and more like she wasn't one of them.

❧—▷

Fallon thought that Robbie had forgotten something when she heard knocking on her door. It had been fifteen minutes since he left, giving her one last hug and dragging a promise out of her to replace the pilling waffle-knit shirt hanging over her desk chair.

The knocking persisted. "Hold on, I'm coming," Fallon yelled. For good measure, she jogged over to the corkboard and unpinned her love fortune. The ticker-tape ribbon curled like a snake around her hand, but she managed to shove it into her pocket before opening the door.

Sebastian stared at her, his hands jammed into the pockets of his gray jacket. "Who was that guy?"

Fallon blinked.

"That guy," he repeated, eyebrows furrowed. "Tall, rich-looking? I say one *slightly* offensive thing about your hair and you've already found someone new."

Fallon didn't know whether to burst out laughing or snap at him. "You and I aren't dating."

"We could be."

She ignored his offer. "That was my brother, Robbie. He came to visit me."

Sebastian exhaled loudly. "Well."

"You believe me?"

"He does look like you, now that you mention it. You both dress like you're going to a yacht club or something."

"For a second there, I thought you were jealous," she teased.

Instead of coming back at her with a snide remark, Sebastian's face paled. He examined his hands as if hoping to find an answer there. "I don't know what jealousy is."

His reaction concerned her. "Of course you do. Girls feel it all the time around you when you're between dating. You can come in if you want. You don't look okay."

Sebastian said nothing but followed her inside. His eyes swept over her plain decorating and neat living room.

Fallon's fingers itched to do something for him. His silence was unnerving after the outburst he'd had at the door. Where had his energy gone? Something she said must have upset him. Part of her wondered why she cared. "Are you cold? I can get you a blanket if you want."

He tore his gaze away from a vintage poster of a pearl-black bistro atop a hill. "Does the blanket have dragons on it, princess?"

A surprised laugh escaped her lips. "I don't think a princess would want to be reminded of the creature keeping her captive."

"Spoken like a true princess."

"I'm not."

Sebastian shook his head and wandered through the

room with a little more energy. He paused at her cassette player. "Nice. Where did you get it?"

"Antique store. It works really well."

Sebastian rubbed his chin. "My grandmother gave me my recorder. I can't imagine being without it." He leaned close to the corkboard to see the photographs of her, Anais, and Nico, and even spent time contemplating each restaurant poster with the seriousness of a museum patron. "Is restaurant inspecting in your future, princess?"

"I hope not."

"Why?"

Because he seemed interested, she answered. "My whole life, I've watched my parents end dreams in the restaurant business. They're only doing their jobs for safety's sake, but I couldn't be brave enough to tell someone they failed an inspection."

Sebastian took a seat on her couch and kicked off his shoes. "What else?"

"There was a boy."

"Seriously?"

She glared at him. "His name was Louis. We sort of dated in the fifth grade, if you could call it that. Holding hands and trading lunches. His parents owned the neighborhood deli. During inspection, my father discovered that the ice machine had been contaminated for quite some time. A rat infestation also ruined the cuts of meat. As you can imagine, an inspection like that made my father famous, but also earned Louis's unending hatred for us Duprees. For me."

Sebastian shifted in his seat. "Do you still pine for Louis?"

"That was fifth grade." Fallon sat in the chair next to the couch. "My point is that a health inspector ruins lives either way. If you don't do your job, people can die from food poisoning. But if you do, the restaurant owners lose their means of making a living."

Sebastian didn't share her pity. "Maybe they weren't meant to cook."

"You sound like my parents."

"I haven't met them, but I'm pretty sure what you just said was a lie." He smirked. "You'll need to lend me an ascot and fitted suit to come close."

Fallon bent over laughing, wiping the tears from her eyes. The only reason why her parents dressed so nicely was because of Robbie's influence, but even they wouldn't wear ascots.

"I didn't come over here to quiz you like a career counselor," he admitted. "Actually, I wanted to apologize."

She recovered from her laughter enough to look up. "For what?"

"What I said the other day about your hair."

"You didn't say anything wrong." She paused. "For once. I don't relish the idea of having my hair cut by a groomer, but it was nice of you to offer."

He huffed. "You're making it too easy for me. Why don't you find something else you don't like about me and be mad? That way, this will matter." He reached into his pocket and pulled out a cassette tape. "It's a copy of the silence we recorded Thursday night."

Fallon took the tape from him and turned it in her hands. Just holding it brought her back to that moment under the bridge.

"You should listen to it when you're stressed," he said.

"Thanks."

Sebastian nodded to himself and stood up. "If that's it, I'll be on my way."

Fallon lingered in the doorway as she watched him leave. He made her laugh. He asked her about her posters and her parents' jobs. Nothing could make her forget his strange reaction to her teasing, though. Sebastian had stood in her apartment, pale and lost, like a wanderer stunned to discover that he'd finally arrived at his destination. Where did that look come from? How had she caused it?

Zita's love fortune burned in her pocket. She took it out and crushed it in her fist.

chapter 10

ON THE DOCK

The next few weeks carried Fallon into October. Trees dropped their leaves faster, causing a symphony of crackling during the morning walks to school. Girls kept their skirts but replaced high socks with stockings to keep warm. Pumpkin-spiced coffee sold on the streets woke her up by smell alone. Winter would tint Grimbaud in blues and grays soon enough. Then spring. You couldn't live in Grimbaud and not love spring.

Sometimes she could pretend that this was just another school year. Her teachers, preoccupied with lesson plans and grading, soon forgot to shoot her pitying looks. Homework covered her desk in piles, textbooks tagged with notes and problems yet to be solved. Working at the library offered its own structure. She learned how to check books out for the few students who read, and caught on to the intricacies of the card catalog. Fallon surprised Anais at the drugstore and joined Nico in the ticket booth when the long hours made him stir-crazy.

Sebastian now had a presence in her life. As the month trundled on, she grew used to seeing him at Femke and Mirthe's charm-making meetings. Sebastian always pulled up a seat next to her and uttered his bored replies to whatever the twins had cooked up. When she sat in her apartment on a lonely, homework-filled night, she held her breath and waited for a knock. But he didn't bother her again at the complex.

"We've been gathering charms long enough," Mirthe said one afternoon. "It's time to find out what everyone's got and move on to the next phase."

She sat with her sister on top of the teacher's desk in the science classroom. Femke nodded and wrote something in her notebook. The twins wore matching purple lipstick and necklaces strung with golden stars.

Fallon breathed a sigh of relief. Since combing through the magazines Anais had let her borrow, she hadn't found any new charms.

Nico checked his bag. "I left my charms at home."

"We're not doing that here," Mirthe said, as if it were obvious. "Too dangerous. Spies could be lurking in the hallways even as we speak."

Sebastian was unmoved by the threat. "No one comes here."

"We can't get too comfortable," Femke said. "That's not good for a budding rebellion."

"Exactly, sister," Mirthe said. She pulled pieces of paper out of her bag and handed them out. The paper was an invitation to come to the twins' house on Saturday. Under the pretense of a party, the club members would bring their charms with them.

"We'll have our party on the dock behind our house. If we're messing with charms anywhere else, our parents are not going to be happy," Mirthe said. Since their house doubled as a weather charm-making shop, decades' worth of weather charms layered the air. If a love charm activated, their parents would sense the change in air pressure—unless the club met on the dock, close to the sea.

"All weather charm-makers know how powerful the sea is. It's got its own charm, more powerful than anything," Femke said.

"Except for Love," Hijiri said quietly.

"Right. We shouldn't offend Love any more than Zita already has." Mirthe bristled. "But I meant that they'll cancel each other out. We won't leave footprints from using the charms we have."

Fallon didn't know anything about the technical side of charms, but she believed the twins and valued the extra safety. "That's good. You don't want to attract attention like I did."

Mirthe placed her hands on her hips, looking every inch like a mother hen. "Out of everyone here, I never suspected you'd do something as careless as use a love charm in public. Zita's spies are everywhere. Obviously anyone working in her shop is one."

Fallon looked down at her lap.

"I'm working on compiling a list of Zita's employees,"

Femke said, "with pictures and corresponding job titles. That way, we'll all know who the enemies are."

"For now, make sure you don't forget the charms," Mirthe said.

On the way home, Sebastian caught up with Fallon. "She didn't need to embarrass you like that," he grumbled. "I was there too."

Fallon slowed her steps. "No, I deserve it. We need to be taking this seriously."

"Still—"

Five girls waited at the entrance. A girl with soft pigtails waved at him and said, "Bastion, what took you so long? We were waiting for you."

"Looks like your new girlfriend is calling you," Fallon said.

Sebastian sighed and hitched up his schoolbag. "Fine. We'll talk later."

For a moment, she could only think about Sebastian and the pigtails girl embracing under a streetlamp or sharing an ice cream cone despite the frigid weather. Fallon rubbed her shoulders. "Go have fun. I'll just see you at the party."

She walked ahead, brushing past the girls. Fallon pressed her hands to her ears as casually as she could to avoid hearing the sound Sebastian's lips would make upon connecting with the girl's.

The blue colonial house with its back to the sea bore years of abuse. Cracked windows on the second floor were repaired with duct tape. A stone sundial was missing the slice for three in the afternoon. The garage on the side of the house was wide-open, revealing an intricate weather charm-making studio.

As Fallon approached, the hairs on her arms rose. Most charm shops made her feel funny, but this one, having been both lived in and used excessively, carried its own sea of memories. Some charm-makers sold their own weather charms to add variety, but the twins' family specialized in this craft for generations. *No wonder Femke and Mirthe are a little strange*, she thought.

Pinwheels spun madly within the shrubs, even though the rest of the town lacked a breeze. Mr. De Keyser, the twins' father, licked his thumb and raised it. "Southerly coming this way," he said to no one. The empty jars lining the back wall of the garage rattled.

"Batten down the hatches," Mirthe teased, appearing at the front door. October's chill couldn't touch her; she wore a chunky sweater that almost hid the fact that there was a swimsuit underneath. Bare-legged, she crossed the front lawn and winked. "Dad's working on a special order for warm winds. The others have already arrived. Let's go around back."

Bemused, Fallon followed. "Your dad looks just like a stranded captain." Mr. De Keyser's navy-blue vest had nautical patches covering it; the white pants torn off at the knees seemed to imply that he had emerged from a sinking ship minutes ago.

"We De Keysers believe that getting as close as we can to the elements makes for a stronger charm, every time. Our great-great-aunt Noor wanted not only to control weather but to become it. She crafted a charm that would deconstruct her body into wind."

"What happened?"

"Didn't work. She ended up falling to her death after attempting to fly." Mirthe sighed. "You see what I mean, though. We come as close as we can to weather. The closer you get, the more powerful the charm."

As dismal as the story was, Fallon noticed the pride evident in Mirthe's voice. At home, she and Femke were accepted. They had a wonderful purpose with a family as strange and kind as they were.

The lawn gave way to sand. Grimbaud wasn't known for beaches; pinching crabs and rocks covered the coastline. Lovers twisted their ankles attempting to climb sand dunes or bruised their backs while reclining near the water. The De Keysers' property had a relatively smooth path to the dock. Fallon took off her sandals.

"Watch out for pinching crabs. You wouldn't want to lose a toe."

"Can that really happen?"

"I have stories."

Fallon believed her.

The dock stretched out from the sand like a crooked

finger. A single rowboat bobbed in the water, tied in place with thick rope. Sebastian, Hijiri, Femke, and Nico sat around a table squeezed onto the narrow dock. The wind rattled the backs of their fold-out chairs. It was a mystery that no one toppled over into the water, what with the table being so big and round and pushing everyone's chairs to the very edge.

"Sorry I'm late," Fallon said as her feet thumped against the wooden boards. "I got stuck in line for the pralines."

They descended upon her offering of raspberry-and-coffee-filled pralines until everyone went quiet, licking their fingers. Fallon settled into the chair between Nico and Sebastian, trying not to think about the chilly water only a breath away from her chair's legs.

"We're going to be very organized about this," Femke said, poised with her notebook and pen at the ready. Just like her sister, she wore a chunky sweater and swimsuit. Neither girl seemed cold, though everyone else shivered in their scarves and boots. Hijiri dabbed her red nose with a tissue and offered to go first with her collected love charms.

"Wait," Mirthe said. "One more minute."

Fallon wasn't sure what they were waiting for, but no one saw fit to argue. She sat with her hands in her lap, ignoring the nipping winds, until she heard Mr. De Keyser's crowing laughter from his workshop.

A new wind crawled through, nudging the other winds away as it slowly blanketed the dock. Fallon breathed deeply, tasting balmy, moist air and shaved coconuts. Her coat felt too stuffy. Her hands began to sweat. She shucked off her coat, hanging it on the back of her chair, and noticed that the others were doing the same.

Femke and Mirthe shed their sweaters, revealing modest one-piece swimsuits. "The southerly has arrived," Mirthe said. "We have some time before Dad bottles it all up."

Nico leaned his elbows on the table and sighed. "How much does your father charge for the heat? I'd love to pocket some for the ticket booth."

"Oh, it won't feel this intense if you buy one," Femke said. "As you can imagine, we have to have a ton of heating charms in stock over the winter. Dad has to split the winds into pieces that go into each charm. The heat's less potent the smaller it is."

"If you've got the money, you'll get a larger piece," Mirthe said.

Nico pouted. "I probably don't."

"There's always electricity," Femke said.

Fallon bit back a laugh. The rest of the world relied on air-conditioning units, yet only in Grimbaud could you think of spending your money on a charm to do the work for you. Too bad charms didn't last as long; you had to keep returning to the shop to buy more before the old ones lost their power.

Eager to use the heat while it lasted, the club started sharing their charms. Fallon went first, opening her binder of the magazine charms. Most of the charms required the user to recite a particular phrase or wear an item (usually an accessory) on a certain day. Despite the sea's protection, Fallon didn't want to try a new one.

"What about the one that promises a boost in stamina?" Sebastian said.

Mirthe let out a snorty laugh. "Stamina for your first date? Did they make that charm for older daters?"

"Wouldn't that come in handy if we confront Zita at night? It could be harder to find her than we thought. We'll need the energy," Sebastian said.

"Yeah, but how do you feel about following its requirements? You must wear a pink ribbon tied to your shoulder on Tuesdays. If we don't find her on a Tuesday, we'll just be wearing useless ribbons." Mirthe tapped her chin. "You may be onto something, though. We should see if any of these lovesick charms can provide us some practical use."

Fallon wanted to assure him that his idea was good, but with their chairs so close together, exchanging a quick smile would have been awkward. Her gaze fell to his hands resting on the table. The blue rubber bracelet he always wore on his wrist was much closer now. She tried to read the cracked lettering.

"What?" His warm breath brushed her cheek.

Fallon twitched. He'd caught her. Part of her didn't care that she was prying. The bracelet was on his wrist for anyone to see. She tugged on the bracelet and rubbed her thumb over the faded black ink of a paw print. "This is from your grandmother's clinic."

Sebastian watched her fingers on his bracelet. "Yes."

"You wouldn't believe the charms I heard about," Nico said, eager to go next.

The sound of his marble notebook hitting the table startled Fallon. She pulled back and hid her hands under the table.

"Tourists don't care at all about rules and norms. They're not afraid of being overheard by Zita's minions. At first, I hadn't been sure how I could help the rebellion, but discovering that I had my own channel of vital information was, well, a huge relief."

Out on the canal, the tourists entertained Nico with love-charm stories. The charms had punch lines, interwoven with little warnings and life lessons, to the point that Nico wondered where the charms began and the tourists' experiences ended. A rather heavyset man wearing a straw hat spent the entire cruise telling Nico about a love charm that got him sent to the hospital with a broken leg. Apparently, it was a painful charm meant to capture the attention of a pretty nurse.

"Breaking his leg over a girl," Sebastian mumbled, shaking his head.

Nico flashed a wry smile. "Now that one, I think, was a con."

"I don't want to think about cons," Hijiri said, her quiet voice sharp. She said that in her hometown, con men pedaling fake charms were a common problem. "I found a charm that could do a good job stunning or distracting. It's called Blinded by Love. You use a mirror and blow a handful of glitter across its surface. The effect causes a flash of light."

Mirthe grinned. "I get why it's called that now."

Hijiri pulled a compact mirror and a bottle of glitter out of her bag. She ignored their stares and shrugged, saying, "It could be useful to us."

Fallon didn't believe her. She was sure that the blinding charm was one of Hijiri's creations.

Mirthe blew a kiss and did as Hijiri had instructed, causing a lightning-like flash that burned Fallon's eyes. They took turns until the glitter was used up, each of them blinking the spots from their visions.

Femke passed out paper glasses with rose-smoked lenses for everyone. "Mirthe and I found these charms during one of our out-of-town trips. They were cheap enough that we bought everyone a pair."

"Thanks," Nico said, "but what are they?"

"Anti-rose-colored glasses," Femke said, slipping them on. "You know how when you're in love, even Grimbaud's dirty bathrooms look shiny and perfect? Well, no matter how in love you are, wearing these glasses strips your lovesick sight away and shows you the truth."

"I imagine this isn't a popular charm," Fallon said. When she put on her glasses, the sparkles on the sea dulled and she saw a hole in Sebastian's shirt collar she hadn't noticed before. The fact that *anything* changed while wearing the glasses made her heart quake. She quickly took them off.

"Take a good look, guys," Mirthe said. "We don't know it yet, but the charms could be useful in the future. Just remember that we can't use them unless there's an emergency. The power wafting off these charms will act as a beacon to Zita's most ardent followers."

"Like the police," Fallon said. "Can you tell me about the pins? They match the color of Zita's shop."

"Then you've already guessed that Zita's sunk her nails in them," Mirthe said proudly. "They turn a blind eye toward her business. They only look into charm-related crimes when the charms used are not love-related. And if someone is causing Zita trouble . . ."

"Our parents told us that the people working on the police force tend to have awfully nice love fortunes," Femke said. "A coincidence?"

"We don't think so." Mirthe crossed her arms.

Sebastian hadn't found a charm they could use, but he told them about what the Maeses had said about the opening of Zita's shop. Only the elderly remembered a time when other love charm-makers worked in Grimbaud, but their memories were hazy as to how and when Zita deftly kicked the other charm-makers out of town. Zita's reconstruction projects had erased old love charms. Even the belfry once had a charm until the largest bell, on which you planted a kiss for a lasting relationship, had been replaced. Fallon sighed. Robbie and Morgane would have been too late to take advantage of that charm.

The southerly's presence began to wane. Femke pulled her sweater back on, but Mirthe ignored the weather and slapped her hands on the table. "You've all done a great job. In the coming weeks, I advise you to think about the charms we've seen and how they may help. We can't rely on charms to stop Zita, but it's better to have some ready for peace of mind."

"In the meantime, we move on to phase two," Femke said.

Mirthe rubbed her hands together. "If we're going to pull this off, we're going to need support."

"What can we do about that?" Sebastian asked. "The majority of the town loves Zita. Even the people born before her reign prefer having her around."

"We can't be the only people in Grimbaud seeking a change," Nico said. "Maybe we're braver by actually doing something about it, but it doesn't mean that everyone else loves her."

"What kind of support are we talking about?" Hijiri asked.

"Whatever we can get," Mirthe said. "When we find Zita, I don't want it to be just us."

However, the plan still had holes. The biggest problem was finding Zita. No one had seen the woman for years. Extra allies would be beneficial in this matter, especially if they were adults, because they'd have a wider scope to roam the town freely, collecting clues.

"Where do we even start looking?" Sebastian said. "It's not like we can put an ad in the paper."

"We have two particular places in mind," Femke said.

Fallon put on her coat as the last of the southerly slipped away; the coat stayed warm as if it had been baked in the sun. The water frothed underneath the wooden boards, shocking her bare feet.

"The Bachelor and Spinster Villas."

For a minute, no one spoke. Fallon's heart thumped in her chest, drowning out the noise of the sea. Just thinking about the Spinster Villas made her ill. "Are you serious?"

The twins raised their eyebrows at the same time. "Why wouldn't we be?" Mirthe said. "They are the rejects. The people we might become. But they also have every reason to hate Zita."

Nico shifted in his seat. Hijiri breathed through her mouth. Sebastian looked the most at ease with the news, but Fallon sat close enough to sense him tense beside her.

"Yes, yes, the villas. It's happening," Mirthe said. "Anyone have other ideas?"

"What about Hard-boiled Hal?" Fallon said, thinking of Anais's love for the radio show. "If we can find out who he is, he might be willing to help us."

"That's good," Mirthe said. "Impossible, but good. We'll be famous for solving the mystery of his identity . . . if we can."

Fallon's teeth started to chatter as the others voiced their ideas. As much as she didn't want to think about the Spinster Villas, she knew she had an advantage. After all, she worked in the library for Ms. Ward, the youngest spinster in Grimbaud.

chapter 11

KISSING

Fallon found a couple making out in the gardening section. They didn't stop when she stomped her feet on the carpet. She cleared her throat, but they only changed positions so that the girl's shoulders pressed painfully against *Flowers and You* and *Weeding for the Ages*. The girl clung to her boyfriend fiercely, digging her nails into his blazer. When she thought she saw a flicker of a tongue, Fallon stumbled out of the row in search of help.

Ms. Ward looked up from the computer at the circulation desk. Her eyes narrowed. "Another one?"

Fallon nodded.

The ruffled blouse underneath Ms. Ward's chin rustled as she got up. She grabbed a newspaper lying on a nearby desk and stalked over to the kissing couple. "The library is not a kissing booth!" She smacked the newspaper against the gardening books as a pet owner would train a new puppy. The couple broke apart, snickering, and dodged her as they raced out of the library. "Out! Out! Out!"

The other students in the library had their laugh too, while Ms. Ward's face flushed bright red. No one seemed sympathetic to the poor librarian. Students weren't allowed to display affection beyond hand-holding and hugs during school hours. As romantically inclined as Grimbaud was, rules needed to be followed. That included the library, though no one seemed to care.

"That's the fifth couple this week," Fallon said as she followed Ms. Ward back to the circulation desk. "What's going on?"

"This happens every year," Ms. Ward said. She settled back behind the computer, her face splotchy with embarrassment.

"What do you mean?"

"Think about Zita's fortunes. You find out the new school year's fortune in September, go buy whatever charms you need from her shop, and start using them by October. As you know, going to Zita's shop is off-limits for me," she said softly, "but I'm willing to bet that one of the charms has to do with the library. Must be cheap too, for so many students to show up here. As if books are only good for pillows."

"I know," Fallon said.

"Of course you do," Ms. Ward said dismissively. "We both have the same problem."

Fallon had shared her love fortune with the librarian after her first day. Their easy friendship made sense; Fallon was next in line to join the spinsters, if her fortune had any truth to it.

"Can you reshelf these books?" Ms. Ward asked, pointing at a cart stacked with returned books.

"Sure."

Fallon didn't enjoy catching the couples either. No matter how many times she saw them, her stomach turned. The worst was when she found them too late, and the couple had gone far beyond kissing. Reflexes dictated that she either shut her eyes or cough up her lunch. She didn't understand how anyone would think rolling around on a fifty-year-old carpet was a good idea. Luckily, they had yet to catch students with their clothes off, but Ms. Ward had three assistant principals on speed dial, just in case.

After being exposed to so many kissing couples, and having entirely too much time on her hands when the library traffic dwindled, Fallon's thoughts went somewhere she hadn't intended: she compared Sebastian's kisses with the boys' she caught in the stacks. He must have learned something from kissing so many girls, because he had a neat, tidy way of kissing. No drooling. No wandering hands. No animal-like noises. He might have kissed coldly, but that was a detail she was willing to forgive after what she'd seen.

If Anais was here, she'd be calling me a prude, Fallon thought wryly. *A messy kiss means love. Not that I'd know.* She pushed the cart down the aisle, past the boy in the headphones tapping his foot to his music.

"Sit over here, Martin, by the window," came Camille's voice.

Fallon flinched. She peered through the cart to see

Camille claim a table near the window. She darted into a row, pretending to be engrossed in shelving. The books felt slippery in her sweaty palms.

Martin carried a box of paperwork. His glasses sat on his nose at a crooked angle and his arms shook from the weight of the box. "Not so loud."

"Why?"

"We're in a library. You have to whisper."

Camille stood on her toes and breathed in his ear. Her question was anything but a whisper. "Like this?"

Martin shivered and almost dropped the box. "We have work to do," he said thickly.

"Nope, only you do." They sat down.

"I could have asked the other officers for help," Martin said, pinching the bridge of his nose.

Camille snorted. "I don't think so. They've got lives."

That was a tactless, hurtful statement, but Martin just seemed to take it. He grabbed the first paper from the stack and sighed. "You're right. I'm the president. I can't give my responsibilities to other people."

Camille sank back in her chair. She took something out of her purse and dabbed her wrists. A strong scent of musk and caramel liqueur made Fallon's nose itch; she pinched it shut to keep from sneezing. "I don't see how serving on student government is going to help us after graduation. I'm only here for you, Martin. I do what I can because I care about you."

Martin opened his mouth, then shut it. He blinked a few

times as if he couldn't focus. "Yes," he mumbled into his paper.

"At least I'm going somewhere at the charm shop."

Fallon stopped shelving. For the rebellion's sake, she needed to pay attention. She knelt down, pretending to read the titles off the bottom of the cart.

"I know Zita's shop intimately," she said, "from every shelved potion to the dust under the counters. While you were moping this summer, I became an assistant manager. Me, a high school student. Zita said I had promise."

Martin looked up. "You talked to her?"

"Over the phone. We have a phone in the break room that's used exclusively for phone calls with Zita. It's pink."

"Pink," he echoed. He returned to his work.

Camille twisted a lock of hair around her finger. "Zita has such a squeaky voice, but there's authority behind it. She told me that she liked how I conducted myself at work. It won't be long before I become a full-fledged manager, and then, perhaps, I could even meet her and learn from her."

Martin signed a sheet of paper and reached for the next one.

"She's as old as my grandma. It's only a matter of time before she retires and hands the shop over to someone else."

Fallon gripped the orchid book in her hands tightly. So this was Camille's aspiration.

Camille smiled fondly at Martin and planted a kiss on his lips that put the sneaking couples to shame. "I'm glad we had this talk," she said, touching his cheek. "We might not be dating anymore, but I can't bear leaving you alone. You're so helpless without me."

Martin touched his lips, slow and stunned, while the pen fell from his hand and rolled onto the floor.

Fallon couldn't watch anymore. As smooth as she could, she stood up, grabbed the cart, and pushed it into another row far from Camille and Martin. *Nico shouldn't hear about this*, she thought. *I can't tell him. He'll only cry.*

The image of the pink phone stuck with her as she finished the shelving. Up until now, she hadn't heard anything about Zita's interactions with people, but the phone made sense. She'd need to keep tabs on her shop to make sure it ran correctly. But where was Zita, that she needed a phone? Maybe the great love charm-maker hopped from train to train, attending private conferences and hiding from cameras. That would explain why no one in Grimbaud had seen her in years.

"Have you finished?" Ms. Ward said, coming around the corner with a handful of books. "I've got more returned books to shelve."

Fallon took them from her.

Ms. Ward hesitated. "If you don't mind my asking, is something wrong? You look upset."

"I'm just tired. I stayed up late doing homework."

Ms. Ward looked unconvinced. "I want you to know that you can confide in me. That may sound silly coming from me, but I remember receiving that fortune at your age and having no one to turn to. It was a miserable time. I wouldn't wish it on anyone."

"Thank you," Fallon said. "I'd like to hear about it sometime."

"It might make you sadder."

"I can handle it."

Ms. Ward smiled warmly. "Good girl. You'll need to be brave. It took me a long time to feel that way."

The librarian's words would have been a bitter comfort if the rebellion hadn't existed. Fallon returned to the shelving, fixated on the prospect of Ms. Ward becoming an ally for the cause. Her sympathy might make her receptive, but in the meantime, Fallon needed to get to know her better.

"Oh, it's almost time," Anais said, clapping her hands. She plugged in the radio and ushered Fallon over to the register. "Thanks for listening with me. It's lonely being here with only Hal's voice for company."

Maybe if you told Bear where you lived, he would stay awake with you, Fallon thought.

The night wound down quickly inside the drugstore. Mr. Jacobs, fully awake this time, let Anais turn up the volume so Hard-boiled Hal's voice reached every corner of the store.

"Mind the register," he warned, carrying a bucket of receipts upstairs to file.

"Okay, Dad," Anais mumbled. Chin on her fists, she waited to be entertained by Hard-boiled Hal's antics.

You won't find anything sappy on our show. Stick around,

*grab a beer, and we'll talk about the other things that matter
in life. Yes, other things* do *matter.*

Hard-boiled Hal's agenda was different that night. He
made jokes about the high school kids spending the last of
their pocket money on charms to make each other miserable. Although he kept his promise of avoiding sappiness,
recent events in town had obviously upset him as well. He
took a deep breath over the radio waves, interrupting his
own rant on last night's baseball game held at the middle
school. *Look, there's something I can't get out of my head.
You're probably thinking about the same thing as me, so we're
going to banish it from our thoughts together. Let's pointedly ignore the statue's removal. Ready? One. Two. Three. Ignored.*

Anais snickered. "He's that upset?"

"Aren't you?"

"Everyone is. But I didn't think that a statue would break
him."

If Robbie could step out of his world of textiles and
clothing to get mad about the statue's removal, then anything was possible.

As late as it was, Fallon was glad that she got to spend
time with Anais while doing work for the rebellion. She'd
need to listen to Hal's show every night if she wanted a
good chance of discovering his identity. Maybe everyone in
the club could take turns. Memorizing his voice was the
best strategy she had. If she could hear him in a crowd . . .

Fallon's eyes widened. Didn't the rebellion already have
a sound expert? Sebastian spent who knows how many
hours each week collecting silence. To the point where

he could probably identify sounds better than the average person. Fallon needed to speak to him about listening for Hal. In her excitement, the temptation to jog back to the complex with the question on her lips was almost irresistible.

The door jingled. Anais tensed, ready to flee in case it was her boyfriend, but only Nico walked into the store. He wore his cutoff jeans, soaked with canal water, and shivered as he approached the counter.

"What's the matter?" Fallon asked, noticing his puffy eyes.

"Did Camille put tacks in your locker?" Anais joked, but she turned down the volume on the radio.

"Worse than that," Nico said. He dried his eyes with the back of his sleeve. "Something's wrong with Martin. I can feel it. My stomach's been in knots all day."

Fallon grabbed a blanket from underneath the counter (in case of spills) and draped it over Nico's shoulders. He was cold to the touch, and not just because of working the night shift at the ticket booth. The episode at the library had happened a few days ago; she hadn't told him about it for fear of upsetting him, but she should have known better. Camille and Martin's continuing relationship wouldn't have escaped Nico for long.

Anais dropped a few dollars into the cash register and poured cups of tasteless coffee. "Many things could be wrong with Martin. He's the president. You'll have to be more specific."

Nico held on to the coffee like an anchor. "I didn't want to believe it at first. I thought that Camille was just being pushy when she made those moves on Martin. We've had an officer meeting every week since September, and only recently have things changed between them. Martin doesn't lead the meetings anymore. Camille does. He just sits there, looking at his paper, like he hasn't been sleeping. And worst of all, he lets Camille push him around. God, when she kisses him . . ." He paused. "She has no shame. And neither does Martin, for that matter. He just lets her kiss him in front us."

"I hate to say it, but your fortune wasn't very positive about you and Martin," Anais said. "Things like this happen. Exes get back together. I'll never understand that, but they do."

"No, wait," Nico said, grabbing Anais's wrist. "I'm not saying it right."

"Try again," Fallon said.

"When Martin's not near her, he seems almost normal. Kind of sick, like he's getting over a cold, but better. He calls me Nicolas." He took a sip of the coffee. "During the officer meetings, he loses himself. And I know Camille spends as much time as she can with him when she's not working at Zita's. When they're together, something hurts him. I know it."

"That can only mean one thing," Anais said.

Fallon's breath caught. "Camille's using a love charm."

chapter 12

SUN

"I saw Martin and Camille in the library," Fallon admitted. "I don't know Martin that well, but after what you've just said, I agree with you. He was very passive with her."

Nico's brow furrowed. "Passive, how?"

As usual, he fished for more details that would hurt his heart further. Fallon had no intention of indulging him. "Along the same lines as what you said happens. So what are we going to do about it?"

Nico took a shaky sip of his coffee.

Anais steepled her fingers in the fashion of a calculating villain. "Oh yes, we're doing something. Camille's gone too far this time."

Fallon thought about what she'd learned so far about love charms. "Manipulation is a fact when it comes to love charms, isn't it? Either you do it to yourself or to someone else. But turning someone into a zombie has to be illegal. The police should get involved."

"That would take too long," Anais said. "Charm crimes aren't that common because there's a fine line between using a charm as it's meant to work and using it for an awful purpose. Remember when Alard Carlier got suspended from school for using a charm to cheat on his final exam in history? He could have gotten expelled if he hadn't claimed his retention charm malfunctioned. Of course, we all knew he tinkered with the charm so that his pen would gravitate toward the right choice on the bubble sheet. The administration believed it, though. If Camille hasn't been caught yet, that means that no one's noticed a problem. It's up to us to help Martin."

Fallon felt a rush of pride for having a friend like Anais. "What should we do first?"

"Isn't it obvious? We go to Zita's shop and look for the deplorable charm."

"Nico and I aren't allowed to buy anything there," Fallon said. Even if Nico tried, they'd deny him any purchases in case he thought about using them in pursuit of Martin.

"My fortune was just fine," Anais said. "I'll go in and find out what I can. You two will wait outside. I can go tomorrow evening. Dad will just have to cover for me."

Nico put his coffee down and hugged Anais tightly. "Thank you."

"No one messes with my friends," Anais said bashfully. "I may be small and cute, but I've got a sharp tongue and I'm not afraid to use it."

Fallon grinned. "We wouldn't expect any less."

Pigeons occupied Verbeke Square the next day. They cooed and picked at the waffle crumbs leftover from the food carts. Fallon sipped milky orange blossom tea at a café overlooking Zita's Lovely Love Charms Shop. The pink-lemonade shop had been busy as usual when Anais went inside.

"She's been in there an awfully long time," Nico said, sitting opposite Fallon. He rubbed the extra salt off his hot pretzel and took a bite.

"She won't find anything," Fallon said, dejected. The plan had been so exciting, so hopeful, when they first formed it, but now she wasn't so sure. Would it really be that easy to find the potion Camille was using on Martin?

"It's good exercise for her," Nico said. "Besides, maybe she'll find something that'll help her open up to Bear."

Fallon almost choked on her tea.

"What?"

"I wish."

Fallon hadn't spent much time thinking about Anais and Bear's relationship—and with good reason. They seemed perfectly happy together. Anais's had the energy and ador-ableness of a lapdog with her fluffy blond hair and big eyes. She fit him in a way opposites do, with her head tucked into his side as they strolled through the school yard. Bear was just her type—big, strong, protective—but it was his gen-tleness that kept Anais interested. If only Anais could show that she trusted him back. Fallon hated to think how Bear would take being lied to.

After half an hour of waiting and another cup of tea, Fallon spotted Anais holding a little pink bag with a devious grin on her face.

Nico chewed the last of his pretzel. "Did you find it?"

"Not really," Anais said, pulling up a chair. "But I can be pretty persuasive when I want to. I had a long conversation with Camille Simmons about ex-boyfriends. As you know, I can't stand spending even a second in the company of a boy I broke up with. But I pretended that I still cared in order to wheedle information out of Camille. And it worked."

When Anais had found Camille, she asked for a charm that would keep her ex-boyfriends interested in her.

"We don't sell anything like that," Camille said, toying with her headset.

"You don't understand how lonely I am without my exes fawning over me," Anais said, batting her eyes. "I know they still love me. They just need a little encouragement. Surely Zita has a charm for that."

Camille tugged her headset off. She crooked a finger for Anais to come closer and whispered, "What would you do if you got their love back?"

"Use them."

Camille smirked. "Are you looking for a job here? You might fit in with that attitude."

"Just the charm, thanks."

"Zita won't sell anything like that," she said, "but I've cooked up a little charm that fills a boy's head with lake fog. Ripe for using. Maybe I'll be able to sell it to you soon."

"Why not now?"

Camille picked up the headset. "I'm not the boss."

Anais stepped back as another customer quizzed Camille on the display of heartache-be-gone potions. She bought a hanging charm that was supposed to enhance peacefulness in torrid relationships ("It smells like chamomile," Anais had said) and left the shop as quickly as she could.

Fallon trembled when the gravity of Anais's discovery hit her. "Camille made the charm herself," she said, sharing a stunned look with her friends. "It isn't Zita's creation. How did she get away with using it without getting in trouble?"

"Camille's quite the businesswoman," Anais said. She snatched Fallon's empty teacup and poured herself some orange blossom tea from the pot. "She had a twinkle in her eye. Some people would call it smugness."

Nico crossed his arms. "Zita, or at least one of the managers, must already know about Camille's love charm. We can't get her in trouble that way."

"That makes sense," Fallon said. Could there be another way? "If we could find out where and how Camille makes the charm, then we can steal the ingredients and prevent her from making more."

Nico pressed his hand to her forehead. "No fever."

"I'm fine."

"You don't sound like the Fallon Dupree I know. Breaking and entering?"

"I like this Fallon," Anais said, "but he's right. We're not thieves. It sounds like something out of an action film."

After leaving Verbeke Square, Fallon asked Nico to walk back to the complex with her. She told him more about what she had seen at the library, though she was careful to leave out the details that would upset him. The pink phone. Camille's desire to succeed Zita's legacy. "Regarding poor Martin, I have another idea."

Nico's thinning hair twisted in the wind. He burrowed into his jacket. "Another one? I'm not surprised. You're just as clever as Anais."

The compliment warmed her. "Thanks. I just have a feeling that Zita's shop won't have all the answers. Lucky for us, our rebellion has a love-charm expert."

"Do you mean the twins?"

"Hijiri, actually. She doesn't want anyone to know, but she actually makes love charms."

His eyes widened. "Would she help?"

"I hope so. That's why I asked you to come with me. We're going to find her right now and see."

The student housing complex lit up like a string of broken lights as night fell, marking who was awake and who had actually turned in for the night. As they approached the gate, a dark figure appeared. Sebastian. He held his tape recorder in his hand.

"What did you catch this time?" she asked.

Sebastian tilted his head, surprised. "You really want to know?"

"I wouldn't be asking if I didn't."

"Hm." He pocketed the recorder and shrugged. "Found some quiet near Verbeke Square. Sometimes that area's dead silent between groups of pub crawlers."

"There's something I'd like to ask you," Fallon said.

"Have you decided to go out with me?"

Her heart scrambled up her throat, choking her words.

"Stop teasing her," Nico said. "We're looking for Hijiri. Do you know where her apartment is?"

"Actually, we're neighbors."

"Really?"

"You can't miss her when the door to her apartment creaks so loudly. Mrs. Smedt hasn't fixed it yet." Sebastian opened the wooden gate and waited until both Fallon and Nico passed through before following. "There's a good chance that she's still awake."

"Good," she said.

"Is that what you wanted to ask me?"

"No."

Sebastian brushed up against her; numb from the cold, she barely felt him, but she heard the scratchy sound their coats made rubbing against each other. "Mind telling me?"

Fallon regained her composure and bumped him back. "It's for the rebellion. We're going to need your keen hearing."

He laughed. "You make me sound like a dog."

"Aren't you?"

Hurt flashed in his eyes. "That's not how I see things."

Fallon reached out for his hand. She hadn't meant it like that. Her stiff fingers met air as Sebastian backed away from her. "I shouldn't have said that."

Sebastian glanced her way, his expression softening. "You wound me, Dupree. But maybe my hearing skills are that good. I should really take it as a compliment."

"I *am* sorry," she said. Hearing him say her last name was a pinprick to her conscience. She had sounded like her parents just then, hadn't she? They rarely held their tongues.

"I know."

Nico coughed behind them. "Guys, it's getting even colder out here. Can we please find the apartment?"

Sebastian strode ahead with his chin down. The ground-floor apartments looked the same on the outside as the higher floors, including the decorations taped to the doors. "Mine's over there," he said, pointing to a door with a paw-print sticker under the number plate, "and Hijiri's is to the right of me."

Hijiri's door had nothing on it, but that was normal for a freshman. She had only been living there for two months. Some students took longer than others to make it a home. Fallon knocked on the door and waited.

After a few minutes, Hijiri appeared, half-asleep and wearing a faded, oversize T-shirt and shorts. "Have you no pity for sleeping people? I was having a good nap," she said, but she didn't sound too angry.

"Can we come in?"

Hijiri glanced at Sebastian and Nico. "Okay."

The heater in her apartment was running full-blast, creating a tropical atmosphere. Fallon shed her coat and left it at the front door. Although clean, the apartment was barren. Standard-issued furnishings did little to take up the gaping space. "I know you didn't want me to tell anyone, but we have an emergency." Fallon started, knowing that she had to get over this part first.

Hijiri plopped down on the worn brown couch. Her hair, more tangled from sleep, covered her round face.

"I'm sorry," Fallon continued.

Hijiri played with the hem of her T-shirt. "What's happening?"

While Nico talked, Fallon stared down at her hands. The guilt of having revealed Hijiri's secret snuck up on her. *The rebellion would have needed to know about her skills eventually*, she thought. But not this way. This wasn't just about the rebellion. No, it was entirely selfish. Fallon had wanted to help Nico, one of her very best friends. However, nothing would compel her to divulge Hijiri's plans to make a true love's kiss charm. Hopefully keeping that a secret still was enough to make up for what she had told the boys.

"So Camille could be more dangerous than we thought," Sebastian said, gripping the back of an empty chair. "It's not just about her almost catching Fallon at the meeting."

Nico sank onto the couch next to Hijiri and put his head in his hands. "I'm having a hard time absorbing all this."

"You're the one who's always hated Camille," Fallon pointed out.

"Naturally. I'd hate anyone dating the boy I love. But this is going too far. I didn't think she'd be this extreme about keeping Martin."

Fallon thought about what Camille had said in the library. "Maybe it's not about Martin. She's ambitious. Camille might want to keep him around for another purpose."

Nico moaned. "That's even worse!"

"And probably true," Sebastian added.

Nico lifted his head and stared at Sebastian. "What do you know about Camille?"

"Me?"

"You've dated her, right? You've dated everyone."

Sebastian's expression darkened. "Camille Simmons stays out of my way. She's a serious girl, like Fallon here. Her standards keep her from wasting time with me."

Fallon flinched at his words. She didn't want to hurt him, but she couldn't possibly date him. His idea of dating was pretending, and even if she tried, he'd break her heart sooner or later.

Hijiri tapped her fingers on the couch. "How much do you love Martin?"

"Very much," Nico said brokenly. "More than I can say."

Fallon breathed through her own tears, pushing them back. Maybe she was just tired. She rarely stayed awake this late at night, and Nico's emotions were affecting her. She caught Sebastian's eye and couldn't smile. Her mouth wasn't working. He looked as upset as she was.

Hijiri's gaze remained on the floor, but she pivoted so that she was facing him. "Okay, I'll help, but you must promise to do what I say. Love charms are powerful, dangerous things when abused. If Martin's as affected as you say, you'll have to draw him out of it."

"But my fortune . . ." Nico said.

"Ignore it." Hijiri frowned. "If you must, think of it as a friend saving a friend."

Fallon buried herself in her sheets, but sleep evaded her. The heater's warmth tickled the back of her neck, gentle as fingers, unlike the restless state of her mind. She had followed through with her nightly routine of laying out her uniform and combing her hair until it shone. Yet her heart pounded against the mattress. Emotions trailed her thoughts like ghosts and none of it made sense.

When she thought of Sebastian the beginning of a head cold shot through her temples, making her ache. Not that anyone at school was sick. This was a sickness entirely of her own making.

"I have school tomorrow," she told the universe, but her tired eyes stayed open.

The mystery of Sebastian Barringer only deepened. He was real. Vulnerable. There were cracks in his armor that

Fallon had discovered by tripping over them, by saying things she'd never guessed had barbs. Even the frenzied excitement of helping Nico failed to distract her from noticing him. Fallon wanted to understand his reactions.

The early hours of the morning dyed her bedroom milky blue. Fallon pulled open the little white drawer on her bedside table. She felt the hard plastic of the cassette tape. Blindly, she popped the tape into her player.

At first, she didn't hear anything. Fallon retreated to her nest of sheets and blankets. She squeezed her eyes shut. Then, like modicums of stars in a cloudy sky, the sounds crept up on her. The gentle gurgle of the canal water. A breeze teasing the grass. If she listened hard enough, she swore she heard her own breathing mixed with Sebastian's as they waited in the darkness for the silence to end.

Her body relaxed. It wasn't until morning, when her alarm went off, that she realized she'd fallen asleep.

Fallon arrived at school early and walked over to her usual meeting place inside the tunnel. She eased into the shadows, adjusting her ears to the vibrations of the students crowded within. Anais waved at her, one arm securely wrapped around Bear's. He carried her bag and textbooks with a pleasant smile on his face, and actually seemed interested in Anais's typical tirade about mosquitoes.

"I got bit three times on my arm yesterday," Anais said, shoving up her sleeve for Bear to see. "It should be impossible. Mosquitos should all be dead at this time of year."

With his free hand, Bear carefully examined the mosquito bites. "I have some cream in my locker that might help."

"You do?"

"The mornings are damp, the perfect time for mosquitoes to attack," he said. "It makes training uncomfortable, but I prefer being outdoors instead of in a gym."

Anais shivered a little. "I'm going to have to leave you alone now, Fallon. These bites are really itchy."

"Don't worry," Sebastian said, strolling into the tunnel, "I won't let her out of my sight."

Anais dug into Bear's arm, moments away from ordering her brawny boyfriend to beat Sebastian up. "You have no business hanging around my friend, Bastion."

Fallon placed her bag on the ground and sighed. "It's okay, Anais. You go on ahead. Nico will be here any minute to protect me from Sebastian."

Bear agreed. "If we don't put that cream on your bites, you'll break skin from all that scratching."

"Fine." Anais glared at Sebastian. "See you later."

Sebastian curled his fingers in a mocking wave. "Feisty friend you've got there."

"She's protective of me."

"Anyone would be."

Fallon blushed.

Sebastian leaned against the tunnel wall. Decades of the stone wall's grime would come off like newspaper ink on the back of his sweater the minute he moved, but he didn't seem to care. Most people didn't.

The tunnel provided a clear view of Grimbaud High's front lawn, plainly covered in trampled grass and benches claimed by the same students day after day. Fallon saw Camille and Martin sitting on a bench facing the building— another oddity for Martin, since Nico insisted that the pallid president used the teacher's lounge as a private study before the first bell rang.

Nico and Hijiri arrived minutes later, whispering to each other in the tunnel. Nico's uniform had seen better days; he wore wrinkled pants and his bright blue eyes were bloodshot. In contrast, Hijiri stood taller than usual. "Tell me where they are, and we'll start," she said.

Nico pointed a shaky finger at the bench. "Right there."

Fallon's stomach dropped. Early as it was, Camille easily held Martin's attention. She climbed up on the bench, her skirt billowing in the wind. She took one step at a time, letting her hair fall prettily in front of her face, and while Martin craned his neck to watch her. His notebooks and pencils slipped out of his hands and fell to the ground. He made no move to pick them up.

Hijiri walked to the edge of the tunnel and pulled out a tiny pair of silver binoculars. The binoculars looked akin to something a devoted birdwatcher would have carried. She spent a good minute watching Camille and Martin through the lens. "There's a charm at work, but I can't tell who has it from here. I need to get closer."

"She'll catch you," Fallon said.

"Will she?" Hijiri shrugged. "I'm a nobody. Sometimes that comes in handy."

Pocketing her binoculars, Hijiri left the safety of the tunnel and blended in with the students on the lawn. Instead of making a beeline for Camille and Martin, she swiveled in between groups of students and hopped over a pair of boys already sleeping in the grass.

"I don't remember ever being so invisible," Sebastian said with admiration.

"Me neither." Fallon caught herself and looked him in the eye. "I meant me. Not since high school began." When the student body labeled her a snob.

Sebastian bumped her shoulder. "I get it. Thanks."

Hijiri wandered close to the bench, just behind a group of girls crossing the lawn. She slowed down, moving with purpose, and circled the bench twice as Camille laughed and stole Martin's glasses. She lifted her head, sniffing the air, and hurried back to the tunnel.

"What did you find?" Nico said.

"There's not much we can do for Martin," Hijiri said, "because the charm is coming from Camille. She wears it like perfume. Martin can't resist her when he's close to her. It binds him."

Nico's face crumbled. He rubbed at his eyes with his sleeves.

"So as long as Camille's with him, he turns into a drooling puddle of boy," Sebastian said, frowning. "Is there a charm that can counteract it?"

"Probably not of Zita's variety," Fallon said. "And we can't risk drawing suspicion. Femke and Mirthe would probably agree."

Hijiri grabbed Nico by the sweater. "Don't spiral now. You can do something about this, Nico."

"I can't compete, even as a friend," Nico said weakly.

"Yes, you can. Now dry your eyes. We have to hurry before the bell rings."

Nico sniffed and smoothed down his sweater.

"This is very simple. I want you to walk over there and tell Martin that he's needed. Whatever excuse you see fit. If he doesn't budge, take him by the hand and lead him away. Okay?"

"Okay."

As Nico left, Hijiri smiled. "Let's follow him. We're going to need to hear this."

A bubble of excitement rose in Fallon's chest as she and Sebastian followed Hijiri onto the lawn. They moved as she did, blending and curving with the students, until she was close enough to overhear Nico as he stopped at the bench.

"Martin," he said, "Mr. Claes is asking for you in the teacher's lounge. He wants to go over last year's budget with us."

"Can't you see we're busy?" Camille said, barely giving

Nico a second glance. She played with Martin's glasses, putting them on and off her face while Martin squinted and feebly reached for them.

Fallon wanted to march over there and slap Camille. She wanted, more than anything, to retrieve those glasses and end Martin's torment, unknown as it was to him. But Nico surprised her. He became almost golden, his tanned skin and electric blue eyes at once penetrating.

"This can't wait." He held out his hand for Martin's glasses. "You know how impatient Mr. Claes is."

Camille snorted and slid the glasses back on Martin's nose. Then she gave him a sound kiss. "He'll have to wait until after school."

Nico bristled. Sunlight made his hair catch gold. "Martin," he said, stronger, "let's go." He grabbed Martin's wrist and tugged him forward—away from the bench, from Camille, from the cloying perfume that turned his brain fuzzy and weak.

That was when Fallon saw what Hijiri was getting at by making Nico go through with this. The moment Nico touched Martin, something snapped and fizzled in the air. Tension leaked. Martin's eyelashes fluttered and he seemed to really breathe for the first time that morning.

"Mr. Claes doesn't appreciate being kept waiting," Martin said softly.

Camille's mouth twisted. She leaned forward. "You can't go."

Martin swayed on his feet.

Nico let go of Martin and turned away from the bench. It looked as if he was giving up. But then he looked over his shoulder and offered his hand again. "Martin?"

And to everyone's surprise, Martin blinked. "Of course. Coming." He stumbled after Nico, rubbing his temples and coughing.

"What just happened?" Sebastian asked.

Hijiri smiled. "It's simple. Nico is like the sun for Martin."

chapter 13

EVERY TIME

I f relationships could be understood with equations, then Nico's position was perfect for obstructing Camille's charm. "From what I understand, Martin doesn't have many friends. He's also dedicated to his position as president," Hijiri said. "So logically, the student government officers have the power to bring him out of Camille's charm."

Fallon couldn't hide her disappointment. "Any one of them?"

"We'd have to test each officer to be sure." Hijiri paused. "Sorry. I know you were hoping for better news."

"I thought Martin's reaction meant he might like Nico."

"I guess I was too poetic with my sun comment. Let me put it another way. At this point, Nico has enough leverage to interfere with the charm because Martin trusts him and respects him as treasurer. Those feelings rise to the surface even when he's in the throes of the charm. Nico's presence burns away the effects of Camille's charm, if only temporarily. You see, friendship has power too. Just perhaps not as strong as love."

"How do you know so much?" Sebastian asked.

Hijiri laughed—it was a soft, whispery sound. "Through observation. You can learn a lot when you're not participating in life."

"You're already a great charm-maker, aren't you?" Fallon said.

Hijiri tucked her chin to her chest. "Not really."

"You are. Thank you for helping us."

Hijiri mumbled a "you're welcome" and darted away as soon as the first bell rang.

Sebastian stretched languidly. His rolled-up pants rose as he balanced on his toes. "How does she see with that hair?"

"Good question." Fallon frowned. She wanted to thank Hijiri for helping somehow.

"Can't be comfortable."

"No." She thought hard.

"Well," Sebastian said, "don't want to be late for class."

The idea came to her in a starburst. She grabbed his bag strap before he could walk away. "Now I have two favors to ask you."

Sebastian, bemused, stopped to listen.

Sebastian said he needed two weeks of listening to *Hard-boiled Hal's Practical Guide to Love* before he could confidently be able to identify the radio show host's voice. "It's all in the pauses between words," he said. "Everyone creates silence differently."

Fallon wondered what gaps she left between her own words. While she folded her laundry and ironed her uniform, she tried out sentences and listened for the spaces. "I talk too slowly," she whispered.

During the week, she took turns visiting both Anais and Nico. Especially Nico. She squeezed into the ticket booth with him, offering what comfort she could while he struggled to accept Hijiri's discovery.

"She said I have a positive effect on him," Nico said, toying with the money in the cash register. "The more I'm in his line of sight, the better. Maybe he'll be able to pull himself out of the charm completely someday."

Someday. That sounded like hundreds of years in the future. Would they grow old and die still prisoners of Zita's fortunes? Fallon buttoned her coat up to her chin to keep out the chill.

"I care so much," Nico said, "but I'm so tired, Fallon."

"I know." She didn't sleep much herself, unless she listened to Sebastian's tape.

Nico slapped the register closed. "You know what? This isn't like me. I'm not going to sit in this stupid booth, crying and lamenting my fate."

"That *is* like you," Fallon teased.

"Nevertheless. Let's get some air. Real air."

She followed Nico to where the rowboats were tied up. "We're going out on the water?"

Nico shushed her. "Not so loud. My dad can't find out."

The rowboat only left ripples as proof of their escape as they traveled down the canal. Mr. Barnes's big boats cruised farther south; since Nico knew the route by heart, they were in no danger of taking the same path. Fallon sat with her hands in her lap, admiring the firefly lights belonging to the coffee shops and antique stores. Adults drank wine on balconies. A string quartet played on the street near the canal while their audience curled up on blankets and ate cakes wrapped in wax paper.

Nico's wiry muscles flexed as he rowed. "Beautiful, isn't it? It almost makes me forget."

Grimbaud filled Fallon's heart and from the tips of her eyelashes to her toes. Gliding down the canals in a tiny boat made the rest of the world feel so far away. Her worries about Zita sank beneath the water. Twisted love fortunes and charms were only nightmares, gone by morning.

From this distance, Grimbaud was a perfect arrangement of smoky heart-rings, rich chocolate, and love neverending. Love in every brick. In every drop of water. It wasn't a trick of the canal.

"We have to save this town," she said, rocking with the boat.

Nico grinned.

On her way back to the complex, Fallon bought three

cherry-filled chocolates and savored them. She ate one over each bridge, daring herself to make the decedent pieces last until her feet touched solid ground again.

While lost in thought, Fallon glanced up to see a troupe of women crossing the street. They were mostly middle-aged, wearing sheer hats and whimsical clothing. She knew them immediately as the residents of the Spinster Villas. Unlike the beautiful women depicted in the villas' pamphlet, the real women staying there became eccentrics as a way of coping with sadness. Some women got tattooed with the names of the men they would never date, while others adopted stray cats. Ms. Ward carried a brown paper bag in the center of the group.

Fallon jogged after the troupe; they moved faster than she imagined, but it was impossible to lose them with their colorful outfits and loneliness that trailed behind them like smoke. "Ms. Ward!" she yelled.

The entire group stopped. Ms. Ward clutched the paper bag close to her chest. She was startled from having heard her name in public. "Hello, Fallon."

As she approached, Fallon noticed the stares she received from the townspeople. They wanted to know why she was talking to the spinsters, being friendly with them and using their names. Although Grimbaud was generally cordial toward them, no one wanted to actively seek out a spinster's or bachelor's friendship—their condition could rub off on them.

"Who's this girl, Emma?" said a woman in her late fifties.

She wore an empress-style dress that dragged in the dirt behind her.

"Fallon Dupree, my volunteer at the school library," Ms. Ward answered.

"Is she one of us?" asked a small woman with blue hair.

Ms. Ward hesitated.

"I could be," Fallon said, "if my fortune doesn't change next year."

"Honey, they never do," said the first woman. She introduced herself as Helena. The small, blue-haired woman was Yasmine.

The troupe peppered her with questions, comfort, and requests to see the dreaded fortune itself. Fallon tried to catch her breath as they drew closer, but she seemed to be missing air. The stench of mothballs and stale perfume filled her lungs. The paper bag crackled when she bumped against Ms. Ward.

"You're crowding the girl," Ms. Ward said, using her librarian voice. "Give her some space."

The spinsters apologized and stepped back, but not before smoothing Fallon's hair and adjusting her bent shirt collar.

"Go on ahead to the bakery," Ms. Ward said, handing Yasmine a clump of money. "I'll join you in a moment."

Fallon sank onto the curb. "Thanks."

Ms. Ward sat down next to her and placed the paper bag between her legs. "They mean well, but they get so excited sometimes."

"I could be a new member," she said. "They have every right to celebrate."

"You *will* be a spinster, no matter what your living arrangements may be," Ms. Ward said. "I learned that the hard way. At the time, I refused to believe the fortune. I tore it up and remained in Grimbaud just long enough to graduate high school."

Fallon rested her hands on her knees. "What happened?"

"I thought I could outrun the fortune by backpacking across the country. I slept among ruins and sketched terrible portraits of the kind strangers I stayed with. The libraries of the world seduced me and I visited every single one I could. I knew my calling was to be a librarian."

"But love?"

"The same pattern happened, again and again. I would meet a boy and, within a few days, everything would fall apart. The longest relationship I had lasted a week, and only because it took him that long to realize that I sleep with paperbacks stuffed inside my pillows."

Fallon couldn't help but laugh. "Why?"

"Paperbacks are soft," she said, "and I like the idea of sleeping with entire worlds beneath my head."

Fallon rested her chin on her knees. "I like that too."

Footsteps echoed on the sidewalk. Bicyclists made their loops. The streetlamps streaked Ms. Ward's glasses with warm light. "Most of the time, I only saw boys in fleeting moments. The busboy who held the door open for me as I left the café. The violinist in the street who whistled when he saw me coming, but vanished moments later when I returned with change. I started hating that feeling of hope, of potential, Fallon." She tightened her fist. "After enough times, I decided to do my best to accept that love wasn't coming my way."

Fallon couldn't imagine what Ms. Ward had to feel guilty about. "There's nothing wrong with wanting to fall in love."

"You don't believe that."

Fallon squeezed her eyes shut. Her brain had a few arguments against love, especially the feelings that pointed her to Sebastian time and time again. Not love. Surely not love. She wasn't that stupid.

"Zita's fortune was right," Ms. Ward said. "Maybe my fate is to live like a broken record, repeating the same encounters over and over. It's certainly felt like that. Better to embrace spinsterhood and focus on life's other pleasures."

Her words drew Fallon away from her own warring thoughts. "Having so many similar encounters isn't normal. What if Zita's messing with you to make sure she's right?"

Ms. Ward tried to laugh, but her voice trembled. "That's ridiculous. I traveled far away from here, and love charms are fickle once outside of Grimbaud. Zita couldn't have the energy or ability to cause what happened to me."

"So it's fate."

"That's right. It took me long enough, but I accepted it." Ms. Ward sighed. "Romance isn't everything. Life is much, much more."

Fallon's gaze fell on the paper bag. "What's that?"

Ms. Ward flushed. "A villa tradition. We're not supposed to be reading romance novels, *really*, but the women agree that these books lift our spirits. It's our secret indulgence. Once a week, we buy a mystery bag of romance novels from the public library. You never know what's inside. Part of the fun. After picking up desserts, we divvy up the books and spend the evening reading."

"Why do you need them?" Fallon asked. "You said romance isn't everything."

Instead of answering, Ms. Ward shook her head. The bag of romance novels, a lifeline only moments before, sat heavy in the librarian's hands.

chapter 14

TERRIBLE SHOES

Fallon couldn't sleep the night after speaking to Ms. Ward, and she didn't want to be soothed by the tape Sebastian had left her. The pillows needed fluffing. She turned on her bedside lamp. The sheets sagged against her body, a deflated balloon, as she shifted into a comfortable position.

Placing her hand over her heart, she searched for the familiar beat. Her heart was a solid drummer, neat and thorough as she was with her own life, but it ached. Not a physical pain—she would have asked Mrs. Smedt to take her to the hospital if she thought it was serious. More so, she was concerned that it didn't act out enough.

"Why don't you flare up?" she wondered, tucking her chin to her chest. "Why aren't you like Ms. Ward's heart, shooting off fireworks at the first sight of love?"

Not everyone's heart worked the same, but the mechanics underneath had to be similar. Nico's nervous heart carried both anxiety and bravery as he fought to remain by Martin's side, no matter how doomed. Anais's heart was stubborn and guarded, but she freely revealed certain parts of it to Bear with intense, confident love.

"I'm a Dupree," she told the night. "We are orderly and clean. We fold our clothes and cook fresh foods and accept that love comes as easily into our lives as making room for another cashmere sweater in the drawer." Generations and generations. Duprees never had to try. They never worried about finding love because it always arrived with blinking signs and Zita's favorable fortunes. Her grandparents had been among the first to receive love fortunes. Her parents fit together. Robbie and Morgane lived in their world of clothing inspections and memories of belfry escapades.

If Fallon really was a Dupree, why was her cool heart sore with impatience? She felt as if there was something she ought to know.

In the morning, Fallon washed her face with her bar of goat's milk soap, a present from her mother, until it was shiny and pink. She sliced an apple for breakfast and buttoned her white blouse slowly. When she picked up her blazer, she lost her grip and the folds unraveled. Crinkled, brown petals scattered on the floor.

At first, she didn't know what she was seeing. She bent down for a closer look. The petals were brittle and had lost their scarlet color long ago, but she realized that they must have belonged to the begonia Sebastian had given her when they went searching for charms. Her stomach flipped when she remembered the warmth of his fingers when he had tucked the begonia behind her ear.

"How did you survive the washer and dryer?" she asked, rolling the dried-up petals in her hand. The blazer pockets weren't generous, so the tight space must not have been properly cleaned during the wash. The poor begonia hadn't deserved dying inside her blazer pocket. She whispered an apology and finished getting ready.

Begonias, a common enough flower in Grimbaud, caught her eye repeatedly on her walk to school.

During homeroom, Fallon erased and rewrote upcoming events in her planner. Papers due. Midterm exams. Student government and charm-maker's club meetings. Her handwriting had been sloppy and, with October's end upon them, she needed to maintain a sense of quality in whatever way she could to be prepared for next month.

Mrs. Heymans took attendance at her desk; today's brooch was a shimmery pink begonia that cast flecks of rainbows on the wall. With the heaters running, the room was stuffy. Nico napped on the desk beside her.

The classroom door opened with a wail. Marlene Dumont accepted her tardiness without as much as a glance in Mrs. Heymans's direction. "You won't believe this," she said furiously. "I was just turned down by Bastion. And I'm not the first girl he's refused."

Nico woke up with a start. Fallon's heart froze and melted.

A boy in the back snickered. "Why would you want to date him, anyway? Don't you girls ever learn?"

Marlene remained undaunted. Despite any embarrassment it might bring, she knew a juicy piece of gossip when she heard it. With the whiteboard behind her, she launched into her explanation of the morning's events. She had found Sebastian standing alone by the basketball court's fence and thought that she needed a little fun. "I wanted to take my mind off of Hamza," she said, referring to her breakup she had dramatized last week. "Sebastian saw me coming, knew what I was going to ask, of course. But he said he was tired of dating. Tired! Can you imagine?"

"He would be, dating every girl in Grimbaud," said another boy.

"That's not the point," Marlene snapped. "Bastion never turns girls down. So why now?"

Nico, annoyed at losing his nap over this, said, "Because he developed a conscience."

"No."

He grimaced. "Do you have a real answer?"

"There's only one reason why Sebastian has changed." Marlene paused for effect. "Obviously, someone's finally stolen his heart."

The boys in the classroom groaned.

"That's enough, Miss Dumont," Mrs. Heymans said. "Take your seat."

But the students continued to talk about Sebastian's decision, including theories about his fortune and the mysterious girl who (maybe) took his heart. Fallon erased with vigor, shedding shavings and wrinkling November's pages.

"You look happy," Nico said, cracking open an eye.

"Do I?"

He nodded and shut his eyes again. "You're smiling."

Brushing off the shavings, Fallon traced her lips to the corners. A smile.

——►

Fallon and Sebastian agreed to meet in Verbeke Square that Saturday to search for Hard-boiled Hal. The sky was dark and gray; she had forgotten her umbrella that morning and concentrated on stepping over puddles.

Sebastian waved at her from where he stood in front of a lace shop. His hair was windblown, his eyebrows pushed together in concentration. "The square is overflowing with people," he whispered in her ear. "It's going to be hard finding Hal with all the noise."

Fallon curled her fingers into a fist to stop herself from touching her ear. "We might get lucky."

"What optimism," he said dryly.

Her eyes flickered over the crowd. Hard-boiled Hal had to be somewhere in the square. After listening to a few of his shows, she'd noticed that he talked a lot about Verbeke Square: the cafés serving the best beers and the shops with the best lace-making, but mainly badmouthing Zita's love charms. He talked so often about her newest charms that Fallon easily pictured him staking out the love-charms shop with binoculars.

Little kids tugged anxiously on their parents' hands, bored and itching to run. Burdened with groceries for evening supper, housewives paused to watch a demonstrator use bobbins to make lace. There were plenty of men in the square. A group of them congregated at an outdoor café, smoking pipes that spewed heart-shaped clouds. Teenage boys hung their legs over the side of the stone walls.

No one particular man made an impression on her. She hardly knew what kind of man Hard-boiled Hal was. She half expected him to be a character, wearing a fedora and trench coat to match the mystery of his show, but that seemed unlikely. Had he dressed like that, his identity would have been discovered long ago.

Standing next to Sebastian reminded Fallon of the night at the bridge. Even without the recorder, she found herself seeking the pockets of silence and noticing the little sounds that snuck through: the shuffling of feet, a sigh, pigeons cooing, and the feedback of the demonstrator's microphone. Occasionally, she stole glances at Sebastian's profile. His smooth skin and straight nose made him look softer than most boys, but she had no trouble picturing him as the restless, impulsive kid he said he'd been.

The usual ache and uneasiness she felt around him wasn't there. Thinking on it, she knew it was because of

Marlene's news. If Sebastian had truly given up his careless dating, the barrier she had built between them had no reason to exist. From the very first time she had seen him at the complex, Fallon had disapproved of his contemptible behavior toward the girls who came and went as he dated and turned them away. But without that, she discovered much to her surprise that she liked Sebastian.

His teasing put her at ease, as annoying as it could be. She wanted to hear more stories about Grandma Marion and the dogs he'd practiced his grooming skills on. Maybe she'd even try something from a food truck. If she researched the place first.

Still, she burned with the same curiosity as the students in homeroom did. Sebastian's fortune was a mystery. Any hints he dropped were lost on her. Fallon didn't know what could be worse than being doomed to spinster- or bachelor-hood, but it had to be *something* bad. He joined the rebellion for a reason.

Street vendors pushed their carts through the crowd, advertising snacks and coffee. The delectable scents tempted her; she was just about to give in and buy a little pink box of pastries when Sebastian stiffened and turned slowly in a circle.

Fallon stayed close to avoid being crushed by the crowd. Children darted through the square, screaming and laughing. Indecipherable talk flooded the air as people passed in a hurry. She didn't know how Sebastian could pick up one particular voice. But he had.

"There," he said, his voice rough with urgency. He grabbed Fallon's hand and pulled her through the crowd.

She didn't know who they were following. Faces blurred as she broke into a run, her feet sliding on the cobblestones as they left the square.

"He's ahead of us," Sebastian barked.

Fallon only saw clumps of people before them, their outlines darkened by the cloudy sky. "How far?"

"Close." He found a gap in the line at the bus stop and ran through it. "He's talking now. You can hear him."

The townspeople were roadblocks. Fallon's hand slipped out of his. The moment they let go, running became easier. She kept her eye on Sebastian's back. Sounds assaulted her from all directions: water splashing, the low rumble behind the clouds, cars screeching, chatty couples scraping forks and knives against plates. But then the thread of conversation came upon her.

". . . glad you agree with me. The drink special had heart-shaped ice cubes. There's no way I was ordering that," said a voice cutting through the cacophony.

The man who spoke had a loud voice. He came from somewhere ahead of them, within a group of rowdy men in a tightly woven pack. If she took away the street and replaced it with Anais's drugstore . . . yes, the voice was familiar. Her pulse quickened. They were so close.

Fallon's foot slipped on the slick pavement. A deep puddle collecting in the gutter cushioned her fall, but soaked through her coat. When she tried pushing herself up, her palms stung—the skin had been scraped off, spotted with pebbles and dirt.

Someone grabbed the back of her coat, tugging her to her feet. Sebastian's worried gaze met hers. "Are you okay?"

Fallon wanted to rub her temples to ease the ringing in her ears, but her hands hurt. She started trembling with cold. "You're going to lose Hal," she said, "keep going."

He shook his head. "No way."

"But the mission . . ."

"I can find Hal again," he said sharply. "You're more important."

Fallon opened her mouth to argue, but her teeth chattered instead. An innocent breeze turned vicious as it sent icy needles up her body. She was sopping wet, her clothes heavy and useless.

Sebastian grabbed her by the elbows and gently led her away from the sidewalk and up against a building, out of the way of foot traffic. He examined her hands, noting the thin trails of blood running from the open wounds, and pulled a tissue out of his pocket. "Sorry," he said, dabbing at the broken skin. It wasn't the most hygienic way of cleaning her wounds, but he did manage to dislodge the bigger pebbles and flecks of dirt.

She flinched when the tissue touched her skin. "No, I'm sorry. We lost Hal because of these terrible shoes. No traction."

Sebastian's mouth twitched. "Aren't those shoes family-approved?"

"Duprees don't run very often."

He laughed and gently stroked the backs of her hands. "We're going to need bandages for this. Should be easy enough to find in one of these shops. But your clothes are another matter. You won't make it back to the complex like this."

Fears of catching pneumonia raced through her head. "What should we do? I didn't bring enough money to cover an entire outfit."

Sebastian sighed loudly. "Fallon, you're the only girl in the entire world who could make me curious about how much a wardrobe costs. A princess like you must have spent entire kingdoms for your coats and dresses."

"I prefer my uniform. It makes things easier."

"I'm sure it does. But a princess in disguise is always discovered in the end." Sebastian winked. "Come along. I can't compete with your high standards, but it's my fault that you were running and fell. I'll pay for a new outfit for you."

Fallon grabbed a fistful of his coat, then cringed from the pain. "You don't have to, really."

Sebastian unpeeled each of her fingers from his coat. Then he pulled her into a hug.

His coat was too thick to hear his heartbeat, but when Fallon rested her ear against his chest, she found the rise and fall of his breathing to be just as comforting. She shivered fiercely and felt his hands at her waist, pressing her closer.

"See?" he said.

She breathed in his scent. Something clean and with a touch of grapefruit. "What?"

"I can't even keep you warm. So new clothes it is."

"Is that the point of this?" she asked.

Sebastian pressed his cheek against hers. "Of course, princess," he said hoarsely. Turning away from her, he pointed at a store down the street. "How about that store? Lots of pink."

Fallon had a feeling that he was lying. Sebastian hadn't needed to hug her—and certainly not with such affection. A strange sensation had burned low in her belly as she clung to him, his breathing as steady as the tide. When he'd rubbed his cheek against hers, her toes curled inside her terrible shoes.

Sebastian was already walking toward the store.

"Wait," she said, hugging her arms to put off the shivers. "That's a baby store."

"No, it's not."

"Use your eyes," she said. "The window display has cribs in it."

Finding a cheap store selling apparel for teenagers wasn't that hard, since Fallon had always been curious about them. She never went into one without Anais. They found a store leaking bright plastic jewelry and sweet pop songs. Evening shoppers darted amid chaotically arranged racks. The clothes hung limply on the hangers. Robbie would disapprove. Her parents, having learned from their son, would also have steered her in the other direction.

But if she didn't give in and buy new clothes, she'd end up with a debilitating cold. For the rebellion's sake (and her own health), she needed to get dry quickly.

With Sebastian at her side, Fallon took a shuddering breath and stepped inside.

chapter 15

MAN BEHIND THE VOICE

Fallon's scrap of bravery fled the moment she examined the clothes. The slacks had loose buttons. Piles of sweaters folded on the sale table had stretched collars. Threads hung loose from sheer blouses hanging on the walls. She didn't dare check the tags for the listing of materials.

Sebastian tracked down an employee and asked for a first aid kit. Since the salesgirl was squeamish, Sebastian cleaned Fallon's hands with alcohol and wrapped the bandages snug. "There," he said, smoothing the last fold of bandage. "Now you're infection-free."

"What?" she asked. The music caused the entire store to throb.

He shook his head. "Let's find you some clothes."

"I don't know."

"You're not scared," he said. It wasn't a question.

"Did you see the loose threads?" she said, gesturing at the blouses. "I can't wear that."

Sebastian smirked. "Can't say I'm surprised. But you need to try harder. This place is like a warehouse. You'll find something you'll like."

Fallon cast a doubtful look.

"You have to. No one's catching a cold on my watch."

She flexed her fingers. The store was heated, but her clothes weren't drying fast enough. The amount of bad clothing overwhelmed her, but she tried not to think like her family. *What do I like? What would I want to wear, no matter what it was made of?*

"Did you see that display over there?" Sebastian said. "Says it's some new brand called Cassiopeia."

The display was shaped like a giant fireplace, cardboard flames bright inside the hearth. The clothing on either side had a different feel than the shop's other items. When Fallon ran her fingers over a dark sweater with neat, geometric patterns, the material felt soft and sturdy.

"You don't wear patterns, do you?" Sebastian said. "Could be worth trying on."

"Yes, I think it is."

He patted the stacks of jeans folded underneath the flames. "Then take one of these too."

"You know, most boys would hate shopping."

He shrugged, his carefully cultivated boredom in place for the first time that day. "When you've had a lot of girl-friends, you learn that it's not about you. It's about making them happy."

The comment stung; she didn't want to think about his

past girlfriends. "It's a good thing you're not dating anyone now. You can be selfish."

Sebastian lowered his eyes. "I've never stopped being selfish."

"What does that mean?"

"It means," he said, sighing, "that you need to go get changed. No more chattering teeth."

Fallon found jeans in her size and took them and the sweater into the changing room. As she undressed, she worried about Sebastian's change in mood. His comment about being selfish bothered her. Just what had he meant by that? It was almost like he wanted her to solve him, but the clues were just too vague.

The Cassiopeia jeans were comfortable and flattering, warming her clammy skin immediately. The sweater almost touched her knees, fashionably long. Fallon rolled the sleeves up past her wrists and turned to the mirror, finding beauty in the triangles that replicated themselves in different shades of green. Her shivering stopped as she stared at herself in the mirror. The clothes made her look like a different person. Someone more relaxed, but self-aware. She looked away only because she knew that Sebastian was waiting.

The tags were snipped, Sebastian handed his money to the salesgirl, and Fallon left the store with her wet clothes in a shopping bag. Now that she was wearing dry clothes again, the cold weather wasn't so bad. "Thanks for the clothes," she said.

"It's the least I could do."

"I seem to be collecting favors from you," Fallon said. "First, you agree to help me thank Hijiri, and now, we have to start all over again with trying to find Hard-boiled Hal."

Sebastian smirked. "Actually, I know exactly where to find Hal."

"You do?"

"He was walking with a group of men ahead of us before you fell. I don't know which one he was, but the group was very familiar to me. Any guy would know who they were."

Fallon gasped. "You mean . . ."

"A bunch of strange men, lonely, eccentric, and uninhibited by decorum," Sebastian said, smirking. "They belong to the Bachelor Villas."

"Then we have to go there."

"Now? In your state?"

"These clothes will keep me warm enough," Fallon said with a thankful smile. "I'd rather we find Hal now. We've got plenty of time before his radio show starts."

The Bachelor Villas were located a few blocks away from the Spinster Villas, but the two communities notoriously ignored each other. As Fallon understood it, neither the men nor women saw any value in getting to know one another when both were doomed to perpetual singlehood.

"It's sad," Fallon murmured.

Sebastian touched her elbow, leading her around another puddle. "What is?"

"How they're just giving up."

"They can't help it."

"I know. But that's why we're doing what we're doing. If we stop Zita," she said, gesturing to the villas, "then we could end this too."

Like their twin, the Bachelor Villas was a courtyard surrounded by squat, connected buildings. Each building was whitewashed with onyx accents. A wall covered the entire perimeter of the property, keeping the townspeople out. Not that anyone would willingly try to visit. Until today.

"There's probably a community center," Sebastian said, laying his hands on the white wall. "We could just be frank with them and ask for Hal. Or, we could claim we want a tour."

"Are you fated to end up here?"

Sebastian pressed his lips together.

"Come on. I need to know if you're going to be convincing."

He seemed to choose his answer carefully. "It could be safer for me to live here after graduation, but no, I'm not doomed to be single. Romance is in my future."

Fallon bit her tongue as more questions bubbled up. "Asking for Hal probably won't work. If he's here, the others must be protecting him. Otherwise, someone would have found him by now. The tour would allow us a better chance at finding him."

Sebastian swung one leg over the wall.

"What are you doing?"

"I have a better idea." He looked over his shoulder. "The walls are paper-thin. We could hear him without having to talk to anybody."

Her stomach clenched at the thought of getting caught, but then she remembered Robbie's request. He'd asked her to do something a little risky and dangerous before graduating. As a freshman, she was starting early. In jeans, she had no trouble climbing over the wall. The villas weren't as quiet as she first thought. The shadow between buildings came from the courtyard, where men could be heard talking. Someone cooked meat on a grill; smoke trailed over the rooftops.

Sebastian found a gap between the buildings for a modest garden; avoiding the unwound hose, he came as close as he could to the front of the building and listened for a few minutes. He shook his head. None of the men in the courtyard were Hard-boiled Hal.

As her eyes adjusted to the growing darkness, Fallon picked out shapes. Bags of garbage languished behind the houses. The bachelors left television sets and yesterday's dinners out on the grass. The wall was too close to the backs of the villas for proper backyards, but the bachelors used the space anyway.

They wandered the perimeter of the villas, careful to listen for anyone who might sound like the radio show host.

Fallon wondered if they were going to get caught. Surely someone was looking out his back window. "What if someone sees us?" she asked.

Or tried to ask. Her lips moved, but nothing came out.

Fallon stopped walking, puzzled. Even though it was chilly out, she felt fine. No pressure or scratchiness in her throat. No oncoming runny nose and croaky coughs. So where had her voice gone? She stepped on an empty soda can—and heard nothing.

Panicking, Fallon grabbed Sebastian by the wrist. "What's going on?" she mouthed.

He said something back, but she couldn't hear him. Sebastian craned his neck, examining the second- and third-floor windows of the villa they stood behind. He then searched the bushes and even checked the side of the house. When he returned, he wore a smile. He crooked his finger, asking her to follow him. They headed back to the wall.

"Sebastian, I don't get it," she said. Her voice, suddenly there, startled her.

"It has a limited range," he explained, leaning against the wall. "As long as we're this close to the wall, we can talk."

"What does?"

"A silencing charm," he said.

"I've used silencing charms before," she said, "and all they do is lower sound to a dull buzz. Not wipe it out completely." She always bought a few during midterms and finals week so that no one could interrupt her study sessions.

"Remember our visit to Femke and Mirthe's house?

They said that if we had the money, we could buy more concentrated charms."

"That would explain it," she said. The man living in this villa had to have a good job to afford such a charm. "But why hang such an expensive charm outside, in the bushes, no less?"

"I know the answer to that one." Sebastian flashed a delicious grin. "This man doesn't want to be overheard. Not by his neighbors. Not by the townspeople on the other side of the walls. Sounds a lot like paranoia, right? But what if he has a secret worth protecting?"

Fallon matched his grin with hers. "Hard-boiled Hal?"

"This could be him."

They plunged back into the silence. This time, it wasn't as frightening. Fallon ignored the heavy weight of the charm's manufactured quiet, focusing on Sebastian's back as he led her around the corner of the villa. He parted the nondescript bush against the building, revealing a copper charm shaped like lips. The lips had been sewn shut and tied at the right-hand corner of the mouth. Next to the bush was a basement window, glowing bright.

Fallon knelt down on her knees beside Sebastian and peered inside. Despite the man's precautions with the silencing charm, he didn't cover the window. The basement had leather furnishings and a wooden table in the center. A man sat at the table, pressing the keys on a black typewriter.

The man was in his twenties, with rather large eyes framed with thick black lashes. He had the body of an ex-athlete, with thick muscled arms and the beginnings of a beer belly. As he typed, he scratched his scruffy beard and grumbled. His T-shirt said something about burping the alphabet.

Sebastian tapped as loudly as he could on the window.

Even though the tapping was silent on their side, the man heard it perfectly. He stood up from the table, his face drained of color.

Sebastian pointed to himself and Fallon, then to his right, indicating that they'd be waiting for him at the front of the villa.

Fallon's heart thudded as they walked to the front. This man could be Hard-boiled Hal. They'd actually found him. She was glad that she'd never been a big fan like Anais— her excitement came from aiding the rebellion, not from meeting a local celebrity.

The man opened the door; he was wearing pajama bottoms patterned with pralines. "Trespassing is a crime—" he started.

"We know you're Hard-boiled Hal," Sebastian said, raising his voice.

The man leaped forward, slapping his hand over Sebastian's mouth. "Quiet down," he said.

"Not unless you let us in," Fallon said.

The man groaned. "Fine, but not one word!"

The inside of the villa was pitiful. The smell of heavy cologne and garbage saturated the living room and kitchen. Crumbs caught between couch cushions. A laundry pile spilled out of the bedroom. They followed the man down to the basement.

"Have a seat," he said reluctantly, gesturing to the two chairs opposite his across the table.

As Fallon sat, she noticed a door she hadn't seen from her angle at the window. It was a white door peppered with juvenile stickers proclaiming KEEP OUT and CAUTION: GENIUS AT WORK.

"That's my studio," the man explained, catching her eye. "No matter how much you offer, you won't see the inside of it. I can't believe the newspaper sent two kids to find me. They have no morals."

"We're not from the paper," Fallon said. "Our intention isn't to reveal your secret identity."

"But if we didn't threaten you, you wouldn't have let us in," Sebastian said.

The man agreed with that. "How did you know it was me?"

"Well, you do kind of look like someone named Hard-boiled Hal," Fallon said, trying to be kind. The cheeky T-shirt certainly fit the radio show host's personality, but she had expected someone more comely.

"Your voice," Sebastian said, crossing his arms. "It's distinctive. You can't completely hide it."

"So what do you want from me?" he said.

"Your name, for starters," Sebastian said.

"Bram De Groote, accountant," he said, "at your service."

"I hope so. We're in need of allies. The way you speak

about love on your radio show makes us believe that you could be receptive to our plans," Fallon said.

Sebastian added, "Basically, we're part of a group that's going to stop Zita."

"What do you mean?"

"No more love fortunes," she said. "And if Zita does have power over us, we're going to end it."

Bram slumped back in his chair, stroking his beard. "You're playing me."

"This is a serious situation. Our lives are at stake," Fallon said, angered by Bram's skepticism.

"I understand. You've been dealt a rotten hand," Bram said. "All the men here have, but we deal with it in different ways. That's what adults do."

"By having a radio show that promotes grossness and bad manners?" Fallon replied. "We may not be the adults here, but I think we have a better understanding of what's going on in this town."

"Other towns don't operate the way Grimbaud does. They don't let one person dictate how they choose to love," Sebastian said.

"We do it because Zita's always right." Bram slammed his fist down on the table. "My distaste for her and everything she represents is obvious. I created this show to spite her, but it's a useless hobby. I'm not making a difference, nor do I expect to. Destined couples marry each year and new spinsters and bachelors move into the villas. The cycle continues."

His bitterness was overwhelming. As cool and unaffected as Hard-boiled Hal was, his real-life counterpart, Bram, suffered from the same rotten feelings that many people felt in Grimbaud. Like them, he wouldn't do anything to change the situation. "What happened to you?" she asked.

"The last fortune I got before I found out I was a bachelor was during my sophomore year," he said sourly. "It said, *an embarrassing rejection awaits you.*' My friends constantly teased me about it. My mother warned me against actually following through with my plans to confess to the girl I loved, but I couldn't hold back. I had to share my feelings with Emma." Bram took a deep, shuddering breath. "The entire school was witness to my confession. They barely held back their laughter as I poured my heart out. Emma was reading a book on one of the benches. When she looked up, it was only to ask me if I would stand a little to the left to block the sun for her. She hadn't heard a word I said."

Fallon pressed her hands in her lap. "Do you mean Emma Ward?"

"That's the one." Bram flashed a careless smile. "She's a spinster now."

"Didn't you try again?" Sebastian asked.

"Of course not," he said. "The entire school was in hysterics. The administration even held the bell so that everyone could compose themselves for homeroom."

"You can put your past behind you," Sebastian said, trying one last time. "If you've ever wanted to change—"

Bram raised his hand. "Stop now. You know that nothing ever changes in this town. I'm sorry you misread me. My alter ego tends to be much more charming than the real man. You'll have to leave now. I must prepare for tonight's show."

Fallon stood up so fast that the chair almost toppled. Her frustration and anger toward Bram was palpable; she wished that she could shake him until he saw reason. She stopped at the bottom of the basement stairs.

"You know," she said, pinning Bram with her eyes, "Ms. Ward suffered too. She's been hurt more than you ever have, but least she's gutsier than you."

She didn't wait to see his reaction.

Fallon hugged her arms during the walk back to the complex, gathering comfort from the large, geometric sweater. Tonight, she lost her temper for the first time in a while. Her skin felt hot, her heart beating loudly as the last of her anger lingered. How could she just sit there and watch their chance at gaining an ally fail? How could she let Bram De Groote imply that Ms. Ward had hurt him on purpose, the one scar he carried while Ms. Ward bore so many?

"Your language must always be quality," her father had always said, giving her and Robbie extra grammar lessons as children. "No dirty words. Keep your sentences short and clear." She usually tried her best to follow those rules, but right now she wanted to curse and rant.

Sebastian seemed affected by the night's events too. He watched her carefully as they crossed a cobblestone bridge and jumped over puddles. "The club's going to be disappointed when they find out that Hard-boiled Hal is a dud," he said.

"I'm glad we tracked him down," she said. "We found out sooner rather than later that he won't help."

Sebastian tapped his ears. "I'm glad my keen sense of hearing saved the day."

"It's pretty amazing."

"Is that a compliment from the princess?" Sebastian said, grinning. They were only a block away from the complex, but he stopped right in the middle of the sidewalk.

"Is that so unusual?" Fallon tried to walk past him, but he stepped in front of her. They stood so close, she could feel the heat radiating off his body.

"Sometimes I think you really mean it," he said with some concern.

Fallon shrugged.

Sebastian's cold fingers touched her chin. He bumped his nose against hers, his mouth so close. "This wasn't the most romantic night," he whispered.

Her heart did a strange dance in her chest. Her hand, holding the shopping bag with her soggy clothes, went numb.

This was a tease. He'd never gone so far as this, tempting a princess with a knave's kiss. But she was no princess—she was the resourceful lady's maid. She knew that he didn't expect her to give in. Sebastian waited for her to push him away or say something prudish that would make him laugh. But Fallon felt that this was a night of changes. She decided to say something of quality.

"You've got a cold kiss," she whispered back. "I want a real one."

chapter 16

WELCOME LOVE

Observation, not experience, had taught Fallon that it would be dangerous to place her heart in Sebastian's hands. She'd buried any attraction she felt for Sebastian and chose to hate him instead. Hate him for the parade of girls he dated. Hate him for holding their hands, kissing them in the shadows, and sharing nothing of himself.

So what was she doing, saying something like that? Wasn't she just the next girl in line, pressing her heart into his palms for safekeeping? The old Fallon, having been pushed into a smaller and smaller space behind her ribs, snarled. The new Fallon knew this was neither stupidity nor weakness. No matter how illogical, this was how she really felt. Her vulnerable heart awaited judgment.

She nudged his nose with hers. "Well?"

Sebastian flinched. "You're not serious."

"You keep questioning my sincerity," Fallon said.

He stepped away from her, taking his warmth with him. "You know how I work. I date casually."

Fallon placed her shopping bag on the ground. "I'm familiar with your policy. Doesn't it get tiring? One of these days, a girl's going to enter your life who you won't want to let go of. I'm not saying that I'm that girl, but maybe I could be."

Sebastian backed up a few more steps, a look of panic on his face. "You weren't supposed to say this to me."

Fallon dug her fingers into her sweater. Her tongue felt heavy, but she forced herself to speak. "I see," she whispered. "I guess I failed you. I should have maintained my role as a prudish Fallon Dupree: the princess who would no sooner open a bag of manufactured cookies than ever have feelings for you."

"Sorry," he said. "I thought you were that strong."

"It's not a matter of being strong," she said. "You're just too lovable."

Sebastian tried to rebuild his wall of boredom. He crossed his arms, dropped his shoulders, and turned slightly away from her. "Stop," he said.

If Fallon concentrated, she bet she could hear both their hearts cracking to pieces. Her mouth kept moving. "The real question is whether you're capable of giving me a cold kiss. Could you press your lips to mine without caring? Somehow, I don't believe you could."

Sebastian's face crumbled. "Stay away from me," he said brokenly. "I know we weren't actually dating, but this is as good as breaking up. Good-bye."

Before she could move, Sebastian ran. She watched him disappear down the street. Her body felt cold, so very cold, and nothing she could have worn would have stopped the shivers from spreading through her veins. She swallowed thickly, picked up her shopping bag, and counted the houses until she made it to the student housing complex.

>—▷

Despite the dry clothing that Sebastian had bought her, Fallon woke up on Sunday morning with a stuffy nose. She blew hard enough into her tissue to pop her ears.

To be fair, this was her fault. She had been the one to insist they find Hard-boiled Hal last night. She'd also been too miserable to take a hot shower when she got home, so the cold that had been kept at bay slipped its way inside her.

Tangled in her sheets, with bluebirds singing outside her window, Fallon crumpled her tissue and cried.

>—▷

Plagued with congestion and a sore throat, Fallon stayed home on Monday and Tuesday. Doing homework made her dizzy and she could only clean the apartment in short spurts before her muscles complained of too much exertion. Mostly, she napped on the couch.

Whenever someone knocked on her door, she woke with a start, her heart twisting painfully in her chest. Could Sebastian be on the other side? She'd make her way to the door gingerly, her blanket wrapped around her shoulders like a shield. But usually Nico was there with her missed home-work. He'd gotten permission from his parents to work later hours at the booth in order to help her.

"Your apartment is still immaculate," Nico said, gawking.

"There are no excuses for a dusty home," Fallon said, quoting her mother. She reclaimed her nest of sheets and pillows on the couch and allowed Nico to make her some hot tea. "What happened at school?"

"The twins are dying for you to get better," he said, fill-ing the teakettle with water. "They want to know if you've made progress on finding Hard-boiled Hal."

Fallon would have thought that Sebastian had told them by now. Even though the next club meeting wasn't until Thursday, a story like that would be hard to keep secret. "Didn't Sebastian tell you?"

"He's been avoiding us."

Fallon sat up, alarmed. "Are you sure?"

"When has Bastion ever been hard to find?" Nico said, turning on the stove. "Now, we're lucky if we see him in the halls. He even ignored the twins when they said hello to him this morning. Mirthe threatened to plant a hurricane charm in his locker, but Sebastian just kept walking as if she wasn't there."

She blew her nose, trying to fight a headache.

After leaving the water to boil, Nico joined her on the couch and searched her face. "Does this have anything to do with you, Fallon?"

She wanted to lie, but tears bubbled up instead. "Oh, Nico."

"We're friends, right? You can tell me what's bothering you."

Rehashing Saturday night started off easily. She glossed over Hal, deciding to save the details for the club. By the time she got to her request for a real kiss, Fallon was crying again. Nothing dramatic, but even the smallest of tears made it hard for her to breathe.

Ignoring the pile of tissues between them, Nico hugged her. He smelled of canal water and sunshine. "Of course you love him," he crooned. "I'm sorry for it. Your fortune is unforgiving."

"You're not surprised?"

"I had my suspicions," Nico said with a grin. "I doubt you would have spent so much time with a boy you actually hated, Fallon Dupree."

She tried to laugh with him, but it came out as a pitiful sob. "Do you think he likes me back?"

Nico handed her a fresh tissue. "Maybe. Why else would he have said those things to you?"

Fallon felt well enough to return to school on Wednesday. When she got dressed in the bathroom, she found that the skin over her heart was red and aggravated. She must have been scratching it in her sleep. November breathed frost on the stone walls and patches of grass.

She didn't know how to act when she saw Sebastian again. Was she supposed to smile? Say hello? Call him by his nickname, accompanied by a slew of curse words? Most girls did the last one.

As it turned out, Fallon didn't need to worry; Sebastian made the choice for her. She didn't see him at all on Wednesday, even though she searched the hallways between classes and stayed behind after school. On her way to history class on Thursday, Sebastian brushed her shoulder. She tried to grab him, but he slid through the students, his legs carrying him far away from her. He didn't come to the charm-making club either, much to the twins' annoyance.

"We can't lose a rebel," Mirthe whined. "Sebastian might be spreading all our secrets at this very moment. Why didn't you think of this, Femke?"

Femke tapped on the jar of pig's eyeballs and shrugged.

Nico said, "Maybe he's just taking a break."

"We don't have time for breaks! This is a rebellion!" Mirthe wrung her hands. "Okay, how about phase two? Please tell me that we've made progress on that."

Hijiri had nothing to report. Fallon assumed as much, since she'd caught Hijiri wandering the complex, snipping specimens for her own secret love charms. Dulling the effects of Camille's charm on Martin preoccupied Nico these days, so he hadn't found allies either. Plus, he thought that asking a sympathetic tourist for help felt wrong; this was Grimbaud's problem, and needed to be solved by Grimbaud alone.

"You guys need to work harder," Mirthe said. "Femke and I can't advance phase two because we're prepping phase three. It's more complicated than we anticipated."

Nico frowned. "What's phase three?"

"We can't tell you until phase two is over."

"We're getting nowhere," he groaned.

Fallon told the club about Hard-boiled Hal's silencing charm and juvenile decorating. Despite Mirthe's prodding for details, she spoke dryly. The story wasn't as exciting without Sebastian there to share the telling. "No matter how much we argued, Bram remained stubborn. He's not on our side."

"All is not lost," Femke said quietly. She consulted her notebook. "Fallon's still made contact with the spinsters."

Fallon nodded. "Ms. Ward seems eager to help me."

Mirthe snapped her fingers. "Then take her up on the offer. Ask for a tour of the Spinster Villas."

"Why?"

"If you spend time with Ms. Ward, she might give in and join us. She could even recruit the other spinsters."

"We're not going to storm Zita's shop with an army of angry spinsters and bachelors, are we?"

"They don't have the guts to follow us where we're going," Mirthe said. "The important part is that we have more spies. More information. People to turn to on the night when we finally face Zita and change Grimbaud."

"We're counting on you, Fallon," Femke said.

The pressure only added to her worries.

Ms. Ward sent Fallon on an errand to deliver a note to the front office regarding a request for new books. Encyclopedias A through K had fallen apart, their spines nothing more than strings and dried glue.

Fallon absorbed the quiet locked in the halls as she walked. Each classroom was a fishbowl of bored students. Outside, a gym class was being held on the basketball court. In order to reach the main office, she had to walk along the lawn between buildings. Students ran drills, dribbling basketballs up and down the court. Sebastian was third in line, resting his hands on his knees as he waited. His gym clothes were dark with sweat. The gym teacher's whistle blew, startling him. Even though Fallon had suffered a cold, Sebastian looked worse. His lips were chapped, his skin wane. His eyelashes kept fluttering as if he was desperate for sleep.

The gym teacher tossed the ball at Sebastian. Sebastian caught it with his face.

The class erupted in laughter as the ball bounced away. Sebastian cradled his cheek, already letting his eyelids droop again, as the gym teacher blew his whistle like an alarm. He grabbed Sebastian by the back of his shirt and ordered him to sit out for the rest of class. Sebastian sank down against the chain-link fence, unaffected by the lingering snickers.

Fallon played with the edges of the note, unsure. Another girl would have laughed at the heartless boy, but she was nervous. Something wasn't right. Sebastian should have been happy that he'd ended things with her.

Sebastian looked behind him and saw Fallon. Despite the bruising on his cheek, he smirked at her. It was gone in a flash. Pain and longing flickered in his eyes until he turned away.

She wanted to stick her fingers through the fence and rub the skin behind his neck. There must have been knots there. If he turned around again, maybe she could stop the bruising on his cheek too. "Stupid Fallon," she muttered to herself.

When she came back from her delivery, Ms. Ward called her over to the circulation desk. "I know that face. You've fallen in love, haven't you?"

Fallon bit her lip, nodding. No use lying.

"Oh, Fallon. These things never work out for people like us," Ms. Ward said.

"I think I would feel better if I could see the villas."

Ms. Ward brightened. "Oh, yes. Of course. Your future home. The other women will be pleased to see you again. We'll have so much fun. Would you like to stay over, to see what it's like?"

That was the last thing she wanted to do, but she said yes anyway.

The following week, Fallon went to her first student government meeting without Sebastian. She searched for him in the back of the round room despite knowing that no one would voluntarily waste a school night there. That night, Mirthe was her companion. The twin's noisy bangles picked up the room's acoustics. Fallon would have loved to skip the meeting, but because Femke had a paper to finish, Mirthe needed another representative.

"Let's sit near the front," Mirthe said, almost jogging to claim her spot in the second row that lined up with the podium.

Fallon sat to her right and opened her notebook. Throughout the meeting, she concentrated on Nico. This was the only time she got to see his struggle to cut between Camille and Martin. Even though Nico hadn't managed to split Camille and Martin up at the table, he implemented a series of distractions for the president. When the other officers presented, Nico found ways to casually touch Martin's wrist while pointing out something on the meeting agenda. He made notes on Martin's agenda and whispered a joke or two that made Martin smile despite his dizzying bondage to the charm.

When it came time for Martin to present at the podium, he left his chair with more poise than he had at the start of the night. Camille's brow furrowed and she discreetly applied more perfume behind her ears.

"I'm sure you're all preparing for our upcoming finals," Martin said slowly. "Midterms have come and gone, but our academic worries always remain. That's why it's important to take the time to celebrate. I'm proud to remind you of our annual fair at the end of January. The Welcome Love

Fair. I'll explain it for the freshmen. Every year, Grimbaud High's clubs put together a fair open to the public, with games and food and midnight fireworks: all of it in honor of welcoming Love back for the spring." He paused to turn a page in his notes.

"The snow's not stopping in February," Mirthe whispered. "Dad says we're going to have snow until April this year. Good business for heating charms."

The weather was much the same every year. Traditionally, the Welcome Love Fair took place right at the end of January so that Love would arrive to melt away the ice and snow for the rest of the school year. Fallon didn't know why the tradition still stood, when the next day, on February first, everyone still woke up to piles of snow on the ground.

"Nicolas will send around a sign-up sheet. Each club needs to choose some activity or food for the fair. If you have a different idea from what's already listed, please consult the officers about it. We'll then take it to the administration for approval," Martin said.

When the paper made it to Fallon, half of the activities had already been taken. "What should we choose?" she asked.

Mirthe wasn't paying attention. Her eyes glittered, a ghost of a grin on her lips. Fallon recognized that look from the rebellion meetings: the twin was brewing an idea. Still, participation in the fair was mandatory. They needed to make a decision. "How about the popcorn machine?"

"Sure, sure."

Fallon didn't know the first thing about manning a popcorn machine, but she knew how messy a cotton-candy machine could be, and that was the other food option. She wrote the club's name next to the popcorn machine and passed it on.

When the meeting ended, Mirthe couldn't get out of her chair fast enough. She dragged Fallon outside as the other students filed out and said, "Femke and I have been searching for the perfect time to confront Zita—and this is it!"

"What are you talking about?"

"The Welcome Love Fair," Mirthe said, laughing. "The entire town is going to be distracted by the fair. There couldn't be a better time. While everyone's enjoying themselves, all the shops and cafés will be closed. So will Zita's shop."

Dread tickled the back of Fallon's neck. "Quiet down. What if someone hears?"

"How can I be quiet when I've found the missing piece?" Mirthe danced on her toes. "Phase three is going to be ready come January. We're going to meet Zita."

Fallon lowered her voice. "We can't just skip the fair. We're going to get in trouble."

"Then you'd better find someone to cover our booth," Mirthe said, "because January thirty-first *will* be the night. We're going to change our fates."

Leaves crunched behind them. Fallon jumped, gasping, and whipped around. "Someone's there."

"Where?"

Fallon scanned the side of the building. The overgrown bushes lining the building trembled in the wind, but she couldn't see anything in the shadows. "I don't know."

"I got carried away," Mirthe said. "You don't know how long Femke and I have been struggling over picking a date."

"It doesn't matter. I can't believe I had to tell *you* to be careful. Say a policeman heard us just now—good-bye, rebellion! Over before even finding Zita."

Mirthe hung her head.

Fallon checked the shadows again. Nothing. A familiar, musky scent lingered in the air, though. She breathed it in deeply and shuddered. *Camille.*

chapter 17

THE FUTURE

After parting ways with Mirthe, Fallon hurried back to the complex. The tip of her nose was numb. She listened for footsteps and kept sniffing the air loudly, trying to detect a trace of Camille. Nothing suspicious. If Camille had overheard them talking, then she had probably already run back to Zita or whoever it was she could squeal to. Getting caught frightened her, but she did her best to sweep it from her mind. Her thoughts inevitably shifted to Sebastian.

She was the only girl she knew who had experienced a breakup without first dating the boy. The magazines she'd spent days reading during her search for love charms advised different approaches for surviving a breakup. Spend time with friends. Burn the presents your ex-boyfriend gave you. Eat ice cream straight from the container.

Fallon had stared at the cassette tape for three days now, but nothing could compel her to burn it. Remembering that night under the bridge still made her happy. So did thinking of Sebastian's jealousy when seeing her with Robbie. And the soft look he'd given her when he tucked the begonia behind her ear.

Your love will never be requited.

So far, Zita's love fortune had come true.

"I'm going to be like Ms. Ward," she murmured, stomping on the leaves so they crackled and burst like fireworks— it reminded her of the first time she'd walked home with Sebastian, when he tried to startle her by doing the same thing. If things didn't change, her life would be a continuous spiral of breakups. Sebastian was only the first.

He wouldn't get out of her head.

Reaching her apartment, Fallon turned the key in the lock and stepped into the darkness. She felt around the wall for the light switch, just as she did every night. But when she turned it on, she found Anais and Nico occupying her couch with grins on their faces.

"Surprise!" they shouted, spilling confetti from their hands. All over her couch. For her to vacuum later.

"Happy breakup," Anais said. She pulled a kazoo out of her pocket and blew on it.

"Shut up," Nico said, jabbing her in the side. "She's not happy about it."

"I am. Bastion is a loser."

Fallon's eyes swept the room. Her friends had hung a pink banner that read WELCOME BACK, SINGLE LADY. They had tied pink balloons to her chairs. The kitchen table, lit with candles, boasted a small dinner of spinach soufflé and a dessert of strawberry shortcake.

"What do you think?" Nico said, tugging on his shirt collar. "The decorations were Anais's idea. I ordered the food from a place that uses organic ingredients, I promise. I can show you the receipt."

Fallon rubbed her nose with the back of her hand, but she couldn't stop the sniffles. Their kindness overwhelmed her. In a second, she felt Nico's and Anais's arms wrap around her.

"It's okay," Nico said, patting her back.

"You're so silly, Fallon," Anais said sharply. "You shouldn't be sad alone. That's why we're here."

She broke into laughter, the kind that rises from the belly like steam. Fallon hugged her friends tightly and thanked them for surprising her. The decorations carried Anais's somewhat crude humor, which made them a precious reminder that her friends cared for her. She was used to being the one solving their problems and lending an ear. Being on the other side wasn't as uncomfortable as she thought.

Before they sat at the table to eat, Anais gave Fallon a stern look. "I should be mad that you didn't tell me about Sebastian."

"I would have. I just didn't see the rush, since you despise him. I'm sorry."

"Falling for Sebastian was a stupid thing to do."

"Because of my fortune."

"No," Anais said. "Because I want you to be happy with

whomever you decide to love. And from what I'd seen of him, Sebastian couldn't make anyone happy. But maybe I'm wrong. You're the most meticulous of us. If you ended up liking Sebastian, you must have had a good reason for it."

"Thanks for trusting me," Fallon said lightly.

Anais passed her a plate with a generous slice of soufflé. "The school's abuzz about Sebastian's odd behavior. Everyone wants to know who's responsible."

"Don't tell me there's going to be a mob."

Nico laughed. "Just gossip. But Bastion's not talking."

"Tell me you have a plan," Anais said.

The soufflé tasted like clouds. Fallon scooped up a bigger chunk. "What kind of plan?"

"To seduce Sebastian," Anais said bluntly.

Fallon almost choked. "What?"

"You want him back, right?"

"I don't know if I can. He's not a thing to be won. If he doesn't want to date me, I can't make him love me. I'm not Camille," she said.

But Anais's demand for a plan kept her awake that night, long after the party ended. She stared at the ridiculous pink banner and ate another slice of strawberry shortcake from the fridge. Sebastian had used his dating rules as an excuse to leave her. Marlene might have been right when she theorized about an exception to his strict dating policy.

"If anyone's an exception, it's me," she said to herself. No matter how confused and hurt she felt, she knew it was the truth.

Robbie always said that duffel bags were the enemies of clothing. Unlike suitcases that had little compartments built within, duffel bags were lazy. No pockets. No sectioning off. Anything you put in a duffel bag got wrinkled and twisted up. Still, Fallon refused to use her suitcase when she packed for her night's stay at the Spinster Villas. Suitcases represented family vacations and giant leaps toward her dreams, like packing her suitcase to attend Grimbaud High. She refused to use a suitcase for this trip.

The afternoon frost mirrored her brittle confidence; it broke underfoot. She wanted to believe that the rebellion would be a success. *This is not my future*, she thought fiercely.

All signs seemed to point otherwise.

It was too easy to imagine the villas as her home, the same way she could picture working in an hazardous kitchen before someone like her parents showed up to close it down. Her feet felt heavy. The townspeople she passed on the street looked impossibly happy.

This was not a trial period. This was an investigation. She was part of a rebellion that could free everyone if the plan came together. Without phase two, there could be no phase three. Femke and Mirthe knew what they were doing. They had to. And she needed to be strong to make this plan a reality.

She entered the courtyard and discovered women playing a game of croquet. The scene looked perfect, the front cover of next year's pamphlet. Innumerable cats patrolled the property. A tuxedo cat with lime-green eyes stalked past her, tail curled up.

"You're here," Ms. Ward said, dropping her croquet mallet. The librarian wore a turtleneck sweater and a long skirt patterned with cats playing with yarn. "You can leave your bag at my place."

The spinsters took better care of the property than their bachelor counterparts, but Fallon saw small signs of decay. Herbs drooped in their hanging posts. Laundry waved like flags between villas: ragged lingerie, muddy jeans, and sweaters damp with cat hair.

The lending library sitting on the bottom step distinguished Ms. Ward's villa from the others. Fashioned from an old cabinet, the lending library came with a waterproof sign-out sheet for anyone intending to borrow a book. Fallon opened the cabinet doors and looked inside, finding weather-beaten travel guides and chick lit.

"Just a warning," Ms. Ward said. "There's a war of smells going on inside. For the past few months, I've been trying to get a horrible stench out of my villa."

Curious, Fallon climbed the rest of the steps and wiped her shoes on the welcome mat. Then she smelled a battle. The dominating scent of mothballs was suffocating; the second scent was the combined chemical army of air fresheners in varying stages of fading. The strongest smelled something like milk and honey. Fallon pinched her nose when Ms. Ward wasn't looking. "Where is it coming from?"

"The carpets, maybe." Ms. Ward crossed her arms. "I can't afford to get new carpeting on my salary, but at least my villa doesn't smell like cat. I can't afford cats either."

Ms. Ward's sense of aesthetics more than made up for the smell. Framed photographs displayed her years of traveling, capturing stunning mountain views and busy city streets. The walls were painted dark, passionate shades of blues and pumpkins; the living room and even the kitchen bore rows of bookshelves that touched the ceilings. The books were arranged by color, forming a dazzling rainbow.

Ms. Ward smiled proudly at the books. "Next month, I'm going to reshelf them by theme."

"Why? It looks wonderful this way."

"I get antsy when they stay one way for too long," she admitted. "My own personal library doesn't need to make sense to anyone but me. And I can't stand them getting dusty, or remaining as still as statues for months on end."

Fallon thought it best not to argue. The books weren't the only things in this house that wanted to change. "Where will I be sleeping?"

"Upstairs. I have a guest room," she said, as if it were a joke. "I finally get to use it."

"Doesn't anyone from your travels come visit you?"

"We stay in touch, but they have their own lives. If they saw me now, they probably wouldn't recognize me as the same girl. It's a sadness I'd rather not indulge in."

The windows were cracked open. The floor creaked.

The guest room was more like a closet, with a slanted ceiling that left Fallon little room to sit up in bed. A spinning globe sat in the corner next to the window. She placed her hands on the cool globe and squinted, reading the countries' names.

"I'll leave you to get comfortable," Ms. Ward said. "Come join us outside when you're ready."

Fallon unzipped her duffel bag. Her nightclothes were already wrinkled, but her clothes for the next morning had hope. She hung them up in the narrow closet and breathed through her mouth. The clashing scents, while not as bad as the odors downstairs, made her nose stuffy.

When she peeked through the curtains, she saw that the croquet game had been interrupted by her arrival. Rather than playing, the spinsters stood around talking, mallets in hand. When Ms. Ward came out, they descended upon her like a pack of vultures, eager for news of the new girl.

"I'm not the new girl," she reminded herself.

Fallon would have preferred spending time alone with Ms. Ward, but she ended up sitting on a lawn chair while the spinsters continued their game of croquet. Yasmine tried talking her into dyeing her hair an outrageous color, like electric green.

"You can't have blue," she said, petting her blue locks. "Only one person per color."

Helena wore a bonnet tied with ribbon underneath her round chin and insisted on playing croquet with a lacy parasol on her wrist.

When the sun began to set, Fallon's legs prickled from sitting for so long. The community center had been prepared ahead of time for dinner and evening entertainment. All the spinsters sat down at a long table, straight out of a gothic romance novel, and passed around plates of mashed potatoes, braised beef, and green beans slathered in butter. The chandelier over their heads tinkled with fake crystals.

Fallon spooned a substantial helping of green beans onto her plate, but wouldn't touch the potatoes because they were powdered.

"Is something wrong with the beef?" said Justine, the woman who cooked the food. She wore a chef's hat everywhere and enjoyed flaunting her valued position in the villas.

"Everything's fine," Fallon said, remembering how touchy people could be with food. "I'm just not hungry. I don't want to waste your great cooking."

Justine blushed. "That's okay, then."

Ms. Ward smiled at Fallon and tucked a piece of beef into her mouth. "I hope you'll have room for dessert."

The spinsters giggled with anticipation. When dinner had all but disappeared, a few women followed Justine back to the kitchen with stacks of dirty plates. The others held hands on their walk to the lounge.

"Evening entertainment?" Fallon asked, wondering what the surprise was.

"Specially planned for you," Ms. Ward said.

She led Fallon toward the back of the community center, passing through the foyer on the way. One big chandelier projected weak, yellowish light. Fallon saw a flash of gold out of the corner of her eye; it came from a golden plaque paired with a photograph.

Ms. Ward paused. "Fallon?"

She approached the plaque and almost bumped into the table bearing the guestbook. The photograph loomed over the guestbook, depicting a delicate woman with shrewd brown eyes and a serrated smile. Her dark hair fell over her shoulders with abandon, and a simple silver heart necklace graced her throat. "Who is that in the photograph?" she asked.

Ms. Ward pursed her lips. "No one knows for certain, but we believe that she is Zita, when she was a young woman. This photograph's been here since the villas opened. The Bachelor Villas has a matching one."

Fallon shivered despite the heating. "What a place to put her," she said. "Her eyes burn right into you."

"We share this book with our guests," Ms. Ward said, flipping to the front of the guestbook where each spinster's name was written with the date she moved in. "So you see, all of us have to face Zita's scrutiny eventually."

"She should be kinder."

"How do you mean?"

"Zita is supposed to be a messenger, delivering us our romantic fortunes on ticker tape. That must require some empathy on her part, but I don't see it when I look at her."

"I'm sure she does care. What a stressful job it must be. Makes me glad I'm just a librarian," Ms. Ward said. "Come along. The others are waiting."

Fallon lingered a moment longer, dropping her eyes from Zita's salient beauty to the golden plaque. It read: A HOME FOR YOUR HEART. Just like on the pamphlet. She didn't know just whose hearts Zita was taking care of, but it wasn't the spinsters'.

Spinsters occupied the chairs and sofas of the lounge, nibbling from a bakery box and sipping from heavy wine-glasses. Fire burned in the hearth. A brown paper bag rested on the coffee table.

"You seemed intrigued by our little ritual when I met you out walking," Ms. Ward said, speaking loud enough for the others. "So we canceled our movie night and decided to have another round of reading romance novels instead."

Apparently, the public library never lacked in grab bags. This one looked bigger than the last. Fallon plucked a cinnamon-dusted cookie wrapped in paper and avoided the wine, knowing that the women hadn't thought to get her something appropriate to drink. Yasmine did the honors of ripping open the bag, letting the books scatter on the table. All the spinsters got up at once and started examining the romance novels, sloshing wine on the covers.

Fallon took dainty bites of her cookie, mesmerized by

the spinsters, who looked like archaeologists picking at dinosaur bones. They sighed and giggled when finding bare-chested men with long-flowing hair and cleft chins on the covers. Any books that had to do with castles, unsavory betrothals, and duels at dawn were fought over.

The romance novels about heroes and heroines with children seemed to upset the spinsters. They lay abandoned on the table. Fallon picked up one of them, the cover showing a blond woman holding hands with a towheaded boy while a handsome man in a suit looked on in the background. The plot involved the man's job as a spy; he had the double challenge of arresting the boy's kidnappers and winning the blond woman's love.

After finishing her cookie, Fallon cracked open the book and pretended to read. She snuck glances at the other women. Yasmine twirled a lock of blue hair and savored her wine as she read a novel with a pirate on the cover. Helena skipped ahead and fanned herself when she read the spicier scenes. Ms. Ward moved her lips as she read, engrossed in navigating the flowery language.

"How are the heroes?" Ms. Ward asked after a few minutes.

"Haven't met mine yet," said a woman chewing on a biscuit.

"Duke Murdock is brooding by the window in his grand estate," Helena said.

Yasmine bragged about Captain Bishop, the middle-aged, scarred hero who entered the novel by pressing his dagger against the heroine's attacker on the high seas.

"Lady Harrison just slew a vampire," said Justine. "My kind of woman."

"My book's hero is Bob," a woman said sheepishly. "I'm only ten pages in, but he's already held the door for an elderly lady."

The spinsters collectively sighed and hugged their books to their chests.

Fallon had thought she would feel pity for these women, but seeing them enjoy the romance novels gave her hope. By reading about characters falling in love, they rebelled against Zita. They were still able to dream.

Their delight was infectious; she wanted to join them, maybe choose a different book and lose herself in it, but then she thought of Sebastian. His face would be stamped on any hero she read about. Her stomach lurched. "I'm not feeling well; I'd like to turn in early," Fallon said.

"If you're sure . . ." Ms. Ward didn't hide her disappointment.

"Thanks for this," she said, gesturing to the torn paper bag, "but I can't stay awake. It's been a long day."

"Give the girl a break," Yasmine said without lifting her eyes from the pages. "Anyone can tell she's broken her heart."

"How insensitive of me," Ms. Ward said, rising. "I was so excited about your visit that I forgot."

"I can walk back on my own."

Ms. Ward glanced longingly at her book and nodded. She told Fallon about the spare key underneath the loose brick on the bottom step. "Another hour and I'll come home."

Fallon left the room, her stomach pains easing from the walk. When she reached the foyer, she took another look at Zita's photograph. The woman appeared to be sneering at her. Fallon hated the idea of Zita's face torturing future guests or new spinsters. It was the kind of hate that made her hands move on their own. She tore the photograph off the wall and carried it under her armpit back to the villa.

chapter 18

SOLVED

The pungent scent of mothballs ruined her chances of sleep, no matter how tightly she squeezed her eyes shut under the covers. Her nightgown got twisted about her legs. Her heart pounded in her ears. She deliberately averted her gaze from Zita's portrait; if anything would give her nightmares, it would be the photograph peeking out of her duffel bag. With a sigh, Fallon threw off the covers and walked over to the window.

Moonlight painted the courtyard, an uninterrupted sea of grass. Fallon wondered when Ms. Ward would return. She squinted, hoping to catch sight of the librarian. After some time, a flicker of movement caught her eye. Someone walked through the abandoned croquet game. It was terribly dark outside, with frost distorting her view, but she knew it was him. "Sebastian," she whispered, steaming the glass.

Her feet moved faster than her brain. She ran barefoot down the stairs and out the door. The cold hit her like a wall, cutting through the silky fabric of her nightgown and straight to her bones. Frost stung her feet. She narrowly avoided a mallet lying in the grass.

Sebastian turned when her hem tore on the end of a wicket.

She didn't care. The tearing sound continued as she shredded the bottom of her gown further, freeing herself from the wicket. "Sebastian," she yelled, fearing he wasn't real.

"Don't give up," he said in a cracked, dry voice. He looked nervous, as if he had rehearsed his words over and over. His hands reached for her, then curled into fists at his sides. "You can't stop fighting. Hiding here isn't going to solve anything."

Fallon slowed her steps.

"I went to your apartment and you weren't there. Hijiri told me where you'd gone. If it's too late . . ."

Realization dawned. Fallon rubbed her arms and smiled. "You're worried for nothing. I'm not living here, Sebastian. This is for the rebellion. I'm investigating. You would have known that if you'd shown up to the meetings."

Sebastian stood still, his breath forming clouds between them. Then his eyes slid to her feet. "You're not wearing shoes."

Fallon would have laughed if she wasn't so cold. "Yes."

He walked over to her and tugged her toward him so that she stood on top of his boots rather than on the frosted grass.

She was now just as tall as Sebastian. His breath melted the cold from her face; she slid her arms around his neck to keep from falling. Her heart went quiet. Waiting.

His mouth opened, and for a moment, it seemed as if a

silencing charm had fallen down his throat. Nothing came out. They stood like that, both trembling from the cold and something more, until he was finally able to speak. "Fallon," he said, "can I kiss you?"

There was no question of what kind of kiss this would be. Fallon nodded, staring at his mouth, wondering how soft it would be. If it would be. She couldn't tell. Heat traveled from her stomach up to her cheeks.

The wind whistled, flattening her nightgown against her back. Her stomach coiled in anticipation and fear as he slowly bent toward her.

A throat cleared. They jerked apart and turned to see the spinsters standing there, watching. Yasmine shivered in her fuzzy blue bathrobe. Helena's lantern burned with hungry flames. They gathered together in the courtyard. Some had tears in their eyes. Others glowered.

"You kids are too young to know when to give up," said a spinster with fried, yellowing hair.

"Know when you are beaten," said another.

Helena shook her head. "Love can't stop fate, honey," she said. "That only happens in books."

"Shut up!" Fallon yelled. Never would she have said such a thing to her elders; her skin burned with shame, despite her growing anger. "We're going to fight it. This is not our fate. We don't want it."

"Doesn't matter if you don't want it," Yasmine said, burrowing into her bathrobe. "We've never had a choice."

"But you could. The only person forcing you to live like this is yourself," Fallon said.

The spinsters muttered, startled. Helena shook her lantern. "Zita kindly informed us that we're destined to never meet our true loves. She's done us a favor, saving us from the heartbreak."

Fallon let go and stroked Sebastian's cheek. She smiled at him and faced the spinsters. "Take a look at your hearts now and tell me they're not broken."

Silence filled the courtyard. Some spinsters looked down at their chests. Yasmine placed her hand over her heart. Helena started bawling.

Ms. Ward pushed through the cluster of women. "Our school system doesn't condone bullying. We're not always good at noticing it, but when we find it, we shut it down."

Fallon blinked, confused.

"I'm starting to see similarities between bullying and what Zita's been doing," she said.

"You don't mean it," Helena whimpered. "Don't let the girl brainwash you."

"None of us wants to be here," Ms. Ward said, patting the older woman's hand. "Think of the creaky floors and that stench that follows us day in and day out. We're not smelly, disreputable women. Zita has simply told us that we are, and so that's what we've become."

The spinsters, not easily convinced, wanted to discuss the matter further.

Ms. Ward said that there would be plenty of time to talk in the morning. The unflattering pajamas failed to diminish her authority. "We're going to help these kids," she stressed. "If you believe otherwise, then you can take it up with me."

Like reprimanded children, the spinsters dragged their feet and retreated back to their villas.

Sebastian flashed a ghost of a smirk. "I think you've just secured us allies."

Fallon pinched the fabric on his coat sleeve, unwilling to break contact with him. "I didn't expect that to work. It didn't with Bram."

"Who's Bram?" Ms. Ward said, approaching.

"He's actually Hard-boiled Hal," Fallon said without guilt. She didn't care about keeping his identity a secret. "We discovered that he's a bachelor. Yet, he's not compelled at all to help."

Ms. Ward wiped her smudged glasses and adjusted them on her nose. "I seem to be missing something, Fallon. I understood your wonderful speech, but I don't know what you're looking for. What kind of help are you seeking and for what purpose?"

"Sebastian and I are part of a rebellion. We're going to end Zita's fortunes for good."

Ms. Ward's eyes flickered from Fallon to Sebastian. "This is better than books," she said.

>—▷

The rickety heater set to work on Fallon's numb limbs once she was inside. She wrapped herself in an old quilt and buried her red toes in the couch cushion underneath her. The toasty villa would warm her up quickly, but Ms. Ward still insisted on brewing spicy pumpkin tea for them before going back to bed.

"I'm sure you both have a lot to talk about," she said, setting up a tray in front of the couch. "I, for one, am going to need a good rest before facing tomorrow. The room is yours."

Sebastian had gotten the same treatment, wrapped like a worm within a cocoon of patchwork quilts. When Ms. Ward left, Fallon shifted over to lean against him. He stared ahead at the television set, his mouth set in a grim line. He refused to look at her. His voice was thick, scared, as he said, "I have something to tell you. I think I'm ready now. I have to be."

"What's wrong?"

Sebastian wriggled out of his blanket cocoon to reach into his pocket. He pulled out a snakelike paper. Ticker tape. He rubbed his eyes and his fingers came away wet. "Here. Read it."

Fallon gingerly took the love fortune from his hands. After she smoothed down the tangled, curly paper, the red letters proclaimed: *You will die if you fall in love. Your sweetheart will cause it.*

⤙→

The words printed on Sebastian's fortune taunted her, ghosting through her mind with possibilities. The next few months unfolded like an accordion, revealing all the ways in which she could blow out his life like a candle. Her homemade food could poison him. He might push her out of the way of a moving car. She might ask him to do something stupid for her, like find her lost golden bracelet at the bottom of a well, where he would drown while searching.

"Fallon," he said gently. He uncurled her hands and pocketed the fortune.

Slowly, she felt herself breathing again. "Why?"

"I don't know."

"How long?"

"Since freshman year," he said.

She looked up at him and discovered that her heart was still a steady engine in her chest.

Sebastian played the calm one badly. His eyes were red with unshed tears. "I don't want to die," he choked.

This was all too painfully real. She had the irrational fear that someone, like Zita, would open a trapdoor, sending Sebastian spiraling out of her life as quickly as he had come. Fallon opened her arms. "You won't die," she said. "I won't let you."

Her arms tightened around him as he nestled into her embrace, resting his cheek against her chest. Fallon's body shook with his muffled cries. She rested her chin on top of his head and squeezed her eyes shut. Eventually, the storm of emotion died down and Fallon reached out to pour the tea. Her hand shook and droplets of tea missed the mugs.

"I don't think these mugs have been washed before," she said, finding a fleck of cat hair stuck to the outside.

Sebastian laughed weakly. "Only you would think of saying something like that."

Her lips twitched with a smile. "Ms. Ward doesn't own cats, and yet they find their way into her villa, just the same."

"They know a friendly person when they see one," he said. "I met cats like that at the clinic, always looking for the hands that offer treats and a good scratch."

"Like you?"

"I get along better with dogs." Another smirk appeared on his lips like a gift. "I am one. You said so yourself."

"Please don't hold that over my head." She took a sip. The tea torched its way down her throat, touching every nerve. The sudden heat caused her body to shake. "Tell me about the fortune."

Sebastian took a generous gulp of his own tea and hissed when it burned his tongue. He rested his arm on the back of the couch, just behind her neck. "I thought it was a joke at first. A prank that Grimbaud plays on its outsiders. But then I noticed that everyone trusted the fortunes they got. And I couldn't argue, since my fortune had been spit up from the same machine as everyone else's.

"From that day, I decided to protect my heart. I swore I'd never give it to anyone. Nightmares of dropping dead on the street after falling in love kept me up at night, so I wandered Grimbaud and started collecting quiet." Sebastian shrugged. "I could have hid among the other would-be bachelors and accepted a safe, loveless life, but I was stubborn. I began to study the boys around me and figured out what made girls like some but not others."

She saw where this was going. "Then you became handsome."

Sebastian winked. "That's right."

He started teasing death. A girl wouldn't kill him, because he'd never surrender his heart . . . but he wanted as much love as he could experience along the way. He began by dating the bored girls who floated between boyfriends. Then the girls who sought out flings. Sebastian explained his dating rules, sometimes writing it down for them to carry in their purses, and kept his thoughts and emotions as detached as possible. When he received love—a kind smile, a warm hand to hold, or a kiss before the first bell—he absorbed it like a weed dying for sunlight.

"Deep down, I started hating people for following their kinder fortunes. They had the luxury of picking themselves back up again after heartbreak, while I would have died if I tried doing the same. Breaking up with the girls grew easier as time passed, because I knew from their fortunes that they'd recover. But the threats from unhappy girls started to worry me. I needed to find a girl strong enough to handle the rules."

Fallon's mouth ran dry. "You don't mean me."

"You were the one," he said with a rush of emotion. "Orientation established your reputation. It was just as widespread as my own. Fallon Dupree would never be interested in someone like me. That was a comfort. When I found out that we were involved in the rebellion together, it seemed like the perfect opportunity to get to know you."

"So you were secretly happy that I kept rejecting you," she said, scarcely able to believe it.

"I tried being obnoxious," he said, counting off with his fingers, "and reminded you as often as I could how rotten and callous I was. But I never considered how badly *I* wanted to be with you."

Fallon recognized that tug-of-war now that she understood where it came from. All those times he grew panicky and distant were moments when he'd almost forgotten Zita's fortune. She didn't agree with how he'd handled dating, but she understood now. And no matter his actions, she couldn't begrudge him for trying to change, or at least bend, such a horrible fate.

Sebastian couldn't belong to her. He was destined to die after finding his true love. She would become a spinster. Tonight shouldn't have happened: her torn nightgown, the frost on her feet, the almost kiss in the courtyard. The rebellion had already worked miracles, but the ending remained to be seen.

"I'm scared to give you my heart," Sebastian said nervously. Hanging on to his quilt, he left the couch and stared at the bookshelves.

Fallon thought of several responses to that, but none of them matched the severity of what he had just confessed. She pushed back the tray, sloshing more tea, and tiptoed behind him. His back was narrow and tense. She walked around so that she stood in front of him. "I know," she said, "but I'll take good care of it."

"Like ironing your uniform or vacuuming your apartment?" he teased.

Fallon frowned. "Exactly."

"I believe you," he whispered.

The heater sputtered and clicked. They stayed awake until morning, drinking the rest of the spicy tea and listening to the villa's silence.

Fallon and Sebastian left the Spinster Villas without breakfast. The washer and dryer back at the apartment could get rid of the mothball scent, but she'd need to toss in everything she'd brought, including the duffel bag. This Sunday felt like any other November day, except that Fallon battled a new heaviness that made the rebellion's goal so much more critical for her. Zita's fortune had sentenced Sebastian to death. That wasn't something she could easily forget, no matter how satisfying it had felt to know what he thought of her and to hear his secrets.

On the way back, Fallon made sure Sebastian walked on the inside of the sidewalk. She held his hand when they crossed traffic. She grabbed his coat sleeve when a bicycle whizzed by, close enough to clip them.

Sebastian smirked and whispered in her ear, "That's enough."

Fallon's cheeks burned. "You're the one who cried last night about dying."

"Protecting me from the dangers of Grimbaud's traffic is a kind sentiment," he said, "but if I remember correctly, you're the one who fell in a puddle, princess."

"Maybe you should lock yourself in a tower until this is all over," she snapped.

"I could die anywhere," he said thoughtfully. "Imagine how gruesome a tower death would be."

She didn't want to.

They stopped at a fruit stand. Sebastian bought a grapefruit and asked her if she wanted anything.

"Do you actually eat fruit or are you just trying to cheer me up?" Fallon asked.

"I'm disappointed that you think I eat grease for breakfast," he said, his mouth curling into a smile. He said that his grandmother ate nothing but grapefruit in the mornings; like recording pockets of silence, he found starting his day the same way comforting. "You know, Grandma Marion helped push me to find you," he said.

"How do you mean?"

He tossed the grapefruit in his hands as they walked. "I never told my grandmother about my fortunes. After I broke up with you," he grimaced at the phrase, "I sulked long enough to realize that she'd be able to pull me out of it. At first, it was so hard to start. I didn't know how to tell her, so I just read the fortunes into the phone and waited."

"What did she say?"

"Nothing, for a long time," Sebastian said. "I knew she was listening, though. That's just her way."

Fallon wished she could have been there for that conversation. She was curious about his grandmother. She also wondered what it would feel like to truly confide in someone—she did that with her friends, but family was different. Lying to them hadn't been as hard as she'd thought it would be.

He had told his grandmother everything he could, talking until his voice grew hoarse. By the time he returned to the phone with a glass of water, his grandmother was ready to impart her wisdom. "She called me an idiot," he said, "and told me to stop wasting my time and yours by moping."

Fallon laughed at that.

Sebastian ran his fingers over the grapefruit's bumpy skin. "Before she hung up, she told me that she needed to see me directly. Grandma's usually calm, but I could hear her agitation through the phone. She says that she knows something about Zita. It's not safe for me to hear about it in Grimbaud, though."

Her pulse quickened. "When are you leaving?"

"I want you to come with me."

Her rational brain kicked in. "It's November, Sebastian. We have exams in a few weeks. I have a paper that needs to be written by next Thursday."

"I could be dead before then," he said carelessly.

"Or you could live and fail all your classes! Need I remind you that being left back a year is bad?"

"I could stay behind a year. We could graduate together."

"That's unromantic."

Sebastian almost dropped his grapefruit, laughing. "Okay. So. What's the plan?"

"Whatever she has to say must wait until we're done with our exams," Fallon said firmly. They didn't know what kind of lead his grandmother had, but Glastonberry was half a day's bus ride away. They'd be cutting it close trying to squeeze that trip into a weekend. "I'll tell my parents that I'm staying at school for winter break."

"Good plan. We can see my grandmother for a day or two and not miss class." He sighed. "Final exams, huh? It seems pointless to think about real life again."

"I find test taking relaxing," she said.

"I'm not surprised. You probably study."

chapter 19

TINS

When Ms. Ward asked Fallon to stay after school on Monday, she wasn't surprised by the request. The library grew busier this time of year. Procrastinating students hunkered down in study groups. The card catalog was in full use, though usually messed up by students shoving cards back in the wrong drawers. During the month of November, the school library's hours extended until dinnertime. When Fallon arrived after the last bell, the library was as noisy as the cafeteria.

"Form a neat, orderly line," Ms. Ward yelled from the circulation desk.

Fallon set to work on reshelving the encyclopedias someone had left on the floor. She saw a few familiar faces from her classes. The most entertaining students to observe were the study group leaders: they conducted the sessions like maestros, hands flapping, guiding the fold. Thankfully, couples kept their hands to themselves; they were no match for the majority of students roaming the stacks, not for stolen kisses, but for secondary sources.

Ten minutes later, Bram De Groote entered the library with a guest pass clipped to his suit. He looked like he came straight from the accounting office. His eyes narrowed when he saw Fallon, but she stared right back. What was he doing there?

Ms. Ward wore a polite smile when he approached the desk. "Excuse me, who are you?" she asked.

Bram flinched as if slapped. "You asked me to come here," he growled.

"Oh, of course. You must be Mr. De Groote. Just a moment." She finished stamping three books and called Fallon over. "Mr. De Groote and I are going to have a chat in my office. Please take care of things until I return."

Fallon's mouth dropped open. "O-Okay."

She wanted to follow and listen in, but the library transformed into a turbulent sea. Fallon quickly took over the circulation desk and faced the snaking line of students waiting to check out. The ink dried out on the green pad, so she switched to blue. By the time she had finished, some study groups had left. The tables were covered with eraser marks and candy wrappers. Fallon tucked her hair behind her ears and grabbed the cleaning spray from under the desk.

She worked on every empty table. The paper towels turned gray with grime and dust. The headphones boy occupied his usual table against the window. Since she didn't eat cafeteria food, she'd never been able to pick out which lunch lady his mother was. Or why he wasn't in middle school with other kids his age. Maybe he was homeschooled.

"I need to clean here," she said, smiling. "I hope you don't mind."

The boy shrugged and bopped his head to the music.

Fallon wiped the table to the beat of the tango blasting from the headphones. As she worked, she caught sight again of the key hanging from his neck. The key blade was cracked up the middle. "What door can that possibly open?" she asked before thinking.

"Home," he said, in an almost pained whisper.

"You should see a locksmith," Fallon said, wishing she could say something less obvious.

"My mistake," the boy said, tapping a finger on the fissure, "but I'll find a way back in. Isn't that your friend?"

He spoke so gravely that his question caught her by surprise. Fallon pushed in the chairs on the other side of the table so she could get to the window. Outside, students lingered on the front lawn, making plans for another study session or waiting for their parents to pick them up. Anais crossed the front lawn, her face tight with anger as she yelled at someone following her.

The woman following Anais wore a shoulder-padded business suit and carried a file folder stamped with Peak & Brown's insignia.

"Oh no," Fallon whispered.

The boy settled back into his seat, closing his eyes and humming to the music blasting through his headphones.

Fallon wished she could run out the door and rescue Anais. Nothing good could come from a Peak & Brown's employee showing up on campus, especially when Anais had no desire to work with the company. Fallon fogged the glass with her breath as she watched the saleswoman corner Anais.

Anais stuck her fingers in her ears and refused to listen to whatever the saleswoman said. Bear came around the corner with his judo teammates, dressed in their gym clothes for afterschool practice, and noticed his girlfriend's distress. He straightened his back and said something to the saleswoman.

Instead of being intimidated by the burly boy, the saleswoman merely laughed. When the saleswoman opened her mouth again, Fallon felt a wave of dread. She couldn't hear anything through the glass, but she still knew that Anais's secret had finally tumbled forth.

Anais's face went slack with shock. Then, she came beautifully to life, launching pebbles and grass at the saleswoman. The saleswoman dodged them easily, and Fallon had to wonder if this kind of confrontation was something the woman was used to.

Bear just stood there, stunned. When Anais took a step in Bear's direction, his teammates surrounded him. He shook his head and left her there.

Fallon headed toward the circulation desk, anxious to help Anais somehow. The library became stifling. She rocked back on her heels. Why wasn't Ms. Ward finished talking to Bram yet? Duty kept her stationed at the desk.

Luckily, Anais knew where to find Fallon. She showed up in the library as a shaking mess, the saleswoman on her tail.

"Peak and Brown's needs your face for our new campaign. The world wants to know what's happened to our dear little biscuit girl," the saleswoman said, loud enough for the entire library to hear. "Promise me you'll consider coming back."

"This is a library," Fallon said, standing as tall as she could. "If you don't have a guest pass, you need to leave campus immediately."

"One minute with Anais, if you don't mind," the saleswoman said.

Fallon grabbed the phone off the circulation desk and held it like a threat. "The assistant principals are on speed dial."

The saleswoman backed down. "Remember what we talked about," she said, shooting Anais one last desperate glance.

"You're okay," Fallon said, approaching her friend. "It's over."

Anais covered her face with her hands. "I can't."

Fallon grabbed her by the shoulders and steered her toward the geography section, presently unoccupied by eavesdroppers. They sat on the ground, surrounded by outdated atlases and tomes on cultures, also outdated.

"You heard enough to know what happened," she said

angrily. "The entire school will be talking about it tomorrow."

"What about Bear?"

Anais rubbed her eyes roughly to stop the tears. "He hates me."

"No, he doesn't."

"You didn't see his face."

"Maybe you should start from the beginning."

Anais wiped her nose on her blazer. Over the weekend, her father had gotten a few calls from Peak & Brown's. The company wanted Anais to return for a new line of biscuits, as well as become their mascot through commercials and interviews. That wasn't the kind of attention she wanted. Anais argued with her father until he finally agreed to turn down the company's offer, but Peak & Brown's didn't give up: The company sent Mrs. Cools, the tenacious saleswoman, to represent their offer in person. The woman had been following her since that morning. "She must have hid in the bushes or something while I was in classes," Anais said, "lying in wait until school was over."

Mrs. Cools cornered Anais right on the lawn. Fallon had seen that. With no teachers or assistant principals around, the saleswoman freely pitched the offer again to Anais. Loudly. When Bear came to help her, he ended up hearing everything.

"He knows everything," she said. "Worse still, the vile woman thought that Bear was unfit to be my boyfriend. Said he wasn't 'biscuit tin material.'"

"She said that?"

"To his face. Right in front of the team."

This was worse than Fallon thought. "What did Bear do?"

"He *believed* her."

"I'm not taking her side," Fallon said gently, "but Bear's position as your boyfriend has always been precarious. I mean, you never told him about the drugstore or the biscuit tins. He must have felt like you were a stranger when he heard Mrs. Cools's accusations."

Anais frowned.

Fallon shook her head. "I hate to say it, but even Zita warned you that this was going to happen."

"I don't want to lose him."

"Did he break up with you?"

She sniffed. "He didn't say."

"Then this could just be a fight." Fallon squeezed her hand. "Bear needs time to digest what he's heard, but you're going to have to be the one to apologize."

She shifted uncomfortably. "I don't know how."

Sometimes Anais atoned for a sharp word or thoughtless act, but never by saying "I'm sorry." She'd buy sweets for Nico after having a heated debate with him, or leave fresh flowers for Fallon after having made a crude comment the day before. This behavior carried over into Anais's dating life. Her high expectations prevented her past boyfriends from lasting long; she broke up with them early enough not to have offended them too badly.

"You love Bear," Fallon said.

Anais nodded.

"Then try to learn. We can practice. You'll be a professional apologizer when I'm done with you."

Anais cracked a smile. "I'm in your hands."

Ms. Ward's office door opened. Bram emerged and shook the librarian's hand. He looked unhappy about it and shot Fallon a begrudging nod on his way out.

"Fallon, why is there a line at the circulation desk?" Ms. Ward said.

"Sorry; I'm coming."

Anais groaned. "That sounded so easy. Why can't I do that?"

Fallon hid her smile as she hurried back to the desk. She took over stamping as Ms. Ward typed in the ID numbers.

"It worked," Ms. Ward whispered giddily.

"What did?"

"You have a whole army behind you now," she said, tapping the enter key too dramatically.

It took a moment for Fallon to realize what she meant.

⋟─▷

November ended buried in paper. Even the rebellion took a backseat as final exams became a reality. Fallon puzzled over take-home quizzes, hunting through her textbooks for the elusive answers. Her essays poured from pencil to paper like sludge. Charms hung from windows and doors. Some were silencing charms, though none of them were expensive enough to obliterate sound like Bram's was. Fallon purchased a focus charm, made from fluorite, a pale, greenish-purple stone that hung from a silver string.

She tried studying with Sebastian, but he wouldn't take it seriously. He was more interested in collecting silence from her apartment, lying on the wood floor with his eyes closed, the recorder capturing the sounds of her pencil scratching forever. When he *did* study, he cracked jokes and chewed on his pen caps. Sometimes their feet brushed under the table and her cheeks grew hot.

It was too much of a distraction. How he passed his exams was a mystery to her.

Between studying, Fallon promised to help Anais work on her absent apology skills. She assigned Anais a new and more challenging task every time they met. The last one was for Anais to bump into three people on the street and give them a quick apology. Somehow, Anais failed to make even one apology. She either snapped at the person she bumped into or just kept walking, forgetting the point of the assignment.

"I'm not a mean person," Anais whined. "Nico's meaner than me."

"That doesn't even make sense," Nico said, joining the fun.

When she took breaks from her homework and studying, Fallon took Zita's photograph out and stared at it. Fallon decided that her first foray into stealing was worth it. She couldn't stand the idea of Zita looking down on every guest and resident. If she had access to the Bachelor Villas, she'd steal theirs too.

***

"This is your big plan? To become a librarian? Honestly, Fallon, I don't know why that job would appeal to you. You're perfectly capable of becoming a house inspector," Mrs. Dupree said.

Fallon bit back a grin and twirled the phone cord. "Being a librarian could be my calling, Mom."

"Stop. You're giving me palpitations."

"If you let me stay at school over break, Ms. Ward promised that she'd show me the inner workings of the library. She'll even give me a behind-the-scenes tour of Grimbaud's public library."

"You *can* stay," Mrs. Dupree said, "but only because you'll discover faster that running a library is not for you."

"We'll see," Fallon said. "I'll miss you. Say hi to Robbie and Morgane for me."

After hanging up the phone, she put her hands on her hips and smiled. Her empty suitcase awaited her.

***

The bus ride to Glastonberry took longer than scheduled because of the snow. The roads hadn't been salted, so the driver trundled through heavy traffic and abandoned country roads. Fallon slept most of the ride, her head tucked into the crook of Sebastian's shoulder. The closer they came to Glastonberry, the more excited Sebastian grew.

"You're going to love the sea," he said.

"In winter?"

"We can't go swimming," he said, "but the view is amazing from the clinic."

The town of Glastonberry lacked the allure of Grimbaud. The buildings hadn't been built with the intention of wowing tourists and locals. High-rise concrete apartments hugged the coast while the bus drove through downtown. Glastonberry reminded her of her own hometown: commonplace and unremarkable. No gregarious cupid and stork statues. No flashy shops or quaint cafés. She looked for canals out of habit, but found none.

People did sell charms, but she didn't see many shops. Fallon read signs that claimed reduced prices and two-for-one deals on heating charms for December only. One old woman's stand had a poster stating that her charms had a 50 percent chance of working—but no refunds if they didn't.

They stayed on the bus until Glastonberry's last stop, closest to the coast. No one got off with beach blankets and sunglasses. Fallon put on her knitted cap and zipped her coat up to her chin.

"Grandma's clinic is five minutes up the road," Sebastian said, grabbing both suitcases.

Fallon wouldn't let him pull hers. "Tell me about

summer here. I'm having a hard time picturing it." To her right, she saw the steel-gray sea below; they were on an incline, heading toward the peak of a cliffside village. Thatched-roof houses emerged amid the undisturbed snow.

"We have sand-sculpture competitions in August," he said. "Do you see that teal building down there, by the sea? That's the aquarium. My grandmother takes me to the dolphin and fireworks shows every year, even though I outgrew it a long time ago."

Fallon had never been to an aquarium before. Her hometown had a few dusty museums, and what she saw of sea life was served on a plate at restaurants. "I can't imagine ever outgrowing fireworks."

"Maybe the dolphins, then," he said, shrugging. "Cats and dogs are friendlier. And, they have ears to scratch."

When they reached the top, the veterinary clinic looked heavenly. Smoke poured from the redbrick chimney. The rustic building had the appearance of a bed-and-breakfast rather than a clinic, but Fallon heard barking coming from the back where the overnight kennels must have been. The cliff's edge was secured with a fence for the sake of the animals.

When an old woman opened the screen door, Sebastian dropped his suitcase and went running. He called out like a little boy to his grandmother. Fallon couldn't help but smile.

Grandma Marion wore a veterinarian coat and a crisp, masculine shirt and trousers underneath. The weather didn't seem to bother her as she stepped outside and embraced Sebastian. A squirrel with a bandaged head sat in her coat pocket.

A blush crept into Fallon's cheeks and she pulled her suitcase. The similarities between Sebastian and his grandmother were striking; they shared the same straight nose and sharp eyebrows. Her salt-and-pepper hair was cut short and neat and she wore no makeup. Old scratch and bite marks crisscrossed her bare hands.

"You must be Fallon," Marion said gruffly.

She stuck out her hand. "Nice to meet you."

Marion's handshake was firm. "Don't be nervous. You've put up with my grandson. I'm thoroughly impressed."

Sebastian grumbled.

"Come inside before you both turn into icicles."

Fallon's skin thawed when they entered the waiting room. The room was decorated with lush purples and greens like a children's playroom, a friendliness that didn't match Marion's surly exterior. A gray cat sat on the front desk, swishing its tail. Three spotted puppies chewed on one another's ears in a basket behind the desk. Jars of dog treats and colorful leashes sat on shelves, waiting to be purchased. Marion's assistants, dressed in purple scrubs, came in and out.

"Take Fallon upstairs," Marion told Sebastian. "I have one more appointment for the day. We'll talk after."

Fallon stiffened, remembering how important this trip was. Marion had information about Zita. The faster they knew, the more time they might have to ensure the rebellion's success.

chapter 20

BORROWED TIME

Upstairs was another kind of waiting room. Fallon fiddled with the zipper on her suitcase. Marion's living room and connected kitchen exuded peace, from the sea-green accents to the shiny wooden floors. The walls weren't cluttered with family photos. Instead, one painting of sand dunes hung in the kitchen. The rest of the walls were eggshell white.

"You grew up here?" she asked.

"I used to think that my grandmother lived in a sanctuary. The calming effects never worked on me. I felt like an outsider," he said.

"That's not true. You're more like her than you realize." She thought about how focused he had been while recording silence and how at ease he had been sharing the morning hours with her at the villas, listening to nothing but the natural sounds of the world awakening.

Sebastian ducked his head, embarrassed. "Let me prove you wrong. Come see my bedroom."

A short walk past the kitchen and he disappeared through a doorway. Fallon shut her eyes, nervous to see something as private as the bedroom he grew up in.

"You coming?" he called.

Fallon opened her eyes and followed his voice.

At first, his room did seem to imitate Marion's minimalist style. The indigo walls made the room smaller, more like a midnight hideaway. Even though the three black-and-white photographs of sailboats were the only decorations, Fallon noticed, upon closer inspection, that the walls were pockmarked.

"As a kid," he explained, "I used to put push pins in the walls instead of using Grandma's corkboard. I hung up anything I could find, like newspaper ads and my graded homework. She'd take everything down each week, and I'd fill the walls back up again."

The tall windows provided a substandard view of the cliff's edge, with the sea too far away to admire as more than a soup bowl of gray. Sebastian's dog-grooming supplies were neatly put away in a container on his desk. The bed had been perfectly tucked in, the covers as dark as the walls.

"I still have to see your apartment to compare," she said, "but for now, yeah, I'm disappointed. She sure patched this room up."

"It looks like a model showroom," Sebastian said.

Fallon walked over to the bedside table. On the floor, next to the outlet, was a photograph lying facedown. "What's this?" she said, picking it up.

Sebastian's expression turned grim when he saw the photo of the couple. "My parents."

"You look like your dad," she said, tracing the slim shoulders in the photo with her finger. Mr. Barringer was softly handsome in the way that Sebastian was, but his mouth had hard brackets around it, as if he didn't use it for laughing. Sebastian's mother had both her arms wrapped around her husband, flashing large white teeth at the camera.

The bed sank with Sebastian's weight as he sat down. "I don't like thinking about them."

"Where are they now?"

"Dad's still in downtown Glastonberry," he said. "His barbershop is his second wife. My mother lives in the next town over, but Grandma tells me that she keeps coming back to bother him. She refuses to sign the divorce papers, says that Zita promised their love is unbreakable."

"That can't be right," Fallon said, sitting next to him. "Your mother must be lying."

"She's not." Sebastian released a dry laugh. "She carries the fortunes in her pockets everywhere. She shows them to everyone she meets."

"Where do you fit into all this?"

"Forgotten."

"I'm sorry."

"Don't be. I want nothing to do with them. They're so wrapped up in themselves. Not even my own birth kept them quiet for long. I remember arguments, broken dishes, hiding. That's why I wandered the neighborhood as kid, causing trouble. If I had control over something else, I felt good, since I couldn't change anything at home."

She didn't press him further. "Show me a picture of you as a kid. You promised."

"I did, didn't I?"

Sebastian opened his closet and searched through his shelves until he pulled out an old photo album. He flipped through a few pages and stopped at one taken of himself at age twelve. He posed on the top of monkey bars, lifting both hands in victory. He had a thin, angry little face, pronounced by his fleeced hair and the parade of bandages on his arms and legs. "That was a good day," he said, smirking. "I outran Big Paul and his henchmen." He pointed to the bandages. "That was all me. Asphalt and I had a loving relationship."

"You were definitely ugly," she said.

Sebastian feigned hurt. "I know I said it was okay for you to say I was ugly, but I changed my mind. You're supposed to adore me."

Fallon laughed. "Since when?"

"Since forever." Sebastian tackled her, tickling her through her sweater. The bed creaked, betraying its age, as they both fought playfully.

Fallon shivered, even as she found a spot underneath his rib cage that made him snort with laughter. Everything about this moment ached with loss. How long could she spend time with Sebastian before he was taken away? Zita's fortunes were ticking time bombs. For now, Fallon committed everything she could to memory. When she ended up underneath him, Fallon wrapped her arms around his neck and hugged him tightly.

"What's the matter?" he whispered against her hair.

"You're not ugly," Fallon said.

"Neither are you, princess."

She continued to hug him, afraid that if he saw her face, he'd know how close she was to crying.

⚬━▷

When Marion joined them in the afternoon, she dropped a box on the kitchen counter. "I unearthed this from the attic," she said, wiping dust off her coat.

Fallon climbed onto the bar stool, which was level with the counter. The box hadn't been touched in years, by the looks of the peeling masking tape and crushed edges.

Sebastian spun the box around until he found someone's name scribbled on the side in marker. "'Dorian,'" he read. "That's Grandpa."

Marion leaned her elbows on the counter. "How much do you remember about your grandfather?"

"Only what you told me," he said, puzzled. Sebastian turned to Fallon. "Grandpa Dorian died after my father was born. I never knew him."

Marion said, "I wish that man was here now. I'd give him a black eye."

"You don't mean that," Sebastian said.

"I loved him very much," she said, "but it seems that he

caused more trouble than I thought. Go on, Sebastian. Open the box. You'll see what I mean."

Sebastian curled his hands into fists. "What does this have to do with Zita?"

"This box contains everything from Dorian's past," she explained instead, picking at the masking tape. "When we moved in together, he brought this box with him and told me never to open it. He wanted to keep the past in the past. I felt the same. When Sebastian told me about those love fortunes, something about how they were written jogged my memory. Dorian once said that his fiancée had been quite the poetess."

"You think there's something in there about his fiancée?" Sebastian asked.

Fallon watched them both, confused. "What fiancée?"

"Maybe you should start from the beginning," Sebastian said to his grandmother. "Fallon doesn't know about Grandpa."

Marion opened the fridge and sniffed a half-empty milk carton. "Dorian Barringer came to Glastonberry as an escape. He was twenty at the time, and I had just started veterinary school. I remember being drawn to his helplessness," she said wistfully. "He got off the bus right where you two did, with too many suitcases and a torn map in his hands.

"At first, Dorian was vehemently against dating, despite the magnetic pull that brought us together. I knew it was right. He did too, but he was honest with me. Before he packed up his old life and rode the bus out as far as he could go, his doctors back in Grimbaud had diagnosed him with lymphoma. He only had six months to live."

Sebastian sat up straighter. "But he lived another two years."

"That's right. Long enough to marry me and give me a son, Etienne."

"He came from Grimbaud?" Fallon asked.

"Born and raised." Marion opened the milk carton and peered inside. "I never understood the appeal of that town. Too noisy and cute for my tastes. But Etienne was mad about it when he was a young man, and so is Sebastian."

Sebastian inhaled and drew the box close. He peeled the layers of masking tape off until the top flaps came free. One by one, he took out each item in the box and placed it on the counter: certificates of achievement from Grimbaud's elementary and middle schools, a vial of canal water, marked-up high school essays, a leather notebook, a deflated basketball, a pair of scissors, and loose photographs.

Marion wrapped ice cubes in a dish towel and pressed it against her temples. "Look for the fiancée."

"What's her name?" Sebastian asked, flipping through the essays.

"Inés Aandekerk."

Fallon started. She recognized the last name from the guidebooks she had studied before coming to Grimbaud. Aandekerk's Lace Shop was notable because of its long history, but Fallon hadn't gone there yet; it was too easy to overlook lace shops when Zita's love charms and fortunes brought the crowds to the square.

Fallon took the leather notebook and opened it to the first page. The book was dedicated to Dorian. Handwritten poems covered the pages, dripping with sweet nothings. The handwriting matched the fortunes. Reading them made her uncomfortable, so she skimmed the pages for Inés's name. On the last page, she found "Inés Aandekerk" underneath a crude sketch of a young woman. The handwriting was different here—maybe Dorian had been the one to draw her. The sketch revealed a teenage girl at her desk, her face in profile. Fallon felt a trickle of dread as she recognized the girl's tumbling dark hair and the silver heart necklace.

Fallon flipped the book upside down and ran to her suitcase. She was glad she thought to bring Zita's photograph, but wished she hadn't needed it. The frame felt cold in her hands as she carried it back to the kitchen. She held up the photo, her voice cracking. "I think she's Zita."

Sebastian grabbed the leather notebook and stared at the sketch. "They do look the same."

"Where is your fortune?"

When Sebastian pulled it out of his pocket, Fallon smoothed the fortune out next to the notebook. "Look at the handwriting."

Sebastian gasped softly. "I always thought the machine printed them."

"A charm?" Marion asked, wrinkling her nose.

Fallon climbed back onto the chair, but her movements were shaky. The connection was there. "No one knows who Zita is," she murmured, "and right here, we're holding a piece of her past in our hands."

Marion dumped the melting remains of ice cubes in the sink. "Dorian said she couldn't handle it."

"Handle what?" Sebastian said.

"He never told her about the lymphoma." Marion's expression hardened. "He didn't leave Grimbaud just because of the illness. His fiancée was an excitable girl, prone to moods and hysterics. He thought the news would stop her heart, and so he cut ties without even a good-bye."

Fallon cradled the leather book in her hands. Inés's poetry traveled dark and sensuous paths. Her mind must have been full of riddles, easily translatable to ticker tape. "Then Zita knows who Sebastian is."

"Use this for your rebellion," Marion said. "Take whatever you need."

Sebastian's eyes flickered over the box's contents. "Grandpa almost married Grimbaud's greatest love charm-maker," he said, stunned.

"If she loved Dorian that much, Zita should be sympathetic. Tell her that you're Dorian's grandson. Maybe she'll allow for some things in that town to change," said Marion.

Fallon placed the book on the table and wiped her hands on her thighs. Sebastian held the key to Zita's secret past. That could come in handy. But the love fortunes still concerned her. Even with Zita's blessing, their futures were set in stone.

Ultimately, Love controlled their fates. Zita only served as messenger.

The next morning, the snow fell heavy, threatening to block the roads. Fallon consulted the bus schedule and found a bus leaving for Grimbaud before lunch. She wished they could stay longer—she wanted to see Sebastian groom one of the dogs at the clinic—but school beckoned. They'd have to take the bus, or else risk being snowed in and stuck for a few days.

After making herself toast in Marion's kitchen, she heard Sebastian emerge from his room. He yawned, pillow creases tattooing his face and arms. "Grandma's gone out?"

Fallon nodded. "She's sitting on the back porch. Said she needed some quiet."

He ran his fingers through his hair and worked on slicing a grapefruit for breakfast. "Nothing bothers her. Not the snow. Not broken cat bones. Not even Zita."

"She has to be upset about Zita."

"You don't know her," Sebastian said, sticking a spoon in his grapefruit. "Grandma lives in the present. She practices the art of stripping away the emotions attached to bad memories. That's what she does when she meditates. It's how she gets through the failed surgeries and putting animals to sleep."

Fallon finished her toast and washed her plate and cup in the sink. "I'm going to go out there."

"Use one of my scarves. They're warmer than what you brought," he said.

"Thanks." Fallon looked over her shoulder. "And don't follow me outside. Today could be the day you discover a hole in the fence."

Sebastian took a bite of grapefruit and made a face. "Not enough sugar."

"I mean it."

"My immediate plans involve a shower," he said, digging around for sugar and finding honey instead.

"Good."

Fallon pulled on a second sweater, her coat, and grabbed one of the scarves hanging in Sebastian's closet. The snow had been ruined early that morning by the dogs boarding at the clinic. Tracks cut up the backyard. She knelt down to examine a tiny paw print in the snow.

Marion sat on a cushion, her feet bare and her arms loose on her knees. She didn't meditate like the books said; she looked too relaxed, her face deliciously slack. "Come sit by me," she said.

Fallon lost her balance and crushed the paw print. "I didn't mean to interrupt."

Marion grumbled and shifted so that there was room for another person on the cushion.

Fallon sat down, careful not to let her shoes touch the cushion. The fog curling on the horizon distorted the gray sea. "I've been thinking about the fortunes."

"They shouldn't exist," Marion said gruffly.

Fallon smiled. Marion would probably get along with the twins.

"I'm supposed to be a spinster. Zita's fortune says that no one will ever love me in return," Fallon said. "But I have Sebastian, and I think . . . part of me hopes that we've already beaten our fortunes."

Fate played cruel tricks on spinsters. Some went through dry spells, where romance novels provided them with heroes, while others had men plucked and pulled from their lives as quickly as a windstorm. Fallon had thought that her own dry spell began with the arrival of her fortune. Then Sebastian surprised her. He had been there all along.

"Fortunes can be tricky," Marion said, opening her eyes.

Fallon sucked in her breath. "You should hate me."

Marion stretched, uncurling one finger at a time. "That seems like a waste of energy."

Fallon looked at her, surprised.

"Would you willingly hurt Sebastian?"

"Never."

"Then don't vilify yourself."

Fallon hugged her knees to her chest. She had been greedily collecting her moments with Sebastian to pack them in a box, much like Dorian had. Deep down, maybe she believed that his fortune would come true. That she couldn't stop it.

"I'm not a poet," Marion said, gentler than she'd sounded before. "I heal and destroy with my hands. Words can be twisted into other meanings."

Fallon lifted her head and looked at the blinding white sky.

chapter 21

TREMORS

When Fallon turned the key, she had trouble opening her door. She pushed a little harder, one hand still gripping her suitcase, until something made a tearing noise at her feet. A piece of paper caught underneath the doorway. Written with a dying pen on blue paper, it simply read:

> You're the one who discovered the pink phone. It's only fair you join us tonight. Meet us behind Zita's shop at 9pm.
> —F and M

Snow turned to slush in Grimbaud. The roads were salted quickly, so as not to interrupt the tourists spending winter in the charming town. Fallon wasn't too cold as she entered

Verbeke Square, recalling how much more intense the snowfall was in Glastonberry. Her navy trench kept her warm enough.

Zita's shop closed by dinnertime during winter break, but that didn't stop the light show. Pink spotlights cast hearts on the outside of the shop. Fairy lights framed the second-story display window.

The other buildings were dark. Fallon saw a policeman sitting in front of an empty café, nearly half-asleep. Before she could step into his line of sight, a pair of hands pulled her into the shadows.

"Don't even think of saying hello to him," Mirthe whispered. "The police aren't our friends tonight."

"I guessed that much," Fallon said. The twins wore black capelets and striped leggings with matching, stuffed backpacks. The robber eye masks were especially telling.

"Phase three will be ready," Mirthe said, "after tonight."

Femke shushed her.

"Fine. Let's get on with it."

After Mirthe's blunder at the student government meeting, Femke had taken over as the paranoid one. Fallon wondered if that was a twin thing—to absorb what the other lacked in order to remain balanced. She mimicked the twins as they used the shadows to travel unnoticed towards Zita's shop.

Every shop had a back door, and Zita's was no different. Fallon huddled with the twins outside of it, waiting for the next move. They were going to break in, but how?

"Our dad has a special collection of squalls," Mirthe whispered. "We're using some tonight."

Mirthe took a small metal object out of her capelet pocket. Femke handed her a vial that whistled and shook in her hand—the squalls. After attaching the vial to the contraption, Mirthe pressed it against the lock and pushed down on a lever every few seconds. The contraption sent concentrated puffs of squalls through the keyhole. The squalls' pressure acted as a key, allowing them entry without leaving fingerprints.

The twins used the last of the squalls to push the door open and slipped inside. Fallon was careful not to brush against the door. The air made her dizzy; she held her breath, fighting the rose scent, until she couldn't any longer. Her mind started to dance away, playing with fantasy dates of her and Sebastian.

"Remember your fortune," Mirthe hissed, pinching the back of Fallon's neck.

Fallon gasped. Her mind cleared, bringing with it fresh heartache. Zita's shop was a hazardous interior at night. She kept her arms tight against her, using the light spilling in through the windows to help her navigate. Forbidden charms and candy machines were tempting distractions.

"Go on, take something," Femke whispered. She held out a pair of black gloves.

"Why? We'll get caught," Fallon said.

Mirthe shook her head. "Doesn't matter what charms we use tonight. Someone's going to know Zita's shop has been broken into. We might as well cause a stir while we're here."

Fallon took the gloves from Femke and put them on. She hadn't come prepared to carry much with her, so she stole a whole packet of paper charm affirmations she could fold up and put in her coat pocket, along with some thumb-size potions promising the drinker a date free from tongue-tied shyness. After taking Zita's portrait from the villas, she should have felt more comfortable, but the charms were heavy in her pockets. She wanted to get rid of them as soon as possible.

The twins took a few charms themselves until Femke found the break area. The pink phone was mounted on the wall near the coffeepots.

Mirthe picked up the handset. "Let's give Zita a call."

Fallon inspected the phone. "It's a direct line. Look. There's no keypad, just one red button."

Mirthe shared a mischievous grin with her sister. "Then we have no chance of dialing the wrong number."

Fallon wasn't following. "We came all this way to prank call Zita?"

The twins raised their eyebrows. "We need the phone," Femke said, "because we need Zita's voice to figure out where she is."

When Mirthe reached into her backpack Fallon expected to see a mysterious weather charm. Something typical of the twins and their sneaky, ingenious ways. So she almost choked on her disappointment when Mirthe pulled out a Sound and Seek toy.

The toy fit in the palm of Mirthe's hand; it was box-shaped with a tiny microphone sticking out of the top like an antenna. A big-eyed, smiling face had been painted on the toy with bright yellows and reds.

"Why do you have that?" Fallon asked weakly. Her parents had made her play with one as a kid to start honing her inspecting skills early. Sold in study charm shops, the Sound and Seek turned a simple game of hide-and-seek into detective work.

Mirthe danced on her toes in excitement. "Whoever created this charm is a genius," she said. "Once you turn the toy on, it latches onto the first voice it hears—presumably the person hiding. It gives you one clue per game, using one of the five senses. Femke and I know this town so well, one clue should be enough for us. We're going to find out where Zita's hiding."

"It's just a kid's toy. The range can't be good."

Mirthe rolled her eyes. "This one covers the whole town. Femke and I stayed up all night tweaking the charm."

Fallon blinked. Of course they did. There was the ingenuity she had missed.

Femke activated the toy, then pressed the button on the phone and held it down. The three girls waited, listening hard for the phone to change its tone.

Hearing Zita's voice for the first time made Fallon's palms sweat. A strange panic flooded her heart. Something dripped in the background, like the inside of a cave. Then Zita asked for Camille, her voice high and sweet in a grandmotherly sort of way. But there was an edge beneath it, like a knife cutting through cake.

Mirthe pressed a finger to her lips and said nothing while Zita grew more agitated by the silence.

"My Camille wouldn't be quiet for so long," Zita said. "I demand to know who's on the line."

Femke released the button. The call died.

"I guess Camille talks to her more than we thought," Mirthe said, hanging the handset back up. "We got what we needed."

The Sound and Seek toy trembled as it printed a square-shaped piece of paper and spit it out onto the floor. Fallon bent to pick it up, but recoiled from the scent wafting from the paper. "What is that?"

Mirthe crinkled her nose. "The clue." She picked it up with two fingers and stuck it in her pocket. "Let's get out of here first."

Fallon tried not to look too relieved. She didn't want to stay in the shop any longer, clue or no clue.

The girls retraced their steps, managing to reach the back door without incident. However, Fallon smelled the familiar musky scent that meant Camille was nearby. Footsteps approached the shop. Two sets. She warned the twins, who seemed to always have one charm or another on their persons. "What do we do?" Fallon whispered.

"Watch this," Mirthe said, tossing a stormy gray capsule into the air. The capsule erupted, spawning a thick cloud that rumbled and glowed bright with a sliver of lightning.

Within seconds, Fallon could barely see a few inches in front of her with the heavy rain falling from the lone cloud, but she squinted and surmised that the two outlines in the rain were Camille and a policeman.

"The forecast said clear skies," the policeman said, swatting at the rain with his baton.

Camille screeched, trying to use her hands to shield her already soaked hair. "It's obviously a trick," she said, "a charm! I told you someone was sneaking around back here!"

The cloud only grew bigger.

Fallon had never been so thankful for a storm; it masked them completely as they ran in the other direction, water pouring down their backs.

"We're safe," Mirthe said after they'd left the square and were back on the streets. The twins peeled off their masks before anyone saw them. They insisted on walking Fallon back to the complex.

"You look so scared," Mirthe teased. "As if you've never broken rules before."

"Not one this big," Fallon grumbled. If she was learning anything during her freshman year, it was that rules broke apart at her feet, whether she liked them or not. "What should we do with the charms we took?"

"Oh, good point," Mirthe said. "We don't want them. Maybe someone else would like free charms."

On the walk, the girls planted the stolen charms in nooks and crevices, outside of houses and along the canals. When they crossed a bridge, Fallon released the stack of love affirmations, watching the wind carry some and let others drop into the water.

When they reached Fallon's apartment, she invited them inside, but they wouldn't stay long enough for her to brew them tea.

Femke toyed with the buttons on her caplet. "This may be hard to believe, but Mirthe and I have no doubt. Zita is underneath Verbeke Square."

Fallon just stared at the twins.

"The sewers," Femke said. "That's what you smelled from the Sound and Seek clue."

When Mirthe handed her the clue again, Fallon tried not to shudder from the smell. The smell found its way from her nose to her tongue—she could taste the damp, dark underground. She handed back the clue, feeling slightly ill and in need of strong mint toothpaste to chase away the cloying scent. "You knew right away. Have you been in the sewers before?"

"It's not a place that anyone would want to explore," Mirthe said. "Even the most devoted lovers of Grimbaud don't think of the sewers. It's just a given, something that all towns and cities have. But there are entrances all over town. Usually, only repairmen have the keys to go down there."

"And our mother," Femke added.

"But you're weather charm-makers. That doesn't make sense," Fallon said.

"Our father's specialty is wind," Mirthe said proudly.

"Our mother happens to be the best at bottling earthquake tremors."

Fallon was stunned. She'd never heard of such a thing. "Why would anyone want tremors?"

Before Mirthe could answer, Femke shushed her sister and blushed. "It's a private market."

"I see." She didn't.

"Since we don't usually have earthquakes here, our mother chases after them in other parts of the world. She's often away for months at a time. Like now," Mirthe said. "But if there was ever an earthquake in Grimbaud, our mother has the keys to go into the sewers and safely collect the tremors. The closer to the earth you are, the easier it is to bottle them."

"We brought along the Sound and Seek toy as confirmation, but Mirthe and I already had our suspicions. We thought that if Zita truly *was* here in town, there was only one place she could be without being seen by the townspeople," Femke said.

Before the raid on Zita's shop, the twins searched their mother's office for her maps of Grimbaud's sewer system and the keys to the various entrances. "What we found," Femke said, "is that the sewer system is connected all throughout town, except in Verbeke Square. The entire area is sealed off. Mom's never been able to get in. Says so in her notes."

"So you suspect that Zita's living underground, in the sewers underneath Verbeke Square," Fallon repeated, just to be sure. Surely someone as rich and respected as Zita must have been living in luxurious hotels and on first-class train cars. The clue wrecked what she had always imagined Zita's lifestyle to be like.

Then Marion's words came back to her. She had described Zita, or Inés, as someone emotionally turbulent. Someone whose heart could be battered as easily as an umbrella caught in a hurricane. Someone like that might prefer to hide in the dark. Fallon couldn't assume anything at this point. "So we're going to find a way into the sewers beneath Verbeke Square on the night of the Welcome Love Fair?"

"That's exactly right." Mirthe smiled. "We've got the right key and map. The entire town will be distracted by the fair. And we're going to find Zita."

"Then let me tell you what Sebastian and I discovered," Fallon said. Her own adventure had been mild in comparison, but her heart fluttered with hope as she told the twins about Inés Aandekerk and how she'd almost married Dorian Barringer, Sebastian's grandfather. "I don't know how she feels about Dorian after all these years," she said, "but Marion seems to believe that seeing Sebastian might make Zita's heart soften toward us. She loved Dorian passionately. Meeting his grandson may be a good experience for her."

"That's amazing," Mirthe said. "I'm all fired up."

"Phase three is looking beautiful," Femke said.

"We have the spinsters and bachelors on our side too,"

Fallon said, catching their excitement. "We're not alone in this."

"Leave ironing out the details to us. We'll have another meeting. All of us." Mirthe flapped her capelet like a bat. "January thirty-first is just around the corner."

With winter break crawling to a close, Fallon had to use her last vacation day wisely by restocking her school supplies. "I can't just wait for the police to arrest me," she said to herself, folding her shopping list in half. "The only crime you're going to be guilty of today is buying cheap loose-leaf paper."

Grimbaud was abuzz about the break-in. No matter what store she walked into, she heard nothing but theories and outrage about the thieves. This was no ordinary robbery attempt. This was a personal attack on the town.

Any anxiety she felt transformed into frustration. The break-in shouldn't have eclipsed the removal of Love's statue. *Whose side are you on?* Fallon thought, staring at the townspeople she passed. The scent of roses was overwhelming.

In Verbeke Square, the pink-lemonade storefront looked no worse for the intrusion. Two brawny officers guarded the front door, while another kept an eye on the love-fortune machine. The lace shops opened their doors, unperturbed by the ruckus caused by the break-in, while the cafés reluctantly fed their customers.

Fallon inspected the area, searching for anything that resembled an entrance into the sewers, but spotted Martin instead. "Hello, Mr. President," she said, jogging to catch up to him.

"Fallon Dupree," he said slowly.

"That's me."

Martin smiled slightly.

"Are you really by yourself?" she asked.

"Running errands." He lifted his bag, revealing random items from a hairbrush to an ear of corn. "My parents thought I needed the fresh air. I would have been sleeping otherwise."

"Do you typically sleep in on the weekends?"

He shook his head. As the early riser in his family, he usually spent his weekend mornings getting student government work done and taking care of his little sisters. "But now, my sisters are the ones poking and prodding me in the mornings. I've been feeling drained lately."

Fallon worried about Martin's health. His constant exposure to Camille's charm could be doing permanent damage. She wished she knew more about charms, like Hijiri and the twins. She felt helpless.

"I see you're school-supply shopping," Martin said.

Fallon nodded. Even though Martin still looked unwell, his eyes were clear. He didn't slur his words. That was a good sign. "I came to see Zita's shop too. That break-in has shaken the town up, hasn't it?"

"Everyone's talking about it," he said politely.

Fallon bit her lip. "What do you think the thieves were after?"

Martin smiled. "Just a few charms were stolen, so that leads me to believe it was a dare. Kids do that sort of thing all the time."

Glancing at Zita's shop once more, Fallon sucked in her breath. The question poured out of her mouth before she could think. "What was your fortune this year?"

Martin raised his eyebrows.

"Sorry. Was that too personal?"

"It's just . . . no one ever asks me. I guess being the president means that I don't appear very human. No one needs to be concerned about me."

Nico's very concerned about you, she wanted to say, but she closed her mouth.

"I don't carry it with me," he said, "not that I need to. It's easy to remember. My fortune said that someone from my past would be coming back into my life."

Fallon stopped walking.

"It couldn't be more obvious," Martin said balefully. "Camille's the one in the fortune. I broke up with her over the summer and she became a piece of my past. Her elbowing her way back into my life for the new school year seems on cue. I honestly don't know anyone else who could fit the fortune. I've lived here all my life. My past is my present."

"You don't?" she almost whispered. "You can't think of anyone?"

"What's the matter?" Martin looked over his shoulder, confused.

Fallon's heart bellowed and her hands shook with a realization that left her dizzy. Maybe this is what Marion had meant when she said that poetry was twisted. The words either contained multiple meanings or meant something else entirely. And the fortune didn't take into account the one person that Martin wouldn't remember. "Do you have time?" she said too loudly. "Can you come with me?"

Martin's eyebrows just about launched themselves into his hairline. "Where to?"

"We're going to see Nicolas," she said, taking firm hold of his hand. "He's got something to say to you."

⁚→

Fallon couldn't reach the Barnes Canal Cruises ticket booth fast enough. Part of this had to do with her excitement, and the other with Martin's lack of endurance. He could tear through an entire stack of student government paperwork in a day, but he wasn't good at running. Martin's face flushed red and sweat trickled down his cheeks despite the snow. But by the time they reached the canal, he looked more awake than usual.

Another tour boat had just launched, full of eager tourists and fidgety children. The engine roared steadily as it pulled away. The mermaid statue on the roof of the booth looked especially fierce in winter, crushing the two hearts in her hands.

Nico wasn't manning the booth. Fallon thought that he might have left on the last cruise, until she saw him tying up a boat. He wore a windbreaker sprayed with canal water. His hair stood stiffly in the wind.

"Okay," she said, turning to Martin. "I lied about the talking thing. Nicolas *does* have something to tell you, but you're going to have to overhear him talking to me about it. Because I don't think he's brave enough to tell you personally yet."

"As student government president, I should be setting an example for the student body," Martin said, frowning. "I can't possibly eavesdrop."

"You're going to want to hear this. I promise."

Martin squeezed his eyes shut and sighed. "Okay."

Fallon ushered him over to the boiled peanuts cart that had been left unoccupied on a lunch break. Martin hid behind the cart, which happened to be within hearing distance from Nico's favorite bench.

She ran over to Nico. "Hey, I'm back!"

"Bet Glastonberry wasn't as exciting as here," Nico said, giving the rope one more tug.

"You're right. It wasn't," she said. "Do you have a minute?"

"Sure." Nico knocked on the ticket booth and asked for a refill on his cup of coffee; in the winter, his parents installed a coffeemaker next to the cash register. They took a seat on the bench.

Fallon casually looked over her shoulder. Martin's plastic bag stuck out from behind the cart; she saw his breath join the steam from the boiled peanuts and knew he was still there. "I need a happy story, Nico."

Nico laughed dryly. "Why would you come to me for that?"

"Because you have one, don't you? I think it's the perfect time to tell me again."

He took a sip of his coffee. "There's no ending to it yet."

"You could be writing it right now. Come on. Indulge me."

Nico's cheeks pinked as he settled back into the bench. "My father allowed me to work on the Sunday night cruise when I turned ten. Grimbaud Elementary had booked the cruise for its own Welcome Love celebration that night. The entire school had been invited. Dad wouldn't let me enjoy the party with my friends. Instead, I spent the evening helping parents and students find their assigned tables on the lower deck for dinner.

"When night fell, the kids ran around on the upper deck while the parents and teachers lingered at the tables. I remember having a hard time seeing that night; the houses didn't have as many lights on and some of the streetlamps flickered and went out. Maybe it was too much sugar or excitement from the cruise, but the kids started fooling around. Pushing each other. Shouting.

"And there was this boy, Martin Pauwels. He was a year older than me. I recognized him from the posterboards at school; he was an honors student and the school liked to boast about him in its newsletters. A couple of kids had circled him, making fun of his crooked glasses and perfect grades. He didn't stand a chance when they put their hands on him."

When someone pushed Martin just hard enough to knock him overboard, kids became frightened and started shouting and crying for their mothers. Nico knew his father couldn't stop the boat in time, and the inky waters looked deeper than usual, as if they could swallow a person whole. "So I climbed over the railing and dived," he said.

The water was January-cold; it climbed up his nose and burned his lungs. He swam back toward the spot where he'd seen Martin fall and sank underneath the water, his hands out, blindly searching. He found a coat, then a wrist, and wrapped his arms around Martin, kicking toward the surface. The older boy had lost his glasses in the water. His eyes were closed. Nico kicked for the bank and hauled them both ashore.

"Dad was inching the boat as close as he could to the bank," Nico said, "and shouted for me to check Martin's pulse. I couldn't feel it."

But Nico had been trained in giving mouth-to-mouth resuscitation. As a Barnes, he'd grown up practicing on a dummy. He panicked for a heartbeat, but pulled himself together and tilted Martin's head back. "I wasn't supposed to feel anything when I pressed my mouth against his," he said, "but it's not like I could help it." Each time he returned to give Martin more air, his lips tingled and his cheeks grew hot. He almost missed it when Martin started breathing again, but he quickly pushed his own confusing feelings aside long enough for the paramedics to arrive.

"He was okay," Nico said, blinking back tears. "I saw him breathing and coughing up the canal water. But he didn't open his eyes. When I went to school the following week, he didn't seem to recognize me. Maybe his parents didn't tell him, but I discovered that I couldn't either. Whenever I tried, my stomach twisted and I started shaking."

Fallon rubbed Nico's shoulder. "You knew it then, didn't you?" This had always been her favorite part.

"Yeah. I loved him."

"Still do," she corrected.

Nico played with the lid on his coffee. "Still do," he echoed.

When Fallon peeked over her shoulder, she didn't see the plastic bag or Martin's cloudy breaths anymore. Her idea had spawned purely from Martin's fortune, but ignoring Nico's fortune had cost her: *Your love will go unnoticed by the one who matters.* If Martin was never to know Nico's feelings, then anything could have pulled him away from his hiding spot behind the cart. He must not have stuck around long enough to hear Nico's full confession.

She wanted to climb onto the bench and yell until she lost her voice. She and Sebastian might have had dooming fortunes, but she had hoped, after speaking with Marion, that she could do something for her friends. Fighting fate was harder than she had imagined.

chapter 22

BELOW

Fallon might have struck out with Nico and Martin, but Hijiri was different. Zita's fortune for Hijiri had insisted that she change to inspire love, but she didn't think Hijiri needed a makeover to do that. Joining the rebellion had allowed her to change for herself and in her own time. Fallon thought of the haircut as a gift only because, like her family, she had an eye for finding quality. She knew that with a little love, Hijiri's hair could be healthy.

Sebastian ran his fingers through Hijiri's hair—or tried to. His fingers kept getting stuck in the knots. "This is no good," he mumbled. "We're just going to have to wash it first."

"You don't have to do this," Hijiri said, flustered.

"Don't be nervous," Sebastian said. "Look at my hair. It's nice, isn't it?"

Hijiri nodded.

"Well, I cut my own hair. So, yours will look nice too."

Sebastian crossed his arms. "This is our thank you. We wanted to do something for you since you helped us with Nico's problem. Though, I shouldn't take the credit here. Fallon's the one who thought of it."

Fallon smiled and leaned her chin on her hands. She came up with the idea months ago, but only now did she and Sebastian get to follow through. With the new semester starting tomorrow, the timing was perfect. "It's an extended apology on my part too. You didn't want anyone to know about your charm-making skills and I didn't consider your feelings."

Hijiri huffed. "It's okay. Really. I forgave you a long time ago. The thing is, I've never had to help anyone before. At home, I kept to myself. I didn't have friends to worry about or do favors for. But after being able to give Nico directions for fighting Camille's charm, I felt happy." She looked at her feet. "I want to be a part of something bigger than me."

"This is the first step," Sebastian said, walking over to his bag to take out the scissors and spray bottle.

Hijiri eyed the scissors like a nervous cat.

"I'm not going to cut off all your hair," he said, laughing. "But you can't dazzle Zita with your charms if you keep pushing your hair out of your face."

"I like hiding behind my hair."

"And you can still do that—just in a more convenient style."

Fallon watched their exchange with amusement. As a

budding dog groomer, he had to have dealt with anxious dogs that tried biting his fingers or escaping the harness. Maybe he gentled them by talking to them, just as he did with Hijiri. Too bad dogs needed their hair in winter; she'd have liked to see him at work.

Sebastian took Hijiri over to the sink and asked her for what she usually washed her hair with. When she returned from her bathroom with two bottles, he looked at both and threw the conditioner in the garbage. "Use the shampoo only," he said, "because conditioner will only clog up your oily hair. Wash twice with the shampoo and try getting in the habit of showering in the morning. Sleeping on wet hair will only make your situation worse."

He demonstrated this by having her lean over the sink so he could wash her hair himself. It wasn't glamorous, like having one's hair washed at a salon. Hijiri complained of the soapsuds in her eyes.

"I know," he said, brows furrowed in concentration. "I'll try to be quick."

Fallon walked over to the sink and watched him rub the shampoo into Hijiri's hair. The suds foamed and swirled down the drain. Sebastian's hands worked tirelessly at loosening the knots and clumps in Hijiri's long hair. The back of Fallon's head tingled. She wondered what it would feel like if Sebastian massaged her scalp. Her skin flushed.

Sebastian caught her eye and smirked. "You want to go next?"

"I don't need a haircut."

"Okay, princess."

Fallon shivered and returned to the couch, having seen quite enough.

Sebastian remained true to his word, concentrating his efforts on trimming the split ends. But when he got to the front, he snipped the air and smiled. "I'm going to give you bangs."

Hijiri stiffened. "Please don't. I've had them before."

"Trust me. These bangs are going to flatter you."

He spent a few minutes crafting her bangs, making tiny snips and measuring the length with his fingers. "There," he said.

Fallon sucked in her breath. "Wow."

"What?" Hijiri said, trembling. She took the hand mirror from Sebastian and stared at her reflection. By opening up her face, Hijiri couldn't hide her eyes, which were as dark as chipped onyx. Her bangs completely covered her eyebrows, almost touching her eyelashes. Her shiny black hair fell over her shoulders. "This is me?"

"You're so pretty," Fallon said.

Hijiri pressed the hand mirror to her chest. "Thanks."

Sebastian rubbed the back of his neck. "There wasn't much to do. You can still hide, if you want to. But people are going to see you once in a while. I hope you're okay with that."

Hijiri struggled to meet Sebastian's eyes. When she did, she smiled. "I think I am."

Fallon knew that Sebastian had cushioned the blow to

ease Hijiri's worry. With that new hairstyle, she couldn't stay invisible.

"Now that we're done," Sebastian said, "how about we meet the twins and Nico for dinner? Our last meal before school starts."

"Don't sound so glum," Fallon said. "You passed your exams, somehow. You can do it again."

"Your faith in me is inspiring," he said dryly.

Hijiri grabbed her bag and almost dragged them out of the apartment. "Let's go. I want to see everyone."

Fallon and Sebastian exchanged smiles and followed her out.

>—▷

This time, when the semester began, Fallon felt like she was playacting her role as student. Her uniform was a costume. Her homework, the script she had to follow. She'd circled January 31 on her calendar and the date rushed to meet her.

As the twins predicted, January was a month of heavy snowfall. Fallon and Sebastian walked to school together, holding hands until they reached Grimbaud High. She relished these moments, even though she couldn't feel the pressure of his hand through their thick gloves.

"If we survive this," he said, "I promise to kiss you in the library."

"I have to see people making out in the stacks every day. I'm not going to be one of them."

He stopped and wiped a snowflake off her blazer collar. His eyes were dark, serious. "Then you must have figured out by now what makes that place so appealing."

She pursed her lips. "Enlighten me."

"I don't know. I was asking you." He smirked. "But if we steal just one kiss in the stacks, we'll be official. It's like a charm."

Her stomach twisted. "We don't need a charm for that."

Sebastian's smirk turned tender. "All right. I'll think of something better."

Her heart thumped louder. She squeezed his hand.

In mid-January, preparations for the Welcome Love Fair began. The club tables would take up the entire front lawn of the school. The administration paid for tents, offering covering in case of snowfall during the fair hours. The student government officers were busy during this time; Nico's parents relieved him of his ticket booth duties temporarily so that he could assist in the construction of the fair. Whenever Fallon saw Martin in the hallways, she felt a pinch of anger and loss. He scurried after Camille, letting her harass him in front of everyone. If only he had stayed to hear Nico's confession. She felt that would have changed things.

When she couldn't concentrate on her homework, she stood outside her apartment on the stairs, searching the rooftops for some sign that Grimbaud knew of the rebellion's plans. The town pulsed with strength and grandeur when she walked its streets. Charms worked here. This place was magic. It deserved to be free as much as they all did, destroying Zita's fortunes forever. She closed her eyes and pictured Grimbaud's many cobblestones and cafés, the Tunnel of Love, the belfry, canals, footbridges, and the whitewashed walls of the villas.

"We're going to save you," she whispered.

The lights in the distance flickered like stars.

A string quartet always played at the Welcome Love Fair. Four of the best students in Grimbaud High's music program tuned their instruments on a tiny stage. The snow went well with the white, pink, and red decorations coloring the lawn. A few of the shops around Grimbaud had donated decorations; wire storks cleaned their feathers between tables, and cupids of all shapes and sizes pointed their arrows at unsuspecting fairgoers.

Grateful that the only mandatory uniform for the event was wearing Love's colors, Fallon had arrived at the fair early in a thick magenta cable-knit sweater over a dress. Black leggings and boots kept her legs warm, along with the exercise that came with preparing the club's table.

"The charm-maker's club," Martin said, consulting his clipboard. "Your popcorn machine is right over there."

Fallon tried not to frown at him. "Okay. Thanks."

Martin opened his mouth, then closed it. "Take care of the machine. It's doesn't work that well."

"President," Nico said, running through the snow. His tanned skin was at odds with his windbreaker and earmuffs.

He pulled another matching pair of earmuffs out of his pocket and handed it to Martin with a smile. "Your ears are red. I thought you might need them."

Martin stared at the earmuffs and slowly took them. "Thanks," he mumbled.

"Treasurer," Camille yelled, mimicking Nico's previous inflection. "Don't forget that your shift at the officer table starts at seven."

Nico shrugged. "I'll be there."

But he wouldn't. No one from the charm-maker's club was sticking around. Fallon found the popcorn machine and pushed. The clunky machine rattled and its wheels got stuck in the snow. She passed other clubs setting up their tables. Part of her wished she could pretend that this was just another fair, that this day was no more important than any other. But the stronger part of her warned her to focus. Her skirt pockets contained the charms from the club: the anti-rose-colored glasses and Hijiri's blinding charm. She had memorized the confidence charm. The fair was not for her. She had a more important goal to achieve than knocking down plastic bowling pins and eating chocolate-drizzled waffles.

Sebastian arrived wearing a wine-red leather jacket and a button-down shirt underneath. He didn't look warm, but Fallon couldn't tear her eyes away from his clothes. "Hey," he said, snapping his fingers. "You'll grow icicles on your nose if you stand so still."

"You look . . ." she started.

"Handsome?"

"Not ugly."

"Whew. I was worried you had changed your mind about me," he teased. "I should be wearing a scarf or something, but I'm actually burning up. Must be nerves."

"You're the one with the connection to Zita," she said. "That's understandable."

Hijiri showed up a few minutes later with charm-theory and construction textbooks. They'd serve as props, another reason to steer the fairgoers away from their table. The twins wore black berets with their hair tucked inside, and sweaters with white cupid's wings stitched on the backs. Mirthe reached into her pocket and dangled a rusty key. "Ms. Ward and Bram agreed to meet us at the entrance. We have fifteen minutes before we make our exit."

"That should be enough time for Anais to get here," Fallon said. She'd promised to man the table.

More than half of the town's police force was in attendance. They watched the booths with their arms crossed, though a few of the younger officers broke down and ate cotton candy and fried dough when they thought no one was looking. Fallon wasn't nervous. She felt safe knowing that the bachelors and the spinsters were patrolling the fair as well, ready to clear a path for the rebellion when the time came to leave.

Burned popcorn poured out of the machine. A few children held out their hands for popcorn, only to spit it out and complain of the taste. The judo club was across from the charm-making club's table; it gathered a sizable crowd as fairgoers watched the boys demonstrate thirty-five different throws on the plastic mats behind the table. Bear used his hips to propel his opponent forward, knocking him onto the mat with a dramatic smack. The crowded cheered and Bear waved bashfully.

Fallon checked her watch. Then she looked up just in time to see Anais Jacobs push through the crowd. Golden ringlets sprang from her head, her lips glistening with bubblegum-pink gloss. The green dress she wore matched the one she'd worn as a child on Peak & Brown's tins with ruffled sleeves and crystals along the bodice. There were shouts of "Oh, look, the biscuit-tin girl" and "Hurry, take her picture," but Anais remained stubbornly trained on Bear. His teammates must have seen the determined look on her face because they stepped out of the way.

"Thom Janssens!" she shouted, her face scrunched up in concentration. "How could you abandon me?"

"Is that an apology?" Sebastian whispered.

Fallon shushed him.

Anais dug her fingers into her dress. "There're mosquito bites all over me. I got rained on because you weren't there with an umbrella. Walking home alone sucks because you're not there. Who told you to leave?"

Bear flinched with each accusation.

"I *heard* you. You said you hate Peake and Brown's biscuits because of what happened with your mother, but I'm not that biscuit girl. I'm normal. Worse than normal. I work at a sticky drugstore and man the cashier in sweats."

He wiped his face with his sleeve. "You lied to me," he

said softly. "That's what it comes down to. I wasn't worth your honesty."

"I thought I'd lose you if I told you the truth. Being with you made me feel special. I never wanted that feeling to end."

The crowd went absolutely still. No one breathed, waiting for Bear's answer, but Anais surprised everyone by continuing.

Her cheeks burned underneath her heavy blush. "I-I'm sorry. Please forgive me."

The hurt and anger fled Bear's face. He gathered her up in his arms and swung her around, pressing kisses to her face.

Fallon grinned so hard her face hurt. She clapped with the other onlookers, bursting with pride for her friend.

"What a distraction," Mirthe said, coming up behind her.

"It's time?"

"Couldn't ask for a better way to leave unnoticed. Good for Anais."

The club split up, weaving through the fairgoers toward the exit. Fallon's heartbeat drummed in her ears. She caught sight of Nico in the other row, pushing his way through clumps of people. The teachers stationed at the entrance worried her, but as she approached, she snuck behind a group of college students leaving the fair. She stood straight and acted like she blended. Somehow, it must have worked, because the sights and sounds of the fair faded away. She joined the others about two blocks away.

"Where do we go from here?" Nico asked.

Mirthe took out the rusty key again and held it in her fist. "Follow me."

They crossed a footbridge and walked through the streets. Fallon stuck close to Sebastian. When they reached Verbeke Square, Femke and Mirthe led them around the back of the lace shops. Although the square was clean, the backs of the buildings wore grime and some of the brickwork was cracked. Lace hung in the dark windows.

"You said to meet here," said an annoyed voice. "But I don't see any secret doors." Bram emerged from the shadows. That night he looked like a parody of Hard-boiled Hal in a fedora, black trench coat, and faded jeans.

"Show some patience," said another voice. Ms. Ward's glasses were fogged over as she approached; she must have been waiting indoors until they arrived.

The two adults glared at each other.

"Where are the others?" Femke said.

Three bachelors emerged from behind Bram, wearing sweat-stained coats and torn jeans. Four spinsters joined the group as well; Fallon recognized Helena by her lace parasol swinging in the darkness. She couldn't recall the other two women's names, but she'd know Yasmine anywhere with that blue hair.

Mirthe appraised the group. She rubbed her chin. "Let's take care of the entrance first. Bram, do you have that silencing charm?"

Bram reluctantly tossed it over.

Each building had a set of stairs that led down to a kitchen door. "The one in the middle is the entrance," Mirthe said.

Bram snorted. "That can't be. Unless you're planning to break into the shop."

"Look closer," Ms. Ward said. "That middle door doesn't belong to either shop."

Fallon squinted. The darkness made it hard to see clearly, but she thought she saw the change in brickwork where both buildings met. The line went straight down, pierced by the middle door. If anyone tried using the door, they could end up in either shop, but more likely, neither. It was the kind of detail you wouldn't recognize on your own. The front of Verbeke Square was what mattered to most people.

Mirthe descended the stairs and turned the rusty key in the lock. The door creaked when she pulled it open, revealing another wall of red bricks. "See? Someone had this entrance sealed off, just like the other ones around the square." Mirthe smirked. "But whoever it is didn't plan on being challenged by weather charm-makers."

Femke took a vial out of her bag and shook it up. "Everyone stand back."

Fallon gripped Sebastian's arm as they waited. Mirthe used putty to stick the silencing charm on the wall beside the entrance. She ran her fingers over the sewn-up lips and tied the thread at the corner. The area filled with silence. Fallon couldn't hear her own breathing.

After Mirthe jogged back up the stairs, Femke threw the vial against the bricked-up entrance; the glass shattered on the bricks, releasing sparks and smoke. The ground trembled, growing more intense by the second. Sebastian wrapped his arms around Fallon, holding her steady. The bricks fell loose, one by one, like broken teeth, until the entryway cleared.

Mirthe removed the silencing charm and untied the thread, ending the charm.

Femke met everyone's astonished faces with a humble shrug. "Tremors aren't normally used that way, but it worked."

"Mom's going to kill us," Mirthe said.

Nico looked slightly green. "You don't seem too upset about that."

Bram took back his charm. "Looks awfully dark in there," he said, peering into the abyss beyond the fallen bricks.

"I brought a flashlight," Ms. Ward said.

"Resourceful," Bram muttered.

"Is everyone ready?" Mirthe said. "We're going to find Zita now."

"I am," said a familiar voice.

Camille calmly approached the group as if she had been invited; her shiny pink suit jacket and black pants gave the impression that she'd just arrived for an interview. "Like my outfit? I think it's appropriate for meeting my boss."

Nico curled his hands into fists. "You don't belong here."

"Oh, I do." Camille examined her nails. "I overheard

your plans that night of the student-government meeting. If you're so clumsy about keeping secrets, then maybe I should invite the whole town to join us."

Mirthe paled. She shot Femke an apologetic look.

Fallon looked behind Camille. "Did you come alone?"

"That would be stupid," she said, snapping her fingers. Martin emerged from the darkness, his hands tucked in his pockets. He still wore the ear muffs Nico had given him, but his glasses sat crooked on his nose, his mouth slack from the perfume. Camille wrapped her arm securely around his waist and said, "He goes where I go. That's what good boyfriends do."

Nico made a strangled sound in his throat.

For a second, Fallon thought she saw Martin's gaze flicker to Nico, but it could have been her imagination.

"Don't let me stop you. I can follow any time I want, since you broke the entrance open," Camille said.

Femke sighed. "We can't waste charms on her."

Camille flashed a smug smile.

Helena twirled her parasol. "You sure you don't want us to come too?"

Ms. Ward smiled. "We need you out here. Someone is going to notice that these kids are missing. If there's anything you can do to delay the search, that will be a big help."

"And we'll need to protect the ladies," said one of the bachelors. He scratched his belly.

Yasmine ignored the man. "The minute we hear anything suspicious, we'll come running. No matter what."

Mirthe nodded and took out her own flashlight. "Everyone, let's stick together. This is uncharted territory."

Pipes snaked along the walls as the group headed down a longer set of stairs. The stench of mildew and moisture hit her nose immediately. The twins had their flashlights, but Ms. Ward passed around portable book lights for everyone else. Fallon wore one pinned to her sweater. Its firefly-like glow was a small comfort. She felt guilty for sinking her nails into Sebastian's leather jacket, but the cryptlike atmosphere scared her.

The stairs finally ended, leading to a deep, cavernous space. Some of the pipes dripped water; spiderwebs hung between them. Mirthe aimed her flashlight ahead, finding another, smaller entrance leading deeper into the sewers. Fallon stomach twisted at the thought of going farther.

"You go on ahead," Sebastian said, suddenly stopping. "I need to tie my shoelaces. Fallon will keep me company."

"Really?" Camille's voice. "How old are we?"

"Hurry up," Femke warned.

After they left, Fallon took a step toward him. "You're not wearing sneakers."

Sebastian looked away from her. He spoke softly, fear tugging at the edges. "I don't know what will happen once we find Zita. We're so close. I know she's here, Fallon."

Fallon steeled her shoulders and raised her chin. She was scared too, they all were, but they couldn't turn back now. "We're going to end your fortune."

Sebastian's head snapped toward her.

"I promised that I would take care of your heart," she said, coming closer.

"Like a set of precious china plates," he whispered.

"Like a rose wrapped in tissue paper," she said.

"Like your favorite sweater," he said, a warm smile spreading on his face.

Fallon laughed and stood on her toes. She brushed her knuckles against his cheek, savoring the heat from his skin. "You can trust me."

Sebastian leaned into her touch. After drawing a shaky breath, he said, "I love you."

Fallon stared up at him. Her book light illuminated his steady gaze and the curl of his lips.

"I love you," he said again, louder, as if he were a little boy daring to say something forbidden. "There. Magic words, just for you. I've never said that to any girl."

Sunlight from somewhere inside her filled her veins, warming her. She knew it was because of him. "I love you too."

His lips inched closer to hers. Then, Sebastian inhaled sharply and drew back, rubbing his chest.

"What?"

"Nothing. I just . . ." he trailed off. "We should catch up with the others."

Fallon nodded, taking his hand. They plunged through the second entrance.

chapter 23

DEAD END

Instead of darkness, Fallon's eyes adjusted to the chips of stained glass on the sewer's ceiling, lit behind with electric bulbs. Someone must have installed the lights years ago because the dusty glass remained undisturbed. There were no pipes. A series of stone walls unfolded before them.

Bram climbed an abandoned pile of cracked stone and scanned the area. "It's a labyrinth," he said.

Camille tapped her foot and looked at her watch. "How can there be a labyrinth underneath Verbeke Square?"

"How would I know?" he snapped. "The center's lit up."

The twins climbed up after him to confirm what he saw.

"It's true," Femke said, puzzled.

"We're not high enough to see what path will take us directly to the center," Mirthe said. "This could take awhile if we get lost."

"Not a problem." Femke took a pen out of her bag and

placed it on the floor. She asked the pen to show her the best answer; it spun, too fast to be natural, and aimed its sharpened edge northwest.

"It's like a compass," Ms. Ward said, impressed.

Martin squinted through his glasses and whispered, "Cheating charm."

"That's right," Mirthe said. "Even the most addled student government officer should know it. Femke and I found Grimbaud High's legendary cheating charm a long time ago. We think this is certainly the occasion to use it."

"Full of surprises, those two," Hijiri said.

Ms. Ward took off her backpack and dug around in the back zippered pocket until she pulled out a stamp and and ink pad. "If I know anything about cheating charms, it's that they stop working once they've found the answer. We want to avoid retracing our steps when we leave, right? I always carry stamps with me in case I want to continue working after school's over. This one says OVERDUE. The ink's bright red, so it should be easy to see if I stamp each dead end so we don't go back that way."

"That's a brilliant idea," Fallon said. No one had come prepared to face a labyrinth, but as a seasoned traveler, Ms. Ward's backpack was probably full of useful items of the non-charm variety.

"Not bad," Bram admitted, shifting his weight.

They entered the labyrinth with the twins in the lead, Femke balancing the pen in the palm of her hand while turned in the right direction. Stained-glass chandeliers hung from the ceiling, burning shades of pink, orange, and blue. Rusted mirrors covered the stone walls. Fallon saw her hollow-eyed, watery reflection again and again as they turned and twisted along through the paths.

Each time they saw a fork in the path, Ms. Ward generously pressed her stamp against the ink pad and left an OVERDUE mark on the path they didn't take.

"Do you think Zita's really at the center?" Sebastian asked.

"She better be." Fallon twined her fingers in his. She hadn't slept much, either, the past few days. No one had. Adrenaline kept her moving as she followed the group. After a few minutes, she heard wings flapping. "Birds?" she whispered.

"I checked every entrance on my mom's map. There shouldn't be another way in," Mirthe said.

Something whizzed past her ear. Nico cried out. Under the green stained glass, Nico clutched his arm; blood dripped between his fingers.

Fallon pushed her way through the group. She saw that something had sliced right through Nico's windbreaker and cut his skin. "Did you brush against anything?" she asked, thinking of the rusted mirrors all around them. Or perhaps a shard from the stained-glass lights fell.

"I haven't touched anything," he said, gritting his teeth.

Ms. Ward came to the rescue again with a first aid kit. She bandaged his arm tight.

The sound of wings came again. This time, Fallon looked up and saw a stone-gray cupid in flight. Its chubby fingers pulled back on a stone arrow. "Look out!" she shouted.

Everyone ducked. The arrow cracked the mirrored wall into thousands of tiny pieces.

"What is that?" Camille said, covering her head with her hands.

Two more cupids hovered over the path, notching arrows.

"This has to be a charm," Mirthe shouted, searching her bag. "Statues can't fly."

But it wasn't an illusion either—Nico's arm was proof of that. Fallon had never heard of a charm capable of levitating an item. Even if she had, she doubted that those same charms could orchestrate an ambush. Another arrow smashed the mirror behind Fallon. Sebastian grabbed her hand and tugged her down the path as Bram and Ms. Ward brought up the rear.

"Doesn't look like Zita's happy to see us," Hijiri said, taking out her mirror and glitter. A flash of light stunned the two paint-splattered cupids on her tail.

Bram skidded as he came to a stop. His trench coat flared as he pulled out a handgun. He pulled the trigger, shattering one cupid's head and another's bow arm. "What?" he said, cocking an eyebrow. "I didn't come entirely unprepared either."

Ms. Ward crossed her arms. "So the rumors are true. You bachelors *did* install a shooting range in the villas."

Bram shot the wing off of the last cupid. "I don't know what you're talking about," he said with a grin.

Mirthe found a small spray bottle in her bag. "If there's any more of them, they won't find us so easily now."

Femke smiled at her sister. "A fog charm. Good thinking."

As soon as Mirthe pressed down on the nozzle, a fine mist, smelling of vinegar and mountain air, filled the labyrinth. Fog steamed up the mirrors. Fallon could just make out Camille's back ahead of her in the heavy fog. She listened for more wings as they continued on, but the sound faded.

Somewhere, hidden pipes dripped. The creaking of metal made Fallon's heart jump. Ms. Ward had stamped two more dead ends before the light grew stronger.

Two storks guarded the entrance to the heart of the labyrinth. The storks had ruby eyes and wire limbs fused to the walls; their beaks crisscrossed like swords. Fallon expected them to attack, just as the cupids had, but they remained dull and lifeless as she walked between them. Her eyes stung from the massive light fixture suspended overhead, illuminating the square-shaped space full of peculiarities.

A miniature replica of Grimbaud sat underneath the light; every detail had been sculpted and arranged to perfection. The belfry was there, along with Verbeke Square, Grimbaud High, and the footbridges. The canals even had running water. Figurines no bigger than ants occupied the expanse of the town. Each figurine had a spider's silk string running from the top of its head to a giant loom suspended over the model.

When her gaze left the mini-town, she began to notice how lived-in the space was. There were rugs on the stone floor, a cot in the back with rumbled sheets. An aged crimson range hood framed a stove covered with potions and junk. Stone cupids of all shapes and colors lined the tops of the walls, salvaged from Grimbaud's ancient buildings; they didn't move, but they were poised to pull the first arrows from their quivers.

A woman sat at a writing desk, her pen moving achingly slow upon crisp white paper. "You deserve a round of applause for finding me," she said without stopping her pen. Her voice was high-pitched and scratchy.

Camille stepped forward, wiping the dust from her blazer. "It's a pleasure to finally meet you, Zita. Maybe you recognize me. I'm Camille Simmons, your prized employee."

Zita angled her chair to see them better. Fallon thought she looked more fragile than in her photograph, with twiglike fingers and her tattered gray dress bunching at her narrow hips. The silver heart necklace hung about her neck. Her hair was thick and loose, her face youthful without a wrinkle.

Camille gasped. "Zita?"

"Love keeps the heart young," Zita said. "So they say."

Camille ate up her words, nodding vigorously. Maybe

she thought that she'd turn out the same way if she took over Zita's job.

Femke and Mirthe stepped forward together. "Thanks for the greeting. Your cupids almost killed us," Mirthe said.

"Oh, did they? I usually keep a few animated. I don't appreciate rat infestations." Zita dotted an "i" with a flourish. "I'm not surprised you're here. You think you've been careful, but I see everything. I've known about your meetings in the science room. The charm-gathering. The growing rebellion. The break-in was fairly clever, though. Maybe I should take up weather charm-making as a hobby next. I've just about exhausted the other fields."

Nothing about this place was right. Fallon had imagined confronting Zita in a stately office, not underneath the earth where her charms pulsed with unknowable power.

"So, who do we have here tonight?" Zita said, ignoring Camille. "Ah. Bram. Mr. Hard-boiled Hal. Your show isn't quite to my liking. If you dare raise your gun again, you'll find an arrow in your throat."

Bram bit back a snarl and placed the gun on the floor. He eyed the cupids.

Zita made a cooing sound, like a doting grandmother. "And is that Emma Ward over there? I'm sure my villas have been a comfortable alternative to your traveling days. Think of all the men who've left you behind. What a pity."

Ms. Ward pressed her hand against her mouth.

Mirthe shook with rage. "You seem to know an awful lot about Ms. Ward's life."

Zita leaned back in her chair and touched the spider's silk strings from the model, eliciting a series of notes that fell over them in waves of heartbreak and desire. "Just what are you accusing me of? I merely report what Love designed. My system is perfect. Every year, you find out exactly what's going to happen in your love life. My fortunes prevent you from making foolish choices. With me in charge, people no longer need to break their hearts."

"That's a lie," Hijiri said with vehemence.

Zita's chair landed back on all four legs with a loud thump. She put her pen to the paper again and chuckled. "Grimbaud belongs to me. Anyone who steps foot in this town is mine." She gestured at the model. "Have you ever felt the pleasure of distorting a phrase so completely that it becomes a riddle? Your love lives are my riddles to make. I twist them when I want. Take Nico. I like his fortune. Of course I do. Wrote it myself."

Nico gripped his injured arm.

"All this time, you thought that Martin would never know your feelings for him. It's a shame how much time you've wasted."

Camille's expression dropped. "Nico and Martin? You must be joking."

Zita let out a bark of a laugh as she continued writing. "Better watch yourself, Nico. Now that Camille knows, you may find yourself at the bottom of the canals."

" 'The one who matters,' " Nico whispered, his eyes wide.

Camille dug her nails into Martin's arm and dragged him

closer; she shot Nico a deadly glare. Dozens of charms seemed to cross her mind, none of them pretty.

"If you know so much about us, you should also know why we're here. We demand you stop printing love fortunes," Mirthe said. "The benefits of letting us see our futures don't outweigh the bad. What about the spinsters and bachelors? They may think they're protecting their hearts by hiding in your villas, but their hearts are breaking every day."

"And you've all but admitted that you're the cause of it," Hijiri added. "These are not Love's fortunes."

"Set us free," Mirthe said, louder.

Fallon found her voice. "Sebastian's here. You must know him. He's Dorian's grandson."

Zita flashed a deadly smile. "Very good, Dupree. Thank you for reminding me that there is a Barringer present in my dwelling. Only . . . you seem to have lost him. He's not standing beside you."

Fallon reached for Sebastian's hand, finding nothing but thin air beside her. She turned around and gasped.

Sebastian was on the ground and back against the stone wall, breathing heavily and clutching his chest.

Fallon's heart froze over. She ran toward him and dropped to her knees, cradling his head in her hands. His skin felt heated and clammy. "What's wrong? Sebastian, tell me."

"Don't know," he whispered. "Something's . . . something's burning in my chest."

Fallon removed his hand and pressed her palm over his heart. She drew back, startled by the heat. "Do something!" she yelled, turning her frantic gaze to Zita. "You know his fortune. You have to help him."

Zita's cool smile betrayed nothing. Her pen spilled red ink.

"Please," Fallon said.

"His fortune is coming true, my dear. I couldn't have spent my energy on a better cause."

Fallon tried to ignore the panic crawling up her throat. She helped Sebastian unbutton his shirt, biting back a sob when she saw that his fingertips were blue. "Keep breathing," she told him.

When she peeled back his shirt, she didn't expect to see red. Words were written over his heart, red as blood and perfectly formed in thick cursive. The words kept appearing, letter by swirling letter. " '*You will die if you fall in love*'," she read. " '*Your sweetheart . . .*' " The rest of the words had yet to appear.

Sebastian struggled to focus on her. His eyelashes kept fluttering.

"Some people die of heartbreak. Others die from too much love. Fallon Dupree, you shouldn't have made him love you so much," Zita said, her voice turning hard and strange. "Sweet nothings mean everything. His confession was his death."

"No," she cried, even as she remembered his words back at the labyrinth entrance. "That can't be true."

Sebastian cupped her face. His lips were as blue as canal water, his brows threaded in determination. "Don't you dare blame yourself," he murmured, "I love you. I'd have said it a million times."

Zita wrote the rest of the fortune on the paper, fast as a breath, as the fortune stained Sebastian's skin.

He made a strangled sound and hit the hard floor, pale and unmoving.

Fallon's heart slammed itself against her rib cage. Again and again and again. Her body was a dark sea, her heart slipping under. Where was the ground beneath her feet? Tears rolled down her cheeks. She choked out his name, running her fingers through his hair.

Zita put down her pen and stood triumphantly. "He wasn't worth loving, but I have to thank you for your role in this. You can have the best of everything in the Spinster Villas. I owe you that much. Your romantic fate was collateral damage."

Fallon lifted her head, too tired to speak. Her fingers found the anti-rose-colored glasses in her bag. She slipped them on and saw Zita change. Purplish dead skin covered her arms. Her teeth were tiny and sharp, the silver heart at her throat rusted with age. For the first time since coming to Grimbaud, Fallon couldn't smell roses.

"Breaching Love's plans was not easy," Zita said. "I've been working on Sebastian's fortune for many years, spending much of my power to craft it. I was worried that it might not come together." She fingered the heart necklace.

"Tonight, I'm finally ending the Barringer line. It's exactly the ending I made for him."

Hijiri sat by Fallon's side, her face red from crying too. But she plucked the anti-rose-colored glasses from Fallon's face and used them to examine Sebastian. "I needed a clear head, free of love to see this," Hijiri said quietly, for Fallon's ears only. "He's not dead. There's still time to save him."

"How can you tell?" Fallon croaked.

"It's a love charm. Deadly, but still a charm. There's a way to overpower it." Hijiri smiled. "This is not your fate."

Zita's words clicked into place. Fallon was collateral damage because she had never once been destined for spinsterhood. Zita assigned that future to her when she tried taking Sebastian's life. This was not fate, Hijiri said. This was murder.

Fallon's heart came roaring back to life.

"She can't have him," Fallon said. She stared past Zita to the model town of Grimbaud. The loom was a torture trap they were all hooked up to. Under no circumstances would she allow Sebastian to stay tied to Zita's power. Stumbling to her feet, she shot the twins a determined look and hoped they got the message. She needed help. "Now!"

Mirthe and Femke reached into their bags, activating another weather charm. This time, a tornado spilled out into the center of the labyrinth, small but wild enough to send everyone ducking for cover. Shards of broken mirror glittered in the air. The wind howled and beat against the stone walls. Hijiri covered Sebastian's body with hers while

Nico shouted a warning as more cupids flexed their wings, awakening to a human infestation. Camille shrieked and clung to Zita, who stood her ground with a look of mild annoyance.

Fallon kept her head down as she raced toward the model. An arrow tore the fabric behind her back. Debris stung her eyes. Her hair whipped wildly around her, getting stuck in her teeth as she focused on dodging the flying cupids. One cupid aimed for her head, but was swiftly knocked into a wall by the wind.

She reached the table bearing the model and quickly searched for Verbeke Square. Only a few figurines were in the square, and she recognized Yasmine's tiny blue head and Helena's parasol. She couldn't find any trace of the rebels' strings below the square. She let out a frustrated growl and barely felt the pebble that cut into her cheek as it sailed past.

Shouts and gunshots surrounded her. Grief gnawed at her, a temptation to just crawl under the table and push everything out. But Sebastian's face hovered behind her eyelids. He would have insisted that princesses never gave up. Neither did clever maids.

chapter 24

THIS IS WHERE IT STARTS

"Confidence, confidence, unveil me," she said against the raging winds.

Just like before, warmth shot energy down to her fingers and toes. An invisible veil lifted away from her face, taking with it her fears and sadness. The effect was only temporary, so she sucked in her breath and examined the model anew.

The model was so eerily accurate that Zita's underground labyrinth had to be present. Fallon avoided another arrow and bent down to examine the miniature shops and streets. There was an indent in the corner of the square. Fallon used her fingernails to loosen it, lifting off the square and revealing the underground labyrinth. Tiny cupids sat undisturbed upon the stone walls, unlike the real ones fighting in the storm. She saw her own figurine bent over a miniature of the model; it made her dizzy. Everyone's silken strings had been coiled underneath the lid, but now that she had taken if off, the strings sprang back into the air like the others, attached to the loom.

Fallon bit back a sob when she saw Hijiri's figurine covering Sebastian's. She gently nudged her off and held Sebastian in her hands. His figurine was pallid, mimicking the real boy. Fallon grabbed hold of the string. As soon as she did, a torrent of feelings burst through her head like fireworks. The string burned her palm, but she held on, tugging as hard as she could. A shriek came from her own throat as the pain blinded her. Everything Sebastian had ever loved pushed itself into her head and heart as it rushed inside her to make a home.

Using both hands, Fallon wrenched the string from the loom with a sickening snap.

She fell back, hitting the ground hard. She turned her head and saw Sebastian's body jerk, as if the string had been tied around his heart.

"Enough," Zita said. The tornado dulled to a mere whimper. She knocked a fluttering cupid out of the way and snarled when she saw the broken string on the floor. She grabbed Fallon by the hair and yanked her to her feet. "Camille!"

Camille smoothed down her hair and brightened. Grime covered her smart clothes. "Yes, Zita?"

"I promised that you would become a star in my company," Zita said, with sweetness too thick to be true. "Your talent with charms has far exceeded my expectations."

"You've noticed?" Camille said breathlessly.

"I wonder if you can create a potion for me. One that could quietly allow its drinker to expire." Zita's firm gaze pinned everyone in the room. "Imagine what the papers will say. Grimbaud's unlucky teenagers, aided by a hapless bachelor and spinster, decided to declare their heartbreak by dying together in the sewers. You forget that love doesn't always mean happy endings. The greatest love comes with tragedy."

Fallon wanted to drag her nails across Zita's face, anything to stop the woman's threats, but the grip on her hair was too tight. Her head throbbed, her hands blistering from the string.

"That stove works? My boyfriend will help me make the potion you want, Zita. He's very attentive," Camille said. She reached into her shirt and pulled out a vial of pink liquid no bigger than her pinkie finger. She dabbed a few drops on her wrists; the heavy stench and tense presence of a charm filled the air.

Martin's nostrils flared. He stared at her adoringly.

"Ex-boyfriend," Nico said.

"What did you say?"

"You heard me." Nico lunged for Camille, the pocket mirror already out and flashing.

Her mouth twitched. Camille picked up a stone arrow and used it to knock the mirror out of Nico's hand. Then she used it like a sword, swiping at him as he dodged and backed into the wall. "Martin is mine," she said, pressing the tip of the arrow against his jaw. "Someone like you doesn't deserve him. Filthy canal boy."

Zita watched with amusement. "Go on. Show me how strong your charm is."

Camille grinned. "Nicolas Barnes is threatening me. Be a good boyfriend and protect me."

Fallon tensed. She saw Bram bend down to reach for his gun, but Ms. Ward put her hand over his.

Martin walked slowly. The light caught his glasses, hiding his eyes.

"Go on," Camille said. "Protect me."

Martin snuck up behind her and wrenched the vial of perfume from her hand. "That's enough," he said in a loud, clear voice. "This is not vice president behavior. I ask that you resign before I take this matter to the administration. Step away from my treasurer."

Camille sputtered.

Nico's eyes widened, amazed.

"Finally, I have the proof I need," Martin said, studying the vial of perfume in his hands. When he looked up, he spoke directly to Nico. "After months of suffering the effects, I didn't want her to suspect her charm stopped working once it did. I kept pretending. For that, I'm sorry." Then he held out his hand.

Nico took his hand and gasped when Martin pulled him into a tight hug.

"Thank you for saving me, Nicolas. Twice now," he said shyly.

Zita took in the scene with disdain. With the flick of her fingers, the stone cupids flapped their wings and notched their arrows. Some cupids aimed at Camille.

Camille laughed nervously. "I can still make that potion, I swear."

"I doubt that." Zita said dryly. "This has gone on long enough; none of you will leave my labyrinth alive."

Fallon squeezed her eyes shut, anticipating the pierce of a stone cupid's arrow, pain far worse than the grip Zita still had on her hair. But no fatal blow came.

Her eyes cracked open just in time to see the stone cupids drop their bows and arrows as a newcomer entered the room. The boy's eyes twinkled; he wore an oversize black jacket that made swishing noises as he walked. Chewed up sneakers. Tape player in hand. The key around his neck was no longer broken. *The boy from the library*, Fallon thought.

"Inés Aandekerk," the boy said.

"Love," Zita said.

Fallon felt Zita's grip on her hair loosen. She pulled free and scrambled back to the group. Ms. Ward tried to look at her hands, but Fallon curled them into fists, still clutching the figurine, as she returned to Sebastian's side. He was barely breathing. The love fortune written into his skin had faded; she traced the words with her eyes, willing them to disappear completely. They didn't.

The boy crossed the room, sliding his eyes over the loom and model. He reached for Sebastian's snapped string and ran it between his fingers. "Taking another's life for your own benefit . . . Inés, you know that's not allowed."

"He deserves to die," Zita spat. "All Barringers deserve it. I should have killed his father and ended the line earlier, but I thought that trapping Etienne Barringer in a loveless marriage would be enough."

"But it wasn't." Love dropped the string. "You're still wearing your wedding dress."

Fallon looked again at Zita's dress. The bodice laced up the back, the sleeves made of the finest lacework now dull and gray with age. At one point, pearls must have hung from the skirts. Maybe there had been a veil and a bouquet of dead roses.

"If Sebastian was awake, I would tell him why you're wearing such a dress." Love walked over to where Zita stood, glaring. "This experiment is a failure, Inés. It was a fool's dream to think that I could save people by telling them how their romantic lives would unfold. I shared my power with you, and the entire time you only wanted to use it for your own revenge."

"He abandoned me," Zita said, "and married another."

Fallon knew who she was talking about. "Sebastian's grandfather was dying. He left you because he knew you couldn't handle it."

"I waited for him at the altar," she said distantly, "and he never showed up."

A look of pity crossed Love's face. "It's time," he said.

He pressed a button on his tape player, flooding the underground with a brooding tango heavy with violins. The music did more than take the air. Zita's skin began to shrivel. Purple and yellow spots marked her delicate collarbone. Her hair grew thin and gray. She backed up into the stone wall, screeching. Camille watched her boss's transformation with a mixture of shock and impatience.

Zita unraveled before their eyes. Thousands of words spilled from her skin like smoke, each sentence matching Zita's red handwriting. Her hands and feet burst into poetry that smelled of roses and bitterness too potent to understand. The red words were fortunes too, spilling from her torso like an overturned bucket of lace. Fallon thought she tasted her own tampered-with fortune as words whizzed by her and escaped through the walls. Nothing was left of Zita afterward.

Love turned off the tape player with a heavy sigh. The last notes from the music echoed in the labyrinth. Love turned to face them, his expression brightening when he saw Hijiri. "I know what you've been working on. The greatest love charm of all."

"I don't know if it'll ever work."

"I'm here now," he said, sitting cross-legged near Sebastian's head.

Hijiri placed a few items on the floor; one Fallon recognized as the fern leaves that Hijiri had gathered from the patio. She saw orange zest, rose petals, and three other liquids that she couldn't place. Hijiri poured the items together and ground them with her knuckles, her bangs covering her eyes.

Love touched Fallon's hand. "Get ready, Miss Dupree. You're going to perform a true-love kiss."

"I am?"

"You saved his life by snapping the string," Love said, "but the fortune's power still has a hold on him. He can't wake without a miracle." A kiss.

Fallon wanted to believe the boy. She looked over at Sebastian's face and her heart withered. His skin was cold, his mouth turned down. Barely breathing.

"Trust your friend's skills," Love said.

"The charm's ready," Hijiri said. She dipped her fingers in the mixture and spread it over Fallon's lips. "This charm works just like the charms in the storybooks do, Fallon. Kiss him, and your love will bring him back."

The charm tingled on her lips. She fought the urge to wipe it off. Fallon tucked her hair behind her ears and hovered over Sebastian's mouth.

"Not there!" Hijiri hissed.

Love snorted.

Fallon stared at her, puzzled.

"Over his heart. One charm counteracts the other."

Fallon sighed, not wanting to argue. She had read enough fairy tales to know it was always a kiss on the lips. But this wasn't a fairy tale. Sebastian was breathing and Love was there, and maybe this wasn't a miracle, but the erasing of a future that wasn't meant to be. One kiss could correct it. Fallon wasn't about to kill the hope swelling inside her.

Before she closed her eyes, she saw the faded love fortune. *Go away,* she thought feverishly. *Don't you dare touch him ever again.* Her lips found the soft skin covering his heart.

Something bright burned beneath her eyelids. Her head began to throb again. She pulled back, expecting to see a change.

He didn't move.

"Just wait," Hijiri said. "This is where it starts."

The love fortune turned from red to gold, then flaked off his skin like paper. Sebastian drew a sharp breath. The blue disappeared from his lips and fingertips. A healthy glow colored his cheeks. When his eyes opened, he looked up at Fallon. "If you're not a princess now . . ." he said faintly, smirking.

Fallon bit her lip, her heart racing. "Close your eyes. Please."

Her hands burned. Her heart pounded. None of that mattered. This was her first kiss, and she was going to make it a proper one. Fallon gingerly touched the back of his neck and brought his mouth to hers.

For someone who smirked so much, Sebastian's lips were soft. When he kissed her back, pulling her close in front of everyone, she didn't care. His hands were warm on her skin as he cupped her face, and she lost herself in the tender way he kissed her.

Sebastian was finally free of Zita's twisted fortune. So was she. Grimbaud would no longer be trapped in Love's name.

Love cleared his throat. His eyes were filled with admiration as he helped Hijiri to her feet. "Grimbaud is going to need a love charm-maker who brings my messages as they are meant to be. You have a loving heart and a noble spirit. I would gladly share my powers with you."

The room went quiet as Hijri digested Love's offer.

"I can take over," Camille said. "I'm responsible. I won't make mistakes like Zita did."

Love curled his lip and turned from her. "What do you say, Hijiri?"

"No one should replace Zita," Hijiri said with a sad smile. "I think your experiment has failed. People shouldn't know their romantic fates. Because the truth is that it changes."

"Depends on the people," Love said.

"Then let people depend on themselves. Let them mend and break their hearts together. Being blind isn't such a bad thing."

Love sighed and swiped the anti-rose-colored glasses from Hijiri's head. He peered into them and laughed. "So be it, then. I'll be here, though you may never know me for who I am."

"I always will," Hijiri said. "I'll become the best love charm-maker. Just you watch."

Love shook her hand. "I'll hold you to it." He addressed the rest of the rebels. "I'll take care of the mess Zita's left behind. The tornado charm caused some damage above-ground; your allies have noticed and they're on their way here. Sebastian and Fallon will need to be carried. They're not going to make it out of this labyrinth on their own feet."

Fallon knew that Sebastian wasn't, but she felt fine. Just a headache. Her hands still stung, but she could ignore it until they got to the surface again. Fallon tried standing, but her world titled slightly. She moaned and rubbed her head.

Love was at her side. "You snapped one of those strings. A human can't touch those."

"I'm fine, really; I'm fine."

"Let them carry you." Love patted her on the head. "Sebastian's lucky to have fallen in love with a Dupree. Generations of strong, stubborn hearts. I couldn't have given you all the answers, but you trusted your instinct enough to get you through."

Love's words gave her strength as they began the long trek out of the labyrinth. Without the cheating charm, they relied on Ms. Ward's stamps. Shouts came from the exit; she recognized Yasmine's voice along with a few more bachelors and spinsters who were searching for them as Love predicted.

"It's not midnight yet," Sebastian teased. "Maybe we can still catch the fireworks."

Fallon's eyes grew heavy. Her fingers slipped out of Sebastian's. Ms. Ward murmured something comforting. She felt herself being lifted and all went dark.

chapter 25

HEART'S SECRET

Fallon snapped awake when she heard the sounds of pots and pans clanking. Her body felt heavy; she struggled for a minute before realizing that someone had tucked her into bed tightly, the sheets taut and the comforter pulled up to her chin.

She was in her apartment back at the complex. Her nose picked up the familiar scent of lavender on her sheets, as well as mouth-watering eggs and freshly squeezed orange juice coming from the kitchen.

Despite the mid-afternoon light drenching the room, she still asked, "Did I miss the fireworks?"

"If by fireworks you mean your parents, then no. They've been here all night taking care of you. Your brother too," Nico said, stepping into the room. He carried a tray of orange juice and toast. "The eggs are on the way."

Fallon sat up in bed. She looked down at her bandaged hands, surprised and pleased when they didn't hurt. She flexed her fingers. "Where's Sebastian?"

Nico lowered his voice, careful not to attract her family's attention from the kitchen. "Bram and the bachelors took him to the hospital last night, just to be safe. The doctors believed he'd had a heart attack."

That was no heart attack. Fallon recalled the love fortune scrawled across his skin and shivered. "So, he's okay now?"

"Discharged this morning. His grandmother's with him," Nico said.

"What about me? Do my parents know what happened?"

"They found you in bed by the time they wrestled the spare keys from Mrs. Smedt. Ms. Ward had brought you home right after you passed out." Nico gave her a wry smile. "You look awful. I'm sure you can come up with a good excuse."

The moment Fallon took a bite of toast, her stomach sprang to life, demanding sustenance. She concentrated on chewing slowly.

"I'd better go," Nico said. "Martin's waiting for me."

"Is he?"

"I should be mad at you for culling that confession out of me," he said sternly, "but I'm too thankful to care."

"You'd never have told him your feelings otherwise. I had to be sneaky." Fallon smiled. She was thrilled to know that Martin had heard Nico after all. That had to have been what had broken Camille's hold over him. "Don't keep me in suspense. How *does* Martin feel about you?"

His expression softened. "He likes me, but the concept of liking a boy is so new to him. He doesn't know how to act. It's kind of cute."

Fallon almost laughed at his words. She'd been friends with Nico long enough to know that he had never dated anyone. If Martin was new at this, so was Nico. "Go on, then. Don't want to keep your boyfriend waiting. Thank you for checking on me."

Nico beamed. "Anais says hi too. She expects to see you at the drugstore once you're feeling better."

Just as he left, her parents emerged from the kitchen with a heaping plate of sunny-side up eggs. Robbie followed behind, untying an apron he'd borrowed from her.

"Fallon Dupree, you've had us worried sick," Mrs. Dupree said.

"Well, not sick, exactly," Mr. Dupree said. "You're the one who's been immobilized by a bad decision."

"So what was it?" Robbie said, more curious than angry. "Sugar-free ice cream? Dirty ice in your soda? Undercooked meat?"

Mrs. Dupree trembled. "Not another word. I'm going to faint."

Fallon sighed, grabbing a blanket and wrapping it around her. So they thought she had food poisoning?

"We were going to surprise you at the Welcome Love Fair," Mr. Dupree explained. He placed the plate of eggs on the tray and handed her a fork, willing her to eat. "When we couldn't find you, we got worried."

"Maybe we should move here, just to watch over her," Mrs. Dupree said. "This town's perfection ends at its health inspectors. Nothing would get past our eyes."

Fallon pierced one of the yokes, scooping the delicious mess on her fork. A Dupree army had cleaned her apartment while she had slept; not a speck of dust hovered in the air. She felt clean and loved, albeit still tired. She wanted to thank them, but her mother had fallen quite deeply into one of her tirades.

"But my daughter isn't concerned with health inspecting anymore," Mrs. Dupree said, sniffing. "Wants to be a librarian now. I suppose you want us to cancel the table decorations for your wedding too. You'd rather have the venue at a dusty old library instead."

"Mom's talking about your imaginary wedding again," Robbie said, laughing.

Fallon yawned. She pressed her forehead against the blanket and wished that they would let her nap. "You always use that against me, Mom."

"You should be happy that your father and I care that much about you. You've been single entirely too long for my liking. Zita must have gotten your fortune wrong."

Robbie gasped in mock outrage. "Mother, that's blasphemy to speak of Zita like that!"

Fallon's chest tightened. She looked up, ready to blame her sudden fatigue on her fake stomach virus, when she noticed that her apartment door was open. Nico must have forgotten to lock it after he left.

Sebastian braced his hand on the doorframe, wearing a wrinkled white undershirt and jeans. He took in the scene with his usual smirk. "Hey, princess," he said softly.

Fallon dropped her blanket. Her cheeks flushed, embarrassed to have her family as an audience, but she didn't hesitate to go to him. "Your heart . . . ?"

"Perfectly sound," he said. Sebastian walked over and gently brushed her hair away from her face. Her gaze fell to his lips. Remembering their first kiss, something low in her belly ached.

Mrs. Dupree cleared her throat. "Fallon, is he . . . is he the one?"

The Dupree family waited, expectant.

Fallon studied the creases on his shirt. "We'll see."

Despite her noncommittal answer, Mrs. Dupree claimed she heard wedding bells.

&—▷

There was no snow on February 1, nor on any day after. People claimed that the Welcome Love Fair finally served its purpose that year by bringing spring early, but Fallon knew the warmer weather marked a new chapter for Grimbaud.

Love Being Cherished had been moved back to its home in the park. A celebration was being held. The town was in the mood to entertain.

On her way to the park, only Fallon seemed to notice how crisp the air tasted in the absence of Zita's cloying rose scent. The shops' electric signs flickered on and off mysteriously in the middle of the day. Heating charms went on sale immediately.

Sebastian bought her truffles from an enthusiastic chocolatier; some bitter like tears, others spicy and sweet. They shared the last one by messily splitting it in half, licking dark chocolate filling off their fingers.

The stone cupids that Zita had charmed were suddenly back at their posts throughout the town; Fallon recognized the paint-splattered cupid that had attacked her in the labyrinth, perched above the art college's front doors.

Fallon had expected the park to be packed with people. She expected children to plunge their hands into the gurgling fountain, trying to grab shiny coins, while their parents sipped from wineglasses and shared their joy over the statue's return. There would be food and drinks while the townspeople took turns at the podium to talk about love. But when Fallon and Sebastian entered the park, they found it near empty.

Ivory cloth-covered tables bore ham-and-endive gratin, white sausages topped with apple compote, and fried sweet dough drizzled with pink chocolate; the caterers fidgeted at their stations, finding ways to keep the untouched food hot. A few town officials wearing their best suits huddled around the podium, discussing whether to cancel the event.

"Where is everyone?" Fallon whispered, searching for their friends.

"Hijiri's over there," Sebastian said, pointing to the girl standing in front of the statue.

Hijiri studied the marble statue with her arms crossed, her long, now-silky hair falling freely down her back. "Love looks so content here," she said once Fallon and Sebastian stood beside her, "but do you think it ever is? Always running around, making sure the people of this world keep loving."

"We're supposed to be celebrating, not dissecting Love," Sebastian teased.

"Well, this isn't much of a party," she said.

The twins came running into the park, their matching silver-sequined dresses sparkling sharper than the coins in the fountain. They wore plastic clips in their hair meant to look like marble.

Fallon was surprised to see Femke and Mirthe. After discovering the missing fog, tornado, and tremor charms, Mr. De Keyser grounded them. Because of their potency, those charms must have cost a fortune. Fallon wasn't sure how many years it would take for the twins to make up the monetary loss, but hopefully their parents were the forgiving sort. Yet, here they were, dressed to attend the statue's party.

"The Square!" shouted Femke and Mirthe at the same time. They stopped just short of the statue, gasping for breath. Sweat beaded at their temples.

"You have to come to Verbeke Square right away," Femke managed first. "Everyone's there."

Everyone. Anais and Bear. Nico and Martin. What were they doing at Verbeke Square when the party was here? Fallon was about to ask, but Mirthe cut her short.

"No time to explain. Let's go," she said.

The urgency in Mirthe's voice stirred her to move. Fallon grabbed Sebastian's hand. With Hijiri in tow, they ran toward the square as fast as their feet would take them.

Policemen sectioned off half of Verbeke Square with barricades. They urged the gawkers to move along. Anger and astonishment peppered the air. Fallon stood on her toes, trying to see what the trouble was over the crowd. That was when she saw Zita's Lovely Love Charms shop in shambles.

The pink building had somehow been split in half, the brickwork crumbling and creaking even as the police swarmed the area. Conflicting scents of broken charms and smashed love potions perfumed the air. Fallon pinched her nose and breathed through her mouth.

A bored policeman looked at his watch and then climbed onto a crate. He used his megaphone to relay a message that he'd probably repeated all day. None of the officers wore pink pins. "There's been an accident of unknown origin. In light of this incident, Zita has come forward with instructions regarding her business. Zita's Lovely Love Charms will not reopen. The property will be reconstructed at a later date."

"What about our fortunes?" bellowed a middle-aged woman.

A chant started. People took their anger and fear out on the policemen, shaking the barricade and demanding Zita's return.

"Love must have kept its promise about it being over," Sebastian said. "No more fortunes. I'm glad."

"Me too." She refused to let the angry crowd ruin her hope for the town. Grimbaud's people had lived comfortably with Zita's monopoly for quite some time. Losing that stability would be devastating—for those who received the good fortunes. Now everyone was left in the dark. They had to fend for themselves, stumble and break their hearts, instead of being given the answers ahead of time. Those secrets belonged once again to Love. Fallon preferred it that way.

"Besides," she said, "this isn't the end of love charms. It's just the last of Zita."

Bram De Groote and Emma Ward climbed on top of a crate, sharing the tiny space with their arms wrapped around each other for balance. Bram had brought his own megaphone and captured the crowd's attention with his particular radio-show voice. "It's time for a change," he said. "Forget Zita. Love is back in charge. And, as much as I complain about love, I could get used to it. Now that, you know, I don't have a bad fortune hanging over my head."

The energy shifted from anger to excitement and curiosity.

"I've forgotten to introduce myself," Bram said with a grin. "Or don't you know me already? Hard-boiled Hal. In the flesh."

A few gasps broke out. People stood on their toes to get a better look at him. Fallon felt their excitement at a long-held mystery solved.

Ms. Ward plucked the megaphone from his hand and added, "The villas are going to be demolished. They were rotten buildings anyway. No more spinsters. No more bachelors."

Yasmine and Helena hooted from somewhere in the crowd. Sebastian started clapping; it spread from one end of the square to the other and grew stronger by the second.

With the tension in the crowd dissipating, Bram had one last thing say. "What are you standing around here for? Love's statue has been returned to us. Go on to the park and celebrate!"

The townspeople cheered.

Fallon's hands stung from clapping so hard. She stood on her toes, searching for the rest of her friends. Bear and Anais were a few feet away. Bear offered her a tin of Peake & Brown's biscuits. Anais looked at him in mock outrage that quickly dissolved into giggles when he kissed her hand. Hijiri moved through the crowd in her usual fluid matter, getting a closer look at the crumbled shop. A few boys turned their heads to watch her, but she seemed not to notice them. Martin sat on top of one of the café tables; Nico used a chair as a boost and joined him. Their hips bumped; Martin looked flustered and adjusted his glasses. Femke and Mirthe grabbed each other by the elbows and danced, their laughter joining the warm February air.

"Look over there," Sebastian said, touching Fallon's shoulder. "Of course she's not clapping."

Camille stood on the edge of the crowd, still red-faced from her very public expulsion from school.

Fallon smiled to herself. Camille's absence from school would be a comfort. Without Zita's tutelage, she'd hopefully find a less treacherous career to pursue. Love charmmakers would be welcome to practice their craft in town again, but that also meant that the charms would have to be policed; others just like Camille might push their manipulations too far. *I wonder if that's something I can do,* she thought. Most towns had detectives, private or public, that specialized in particular types of charm crimes. If Fallon started studying love charms now, perhaps she'd have the makings of a great love-charm detective by the time she graduated.

After the police took Bram's megaphone, the crowd began thinning out. Most headed in the direction of the park, while a few stayed behind to say heartfelt good-byes to Zita's shop.

Sebastian's breath warmed her ear. "Come with me after the party," he said. "I've got a promise to keep."

Fallon wondered what he'd come up with instead of a stolen kiss in the school library. Her cheeks flushed pink. "I'm looking forward to it," she said before tugging him over to join their friends.

The Tunnel of Love was a twenty-four-hour tourist attraction. Still, with the majority of the town celebrating the statue's return, Fallon was surprised to see someone operating the ticket booth. The wizened old man wearing a newsboy cap refused to take Sebastian's money.

"Why not?" Sebastian asked, curious. "What makes us different than the next couple?"

The old man ignored his question and left the booth, jingling a key ring as he walked. One particular key drew Fallon's attention: it shimmered, larger than the rest. She felt as if she knew that key, but the thought was gone as soon as it came.

"Enjoy the ride," he said, turning the key inside the control box next to the ride. A seductive tango suddenly filled the dark tunnel, beckoning them inside.

The Tunnel of Love's entrance was heart-shaped. Fallon climbed into the boat first, sinking into the cushioned seat. Sebastian joined her with a boyish grin on his face. "I've never done this before."

"Me neither. I didn't want to go alone," she said, blushing.

Sebastian rested his arm against the back of the seat. He twisted a lock of her hair around his finger; the gentle tugging made her skin tingle.

The boat moved forward on a track, meandering through the smooth canal water. As relaxing as the gentle boat ride was, the decorations were excessive. Cupid dolls with fuzzy, plush faces and googly eyes hung from the ceiling, pointing their arrows at each other in a silent war. Love letters, scanned and printed to poster size, showcased happy couples writing sweet words to each other over the years. Porcelain couples embraced under pink lights. Fallon leaned forward to see hundreds of chocolate boxes, fake flowers, and a zoo's worth of animals wearing suits and dresses, handing candy hearts to their loves.

When the tunnel darkened, the love letters on the tunnel walls turned into reproductions of Zita's loveliest fortunes. A wave of panic pierced her heart. Fallon stuck her hand underneath Sebastian's shirt, searching until she felt his heart beating beneath her fingers. Not a trace of the fortune left.

"Fallon?" he said huskily.

"Just checking," she said.

Sebastian shifted so that he was facing her. The boat rocked, but he held her steady by the waist. "I thought love would kill me," he said, his expression solemn. "That was never my future, but it could take a long time for it to sink in."

"Get used to it. I'm never going to be a spinster."

Sebastian cracked a smile. "That, my princess, may be a good alternative for when you get sick of me."

Fallon tucked her hair behind her ears, raising her chin. "Don't be silly. I am the girl who stole Bastion's heart. That's not a role I'm willing to give up, not for anything."

"You didn't have to steal it," he whispered.

They fell into silence as the music ended. The water lapped at the sides of the tunnel. Wheels and cogs creaked as the plastic people and animals continued dancing, giving flowers, blushing with the help of painted cheeks and electric bulbs.

This is the boy I love, she thought, memorizing the slant of his eyebrows, his dark bangs falling across his forehead.

The dim, glowing lights made him look dreamlike, and she supposed she looked the same.

This time Fallon didn't need to touch his heart to know it was still beating. Instead, she buried her fingers in his hair. His kiss was better than pressing the last wrinkle out of a blouse.

Acknowledgments

Without Swoon Reads, this book simply wouldn't exist.
Thank you, Jean Feiwel and the Swoon Reads staff for falling in love with Fallon Dupree and Grimbaud. My editor,
Holly West, is pure magic. I like to imagine her wearing an
Indiana Jones hat as she found her way through my prose,
cutting away the overgrowth and excavating the gems underneath. Special thanks to Christine Barcellona for being
a great brainstorming partner during my first revision meeting. There are no words to express my joy over the charming cover designed by Richard Deas and illustrated by Zara
Picken. It's the stuff of dreams. I could not have felt more
welcomed when I had the privilege of visiting Swoon Head-
quarters. As wonderful as the staff is, I wouldn't be here
without the Swoon Reads community. Thank you for the
votes, feedback, and support. And a big, warm hello to my
fellow sister-authors: Sandy Hall, Jenny Elliott, Katie Van
Ark, Temple West, and Karole Cozzo.

Many thanks to the readers who saw this book change
and grow. First, Figgies Underground, a motley crew of tal-
ented writers and precious friends, including: Lydia Albano,
Kristin Yuki, Cara Clayton Olsen, Emily Rose Warren,

Hannah Horinek, LiAnn Yim, Samantha Chaffin, Patrick and Janelle Labelle, Savannah Finger, Reagan Dyer, and Enaam Alnaggar. Christina Im and Maria Dones, for the constant support in the form of funny, delightful e-mails. Don and Valarie Eckhart, for making the long days at the office fun. Christina Pletchan, for asking the hard questions during my early draft and feeding me peanut butter cup cookies. Steven Georgeson, for being patient with my questions about hearts. Also to Lauren Christian, a friendship I could never do without.

I owe a lot to my readers from figment.com for believing in me. Without you, I could not have been as tenacious, brave, and unfailingly strange with the stories I spun and shared with you.

Thanks to my professors Rita Ciresi, John Henry Fleming, and Ira Sukrungruang for advice and three full years of eating, sleeping, and breathing the craft of fiction. My University of South Florida MFA cohorts, you know who you are, for providing critical eyes and companionship as we all continue to follow our dreams. Phillippe Diederich, my author photo is stunning thanks to you; I keep looking forward to our friendly who-wrote-the-most-this-week competitions.

To my friends and fellow English majors from Florida Southern College: I didn't know at the time that ripping open a mystery bag of romance books would have led to a novel, but I'm glad we did it. Thank you for many nights of silly conversations held over our dog-eared literature textbooks.

Then there's my family. Even though he lives hours away, my brother, Bill Karalius, deserves my heartfelt thanks for listening when I rambled about charms and chocolate over the phone. This book has surely benefited from my dog, Misty, who fell asleep on my lap while I typed. My parents—my practical father and creative mother—have always supported my dreams, even though I was a weird kid. I couldn't ask for anything more.

Turn the page for some

Sw♥♥nworthy

Extras...

Sebastian's Dating Rules

1. You will not fall in love with me.*
2. Failing Rule #1 results in an immediate breakup.
3. If you're dating me with ulterior motives, tell me. I prefer being prepared.**
4. I'm kind to you because I like to be kind, not because I'm in love with you.
5. I will not go further than kissing. This is nonnegotiable.
6. In the event of a breakup, stop keeping vigil outside my door.

* If you fall in love with me, I will know. There are many ways this can happen: confessing your love to me in person, writing me a letter, leaving me thoughtful presents, looking at me funny, trying to claim I bought you an engagement ring, or candlelit dinners.

** I'm fine with you dating me to get back at your ex, make your parents angry, or annoy your friends. But since those people would potentially lash out at me, I'd rather know ahead of time so I can plan for it.

A Coffee Date

with author Kimberly Karalius and her editor, Holly West

"About the Author"

Holly West (HW): What's your very favorite way to spend a rainy day?

Kimberly Karalius (KK): Usually when it's rainy out, the house cools down, which is something you notice in Florida because it's always so hot all the time. I like sitting on the floor with a blanket playing really old board games like Candy Land. I love playing them because they are kind of goofball-y—nothing too challenging, but always fun.

HW: If you were a superhero, what would your superpower be?

KK: The most practical thing for me would be the ability to change my size at any time. I could become tall enough to reach the highest shelf on the bookshelf with no problem, because I'm a really short person. Or become small enough to go explore dollhouses and things like that.

HW: That's an interesting choice. I like that. Do you have any hobbies?

KK: Besides, of course, reading and writing, I watch silent films. Anything with Buster Keaton is an instant favorite for me. Then there are cartoons too. Nineties cartoons hold a special place in my heart, having grown up watching them, but I just can't get enough. If it's animated, I'm interested! And, of course, I love going to theme parks, especially Disney, but I don't discriminate.

SwoonReads

HW: How did you first learn about the site?

KK: I read an article on its launch on *GalleyCat* in September, because I'd made it a habit to always give my creative-writing students news about what was going on in the creative-writing world. When I saw that article I got really excited, because Swoon Reads was definitely something I wanted to participate in as soon as I had a novel that I thought fit.

HW: That probably answers the "when did you decide to post your manuscript up" question too.

KK: Well, I did write *Love Fortunes* specifically for Swoon Reads. My other manuscripts have romance in them, but not as a central focus. So I felt like I had to write something new. I ran through the first draft as quickly and safely as possible, revised it a few times, and then put it up as soon as I felt like it was ready.

HW: I love it when the books are written specifically for us. Before you were chosen, what was your experience like on the site?

KK: I really enjoyed it because it was so different from my other experiences posting, sharing, and writing online. I came from Figment first, and that was really fun because it was like play-by-play comments. I would post a chapter and see what everybody was thinking and sort of plan it like, "This is what I want to happen, but they said this and it's interesting, so let me see if I can do that too." But with Swoon Reads, the entire manuscript was finished, so I got to find out from readers what they thought of the entire story on its own. That was a completely different type of critique and I enjoyed getting those comments. It was always exciting to log in and see if I had gotten any new ratings or comments, and also, of course, to read other people's manuscripts.

"About the Book"

HW: So let's talk about *Love Fortunes*. I know that you wrote it specifically for Swoon, but how did you get the idea for this book?
KK: *Love Fortunes* came from an idea that I've always wanted to put into a novel, but since I tend to write YA, it had been a challenge to think of how it could fit. When I hung out with my college friends, we would talk about literature studies. We read a lot of classic literature, so the word "spinster" wasn't scary to us. We used it all the time. We used to joke that since we had a shortage of boys on our campus, we were going to graduate and become glamorous spinsters. We would all have mansions. I would have one hundred dogs, because I'm a dog person, so no cats. And we'd have butlers, of course. Trying to put some germ of those discussions into a YA novel was tough. But I wondered, "Spinsters are usually older women, right? Why would a teenager be concerned about that?" And then I started asking more questions like, "OK, well, what if somebody told her that she was going to be one and there was no way to change that?" *Love Fortunes* took off from there.

HW: So how does the revision process work for you? When you get your giant edit letter and you have to go back and face the manuscript again, how do you do it?
KK: I went through the edit letter and marked down all of the smaller changes to make. So the more specific you were in your

edit letter, the easier it was for me to revise those. The larger-scale changes were the ones I saved for last. I needed time to think them over before actually unstitching those parts of the narrative. And when I couldn't solve it, I knew I needed to brainstorm with you. So I kind of went with revising the small, concrete issues first, then tackling the global issues later in the process.

"The Writing Life"

HW: Where do you write? Do you have a specific place or any specific writing rituals that you do when you're writing?

KK: In terms of where I write, I prefer couches. They're big and soft, and I can tuck my feet underneath me while I write. After college, I feel like I can write anywhere. The less desk-like, the better. But I do have a nice pull-out secretary writing desk that I write on when I'm serious, and nobody bothers me if I have my headphones in. I also like to listen to music when I'm writing. A lot of times sound tracks help me focus and also set the mood for whatever scene I'm working on.

In terms of writing rituals, I've always wanted them, but I don't think I've really formed any. The only thing I can think of is technical. When I'm writing, I like to zoom my Word document out to 60 to 70 percent. Being at 100 percent is too close to the trenches for me when I'm writing a first draft. I like being able to see more of the page while I'm working—a bird's-eye view of the manuscript. If I can't adjust the zoom, I'm totally guilty of shrinking the text to ten point.

HW: What's your process? Are you an outliner or do you just make it up as you go?

KK: Usually I vaguely set up some parameters in my head in terms of what I want the story to be about, including the major characters and how I want it to end. But I learned from early on that if I plan too much, it stifles that improv sort of feeling I get when I'm writing. I never finished the first novel I started in college because I overplanned. I had every single scene laid out, I had pieces of dialogue, and a giant binder with magazine cutouts. When it came time to actually write the novel, it went stale. I felt like someone else had already done all the work, and there wasn't much use in repeating it.

Usually I have to get maybe fifteen thousand words into a story before I start outlining, and when I do I only outline two or three chapters ahead of where I am. Bullet points are the best; they keep me brief in my outlines so I don't overwrite. Working this way helps me stay on track, but it still gives me room to just freely write as I go along.

HW: What's the best writing advice you've ever heard?

KK: It was advice that I heard recently, and I think it goes back to that improv thing that works for me. An author named Elizabeth Sims came to speak at my local writing group. Basically her idea was that you only need two words in order to sit down and write: "Yes, and?" When you're writing, you should never tell yourself no, even if it's a really weird idea and you don't know how to proceed. You play along with the idea just like an actor would with improv. Just keep going and you figure the rest out later when you're going back to revise. Telling yourself no is what brings on writer's block and other writerly problems, at least in my experience. Sims's two simple words encapsulate that concept so well. I know I'll be using those words when I face the blank page again!

LOVE FORTUNES AND OTHER DISASTERS
Discussion Questions

1. At first, Fallon had a low opinion of Sebastian, based on his reputation. At what point would you say her opinion of him started to change? Which turning points would you identify in their relationship? Has your opinion of someone ever changed like that?

2. The twins made a deliberate choice not to patronize Zita's shop. If you had the chance to receive a love fortune, would you? Why or why not?

3. Do you think Fallon and Sebastian are fated to be together, or do you think they're creating their own fate by choosing to be together? Why or why not?

4. What do you think of Sebastian's practice of recording silence? What does it say about his character? If you recorded the silence in the town where you live, what do you think you would hear?

5. Knowing Zita's history, can you sympathize with her and understand what drove her to behave how she does? Why or why not?

6. If you received a love fortune, what do you think your fortune would be? Do you think it would change the way you behave in romantic situations and think about romance, or do you think you would continue acting the way you do?

7. If you could use (or invent) any love charm, what would it be?

SwoonReads

8. Nico refused to give up on Martin despite the numerous obstacles in his way. What does that say about Nico? Would you have made the same choice?

9. If you could ask Love any question, what would it be?

10. What do you think will happen to Grimbaud with Zita gone?

Want to host your own
Swoon Reads Book Club Party?
Download our *free* event kit at
www.swoonreads.com/partykit!

First rule of dealing with vampire bodyguards?
Don't fall in love!

Caitlin has seen too much death. Adrian cannot die.
Sparks will fly in this steamy vampire romance!

H ey, de la Mara, you're coming, right?"

Without meaning to, I looked up, right at Adrian. And for some reason, he looked right back at me, just for a moment.

"I don't know yet." He said it quietly, but his voice somehow carried so everyone could hear. Underneath his coat, he was wearing a thick green sweater with a wooden clasp holding the neck loosely closed. It looked cozy, and expensive.

And totally confirmed my suspicions.

"Aw, come on, man; you gotta go!" a senior protested. "You're graduating! And what you did last year at initiation was sick."

There was a general chorus of agreements. Around us, I could see the other tables quiet down as they caught on to the gist of the conversation, and that it was now revolving around Adrian. Freshman girls—all of them but Norah, anyway—were craning their necks to see him, which just struck me as funny. Did no one else see the obvious? Trish was definitely going to win the pool.

Aware that the whole table was looking at him, he cleared his throat. "I'll probably show up."

Content with this answer, the normal buzz of conversation resumed. I turned to Trish and whispered, "What did he do last year at initiation?"

She leaned in. "I'm not sure, because only juniors and seniors are allowed to go and I was a sophomore, but I heard it had to do with jumping off a balcony or something."

I stared at her. "He jumped off a balcony?"

"Yeah. Like an Olympian. I heard he did, like, six flips in the air."

"Seriously?" I asked.

She grinned. "Guess we'll see this weekend."

History passed by quickly. We were going through the industrial revolution and Mr. Warren was showing us a series of documentaries. It was only my second day, but he was quickly becoming my favorite teacher. Music with Mrs. Leckenby was mostly painless, but a little smelly—the entire high school was stuck in one room and had to sing for forty-five minutes and the ventilation sucked. Seventh period rolled around. I headed to the library and sat down in my secluded little corner behind the bookshelves.

Looking forward to a nap, I'd just propped my feet next to a row of encyclopedias when I saw movement out of the corner of my eye. I looked up, and there was Adrian.

"May I?" he asked, nodding at the empty chair.

I shrugged. The table barely fit two, but he seemed comfortable as he set his backpack on the floor and took the seat opposite me. Now that I'd confirmed, in my own mind at least, that he was definitely not straight, my earlier nervousness evaporated—but that didn't make the growing silence any less awkward. As I sat staring at him, he finally cleared his throat and asked, "How are you?"

"Good," I said slowly, wondering where this was going. And then because he didn't seem like he was going to say anything else, I asked, "How are you?"

He smiled and murmured, "Good." And then the smile faltered and he rubbed a hand over his eyes.

I frowned. "Do you get headaches a lot?"

He looked up at me sharply. "What?"

I pointed a finger at his head. "You keep rubbing your eyes like you have a headache."

"Oh," he said, relaxing. "No, I don't get them often." He looked up at me again with a soft smile. "All better."

I smiled back awkwardly, but the silence stretched.

"So," I said, searching for a safe topic to break the weirdness, "I heard you had an impressive initiation last year at the Halloween Hoedown."

His mouth quirked up at the corner in a half smile, but he didn't say anything.

"I heard you somersaulted off a balcony about a dozen times," I prompted.

"Did you?"

"I did."

I stared at him, trying to get a read on his expression. He just stared back evenly. For a second, my conviction about him wavered, but then I looked at his flawless skin, the eight-hundred-dollar sweater. Maybe in New York he could merely be a meticulous dresser, but not here. Not in Stony Creek. Honestly, what was someone like him doing in a place like this, anyway? Trish had said he'd been here since sixth grade. Add that to the fact that he was a senior and had never gone on a date—no way was he straight. It felt safe to stare right back at him without worrying that he would consider it flirtatious.

Finally, he smiled. "I guess you'll just have to wait and find out."

I smiled despite myself, rolled my eyes, and settled back in my chair for my nap. I heard him open a book, but I was asleep after a few moments.

Half an hour later, the bell rang and I jolted awake to the sight of Norah hovering over me. Adrian quietly packed up his books to my left as I sat up and tried to remember where I was.

"Hey," she said. "Mom called the office. She and Dad are having a problem with one of the horses, so they can't come pick us up. I usually throw my bike in the back of Molly's mom's truck and she said she could take you, too."

Before I could respond, Adrian stood. "Actually, if you don't mind, I was going to take Caitlin home."

We looked in tandem at Adrian. Then Norah turned to me, obviously expecting an explanation.

"Uh, yeah," I said, belatedly. "Tell Molly I said thanks, though."

"All right, well—see you at home." Norah was wide-eyed as she walked off.

As we left the library, snaking our way through the rush of students, it took about point-three seconds for everyone to notice that I was walking with Adrian. And I mean *everyone*: parents, students, even the faculty heading toward their busted up cars. I very much got the impression that Adrian was a big deal here— and Adrian deviating from the norm was practically unheard of, based on everyone's reactions. Distracted by our audience, it took me about six seconds to realize what vehicle Adrian was heading toward. I stopped dead.

"You're kidding me."

Ignoring me, he unlocked a helmet from the seat of a matte black Harley-Davidson. I walked up to him, knowing and not caring that everyone had stopped to watch us.

"You drive a motorcycle."

"Yeah." He put his sunglasses on.

I couldn't stop staring. "You drive a *Harley*."

He handed me a helmet as he settled onto the bike. "Yeah."

I took it, dumbfounded. This was not what I had expected when he offered to give me a ride. The bike was huge, which made sense since he was at least six feet tall, which in turn meant the backseat, where I imagined I was supposed to go, was almost at waist level.

"Hey, Adrian," I said casually, testing out his name in his presence for the first time. "How do I, y'know, get on?"

He pointed at the back foot rest. "Step there, hold on to my shoulder, swing over."

I stalled. "What if the bike falls over?"

"The bike will not fall over."

"How do you know the bike will not fall over?"

He stared down at me. "Because I'm on it."

Good point.

"When we're on the road," he continued, "lean when I lean. Don't ever lean the opposite direction. If there's some emergency, tap my chest. I don't have mics in the helmets, so we can't really talk once we get going."

I could feel dozens of eyes on us as I put my foot on the back pedal, used his shoulder to brace myself, and swung my leg over the seat ungracefully, wriggling into place behind him. The passenger seat was shallow and backless, which meant if I wasn't basically spooning him from thigh to neck, I would fall off. Not really wanting to touch him, but seeing nothing else to hold on to, I rested my hands lightly on the sides of his waist and leaned back so at least my chest wasn't plastered to his spine.

He stuck the key in the ignition. "You planning on staying on the bike?"

I nodded vigorously. "Yes."

He started the engine. "Then hold on. I don't bite."

Looking for something else to make you swoon? Check out these other great Swoon Reads titles!

Fourteen viewpoints.
One love story.

Even her guardian angel
might have trouble
saving Cara . . .

Partners for life, or
just on the ice?

Words are strong.
Love is stronger.

Phillippe Diederich

Kimberly Karalius holds an MFA in fiction from the University of South Florida and has been sharing stories on Figment.com with a strong following of enthusiastic readers since the site's conception. Although Kimberly lives in sunny Florida, she prefers to stay indoors and sometimes buys a scarf in the hopes of snow. She loves watching really old cartoons and silent films. Being in Florida certainly has one big perk: going to Disney World. Which she does. Frequently. *Love Fortunes and Other Disasters* is her debut novel.